I0600022

WALK OF FAME

FAME SERIES
BOOK 1

CHRISTINA CAPRI

Copyright © 2026 Christina Capri
All rights reserved.

No part of this book may be reproduced, transmitted, or used in any manner without written permission of the publisher/author, except for the use of quotations in a book review.

This novel is a work of fiction. Names, characters, businesses, events and incidents portrayed are the work of the author's imagination; certain long-standing institutions and businesses are mentioned, but the characters involved are wholly imaginary. Any resemblance to actual persons, living or dead, events or localities is purely coincidental.

Just One More Chapter Publishing LLC

ISBN: 979-8-9936961-1-9 (Paperback edition)

www.christinacapri.com

For Denny, who showed me within three weeks of meeting that the type of love I'd always wondered about existing absolutely does.

*And for my fellow spicy romance lovers, this is for you. I see you because I **am** you.*

PS-Book boyfriends do exist. I married one.

PROLOGUE
JAKE

There has to be more.

"Okay now try to make your pecs do that little jump thing but make it subtle, like it just happens naturally when you move your arms," the director calls out.

There. Has. To. Be. More.

I shift on my feet and look down as I flex my pecs and deliver my lines. "You *know* it's always great to see you, Shannon. Hopefully we'll see each other again...*soon*."

"Wink at her!"

I wink at her. Then I turn to jog down the beach to my group of "friends"—or more accurately a group of extras who are thrilled to spend the day with the actors of their favorite soap dressed *down* in as little clothing as possible.

"Alright let's run that again. From the top!"

The hair and makeup team runs over and pats some more oil on my upper body. They "touch up" my hair, leaving it just as it was before, because it has to look exactly the same for continuity sake. So they basically move a single strand and then puff some salt spray around it. Not even *on* it, just *around* it. They scurry back off to the side and I take my mark.

Claudia, my costar, leans back on her towel and resets. She arches her back slightly, enough for me to sense the movement, but I don't acknowledge that I noticed as I stand beside her and look anywhere but at her. She's playing Shannon, a character brought on the show last season solely to create a tension-filled love triangle between my character Sean and Sean's longtime crush Sam.

"Remember the pecs and wink. Claudia, bigger smirk at the end when you nod. Andddd....action!"

My eyes shift to Claudia and I rake my eyes over her longingly. But that's just because it's my *job* to look at her longingly. In real life, I do not long for this woman.

"You *know* it's always great to see you, Shannon. Hopefully we'll see each other again...*soon*," I say as I pop my pecs and wink before turning to jog off.

"Cut. Okay we got it." The director nods. "Let's move on."

Yes, let's do is all I can think.

1

EMMA

I didn't grow up wanting to be an actress. In fact I never once thought of it. I mean sure, maybe when I was a little girl I'd watch a movie and want to be the star. But less in an *I-want-to-be-that-actress* way and more in an *I-want-to-be-that-cartoon-mermaid* way, you know?

Acting just seems so glamorous and my life has been anything but that. I mean, I have an okay life. I'd even dare to call it a good one. But take that with a grain of salt because I'm definitely a glass half full kind of girl. At some point, it became survival mode for me to picture the glass as half full and not half empty. Plus, a half empty cup implies that it was once full. That was never the case for me. It's much easier to think of my life as a glass that just isn't full...*yet*. But either way, I feel confident that no one has ever looked at me or my life and thought either to be *glamorous*.

Which is why I'm not sure how I find myself with a glamorous life and a glass that is so full it's about to overflow, but here I am.

Actually that's a lie, I know *exactly* how I found myself here.

DRIVING HOME from my shift at the casino bar I catch a radio spot about a casting call for paid background talent on a movie filming in the area. One word makes me pause: *paid.* But I keep driving, because I don't know anything about casting calls and I don't even know what "background talent" is. The commercial says *from 2:00-4:00 today* and I reflexively glance down at the clock. 2:14 p.m. Weird. I tune back into the ad just in time to catch *Exit 111 on Hwy. 10 East toward Palm Springs* and I swear that's one exit from mine. And I just passed Exit 108.

It has to be a sign, right? I mean yes, it was a *literal* road sign, but I have to think it might also be a figurative sign? It's too coincidental not to be.

At least that's what I tell myself as I throw on my blinker and pass my usual Exit 110, thinking maybe I've lost my mind. What am I even doing? I have a good enough job, I'm making it. But my life is basically groundhog day. There aren't a lot of exciting opportunities in this town. Why on earth a movie would be shooting around here is beyond me, unless they're wanting some small town charm. And in that case, we do have that. Well, the small town part at least. We have that in spades in good ole Whitewater, Californ-I-A. The charm? I sure haven't found it yet.

I take Exit 111 and follow the CASTING signs stuck in the ground all over the place, thinking to myself that this might be some kind of trap because those signs sure don't look official. They look exceedingly generic, like I could've grabbed them at Staples. I end up in the parking lot of a nondescript building in what seems to be a strip mall of sorts, turn my car off, and just sit there.

And sit.

Ten minutes later I'm *still* sitting in my car, wondering what possessed me to listen to a radio ad to the point of coming to something I have no business being at. I'm usually not a sucker for commercials, except maybe that Sarah McLachlan one because the combination of that song and those shaking dogs used to get me every time.

I'm also wondering if perhaps I'm about to walk into a derelict space with shady people and shadier intentions, but I convince myself that won't be the case because what kind of bad guys spend money on public radio ads that give their location away?

I take a deep breath and hold it as long as I can before letting it out slowly and then subsequently gasping for air because I held my breath *too* long. I don't know who decided breathing like that was a calming technique, but I do know it doesn't work for me. I take an underrated *normal* breath, clap my hands together like I'm cheering myself on, hop out and just...walk in, not knowing *what* I'm actually doing but fully knowing *why* I'm doing it. (For the record, I never liked the movie *Groundhog Day.*) Your girl needs a change.

I fill out a few forms and they ask for my headshot. Of course I don't have one. What have I ever needed a headshot for? Do people actually walk around with those? Is that a thing? I look around at the others who showed up for the casting call, and apparently *yes*, yes people do walk around with their headshots. It's very much a thing. Who knew? Since I don't have one, the casting people just take a snapshot of me and I'm on my way.

I'm in there all of ten minutes. I'm not sure what I expected but it wasn't that. No reading lines, no answering questions, just literally a picture and disclosing my physical characteristics like height, weight and hair color, plus my contact info. That's it. It feels remarkably superficial and I find myself wishing I had at least redone my ponytail.

I get back in my car and immediately look up *background talent*. Okay. Okay. So that just means extras, like the people who round out a scene by just being there. Like the crowd at a football game or something. Google tells me that background talent doesn't usually even speak, so I guess that makes sense why there were no lines. I laugh to myself because I find it hilarious they call it background "talent." I mean, what talent does it take to just stand there and act normal? I can't decide if it sounds fun or boring, but it sounds *paid*, and paid sounds good, so I'm here for it.

THE NEXT DAY my phone rings and I almost ignore it because I don't recognize the number, and if I'm being honest I never answer phone calls anyway. And if I'm being *really* honest that's probably because I never actually *get* any phone calls. But something (okay a tiny sliver of hope I've been trying not to acknowledge) pushes me to answer it. And sure enough, it's the casting office. They want me to be the stand-in for the female lead, Amy Lawton. She is an actual star. A superstar. A *beautiful* superstar.

I almost drop the phone.

I am ridiculously flattered. I'm also ridiculously clueless. I have no idea what a stand-in is. I literally didn't even know something called a "stand-in" existed thirty seconds ago. I put my phone on speaker so I can still hear and search *movie stand-in* while the casting assistant is still talking to me. Alright, so it's someone who stands there so the actor doesn't have to stand there while they get the lights set up and block the scene and stuff. Sounds kind of dull. Like a placeholder. I zone out a bit while thinking through that and catch bits and pieces of *shooting for three months...provide your own lodging...SAG-AFTRA stand-in pay*. And now I'm Googling "SAG-AFTRA stand-in pay" and holy shit, that's real money.

Where do I sign? And can I use a Sharpie? Or maybe my blood? No take backs.

Because things like this don't happen to me. In my life, whenever something sounds too good to be true...it is.

2

JAKE

It's not that I'm not grateful. I am so fucking grateful. I have one of the coolest jobs in the world. I'm an actor and I don't know how to convey this without sounding like an absolute douche, but I'm kind of having my "moment" right now. Yes I know how lame that sounds. But I also know it's a very real thing. I know that because I'm living it.

I've been acting for ten years. I've had some okay parts over the years, but only in the past year or so have I reached major "star" status. I'm *sent* scripts now. I'm *asked* to be part of productions. I no longer have to audition. I just keep getting parts handed my way. For a guy who used to be "Friend Number Two" in more features than I can count, it's pretty mind-blowing to be begged to sign on to a project.

Like I said, I'm grateful. And lucky. But my moment didn't really begin until after my third season on an Aussie soap. Yeah, I had to leave the country to get a role that was more than a glorified extra with a couple lines. I'd worked in L.A. for over half a decade before I left the States, and when I left I was "that guy who was in that movie." Like you might recognize me but you'd never be able to place me or the movie I was in. Not stellar. So I took a chance on *Sunset Cove* (an Australian evening soap opera a la *The O.C.*, if the name doesn't give that away). The money was good and I thought at least I'd get to experience Australia and shrimp on the barbie and terrifying human-sized spiders and all that good stuff.

My character Sean was immediately well-received and my one season got extended to two and then I got offered a contract for two more years before the second season even aired—thanks to some leaked pictures of me joining the *Sunset Cove* lifeguard team. Turns out the *Baywatch* effect is real. Those images blew up and the producers decided I was worth keeping a little longer.

And then, season three happened.

I shot a scene where I had to stop an attack on my character's crush Sam and I got to flex my action muscles. It was my favorite scene I'd ever filmed. Instead of the usual "flirt with the damsel in no distress" they always wrote for me, this time I finally got to save the damsel in actual distress. The scene had meat. And grit. I got to chase, punch, and generally destroy two characters who were attacking my crush, Sam. In the scene, she had been knocked unconscious and once I beat her attackers to that same lack of consciousness, I scooped her up and as I carried her away I whispered, "I love you, Sam" since she was out cold and I knew she couldn't hear me.

And just as the episode closed there was a shot of her blinking her eyes open. She'd heard me.

That was the season three finale. It was perfection. Fans went WILD. We'd finally given them the satisfaction of these two characters coming together. Very Ross and Rachel-esque. Clips of me going apeshit on her attackers and then carrying her away like that went viral. Like *insanely* viral. Some TikTok guy edited the action sequence with the caption "Make this guy the next Bond" and it got shared seventeen million times. For a guy who had 140,000 Instagram followers at the time, it was insanity. Of course the comments were riddled with "stfu he's not even British" but who cares? Not me. Because it didn't stop people from sharing it and didn't stop me from drowning in calls.

Sunset Cove got picked up for syndication in the States and suddenly I was "the guy to cast."

It was amazing. Humbling. Exciting.

Until it wasn't.

I got the season four script and threw it against the wall. It was shit. *Bullshit* to be exact.

It was clear the writers were trying to up the ante now that our show had received all this hype. Now that *I* had received all this attention. I know they were just trying to capitalize on that, but they cheapened our story, if cheapening a soap opera is even possible (turns out it is). Suddenly, I was to be shirtless in nearly every scene. That's fine, I could deal with that. My best friend Timbo is my trainer so it just means working out with him a little harder to make sure I stay at the top of my pec-bouncing game. No problem.

But there *was* a problem, and it's that instead of letting Sean and Sam be together like we'd hinted at for three seasons since I joined the show, they messed with that sacred dynamic and doubled down on a love triangle with Shannon, the character played by Claudia that they'd brought in midway through season three. I hated it. Alissa—the actress who plays Sam—hated it. We begged the show runners to rethink it. We warned that it would betray the viewers. We told them the reason that the season three finale had received a record number of viewers was because of one thing—we'd given them what they wanted. We'd foreshadowed them finally being together. Our viewers were chomping at the bit for season four if only to see Sean and Sam *finally* together.

We got overruled. It was like they'd struck gold and instead of running with that gold, they threw it back to see if they could find something better than gold.

Spoiler alert: Gold is pretty damn great. It's worth holding onto.

Alissa is contracted for another season but this is my last. Of course they offered me a multi-season extension at a huge number amidst all the fanfare following season three, but after I saw the season four script I declined. Then they offered me an astronomical amount for just *one* more season, so Alissa and I could end our arcs on the show together. I almost took it because I adore her and had always planned to leave when she left, plus I wanted to do justice to Sean and Sam. The insane amount of money was definitely enticing, but the *Sunset Cove* writers wouldn't guarantee me they'd do our characters justice. They wouldn't commit to anything regarding the Sean/Sam/Shannon triangle, so I wouldn't commit to them.

This is my last season.

And to really make a now uncomfortable set even more uncomfortable, Claudia both hates me and wants me. It's awkward because we're supposed to be flirtatious and all *will-they-or-won't-they* and well, we already did and we most definitely won't again. Yes, I slept with her last season. But only because I thought her character was leaving the show. And, well, because she's crazy hot. Things were super hot for about three weeks before they were super cold. I didn't want more. She did. So we stopped hooking up, and then I found out they were bringing her back for the next season. I didn't know that was even a consideration when we got together. Things have been weird ever since. I *dread* shooting with her.

And I now have a *no-coworkers-unless-they're-a-day-player* rule. Because continuing to shoot with someone who is angry at you because they can't have you weirdly only makes them want you more...which makes them come onto you only for you to politely decline them again which makes them despise you even more...it's a shitty cycle and I feel like I'm on a hamster wheel I can't get off. My life feels very *Groundhog Day*-esque, and that's always been my least favorite Bill Murray movie.

At this point, I'm just ready to get the heck out of here and off this show. I'm basically just a living piece of eye candy now thanks to the powers that be on *Sunset Cove*, and I hate it. But we wrap filming in six weeks and Timbo and I are headed back to Los Angeles and I can't fucking wait. Never thought I'd be happy to get back to Los Angeles, a city that can be disturbingly vapid on even the best of days.

But I've had enough of the Outback for now.

As soon as I get back to L.A. I have meetings about a new series called *Hierarchy* they want me to star in and they're offering executive producer status. I've never been offered that. Never even had the chance to consider it. When I left the States for down under, I was completely nameless. My parts weren't memorable and honestly neither was I.

I definitely wasn't planning to jump right into another series after shooting one for the past four years, but damn if I don't think I'm going to sign on. They claim that they want my "creative input" and for me to help select the female lead. It's being adapted from a hugely popular book series and there is tons of press around it. I'd imagined myself coming back and shifting into film, maybe even parlaying my newfound fame to join a superhero franchise because I'm in no way above making buckets of money to play a superhero I admired as a kid. That sounds freaking epic. But, I'm kind of a homebody and I don't really want to travel every few months for a new film. I like to have some rhythm and routine to my life. And after experiencing what it feels like to have no control on a show I was so invested in, the thought of having some say on set is appealing.

So appealing I'm not sure I can turn it down.

3

EMMA

It turns out being a stand-in is freaking fun. *So* fun actually. I get to learn all the behind the scenes secrets, work with a renowned director, hang with movie stars, and make some money while I'm at it. How is this a real job? Sure, it's a *lot* in some ways. I'm on set for sixteen hours a day sometimes. But I'm usually just watching. And waiting for them to need me. Andddd occasionally napping on set when they don't. Or snacking all day because the craft services tent is so legit. I've always been a sucker for a buffet. Ryan's and Shoney's were the pinnacle for me growing up.

I'm two months into my three month stand-in stint and getting fitted in the wardrobe trailer when the first assistant director, Laura, walks in and asks to speak to me.

"Emma, how would you feel about working as Amy's stunt double?"

"Are there even any stunts in this movie?" I ask, honestly

wondering. It's not like we're filming an action movie here. This is a romantic comedy and there's zero physical humor.

"She will be roller skating in a couple of scenes and riding on the back of Ted's motorcycle in another scene. Nothing too crazy."

"So...you just want me to ride on the back of a motorcycle and roller skate?" I ask incredulously.

"Basically."

I want to ask my next question but I don't want it to come off as insulting. So I try to phrase it gingerly. "I don't mean this sarcastically, I just genuinely want to understand..." I trail off, shifting on my feet. "Why does that require a stunt double? Wouldn't *Amy* just film those parts? They're so minor and don't seem dangerous."

Laura nods, like she understands why I'm a little confused. "On the motorcycle you won't wear a helmet and it's a distance shot. She doesn't want to do it, and since it's not a close up we don't need her."

I bite my tongue because all I want to do is ask why they won't just let her wear a helmet. But I know it's not my place to ask that so I keep listening.

"And for the roller skating shots, we will get some with her in skates, too, but Dante wants some close ups of the footwork and since it will just be waist down for those shots we don't need her." She clears her throat. "You don't have to do it, we just wanted to ask you first. You'd get stunt pay on top of stand-in pay on the days you work stunts. And we'd have you work with a coach on the skates so you'd get paid stunt pay on those days you train, too."

How absurd is all I can think.

The film world is *insane*. I stand around all day on set so the actress doesn't waste her time standing around on set. And now they want to pay me so the actress doesn't have to spend a little extra time roller skating. And they want to actually *train* me to skate? No wonder movie stars seem like they're living in a different world. They *are.*

I smile and say, "Count me in."

"Great, you'll need to see the hair team so they can match your hair to Amy's. Other than that, we'll get the contract to you and go from there."

Wait, what? I hold my hand out, pausing her from leaving. "Wait. You mean I have to cut my hair?" Amy's hair falls just at her shoulders and mine reaches halfway down my back. It would take a pretty big cut to match her hair.

"Yeah, we need you to look just like she does, same length and color."

I hesitate. My hair is about nine inches longer than Amy's right now. She cut her hair off for this film. My hair is dark blonde with years of natural sun highlights. I've never colored it. Her hair is currently an ashy brown with no dimension. I've literally heard them refer to it as a "mousy" brown. They dyed it for the movie because she's playing a "small town girl." (And I just have to say it—what a diss to small town girls everywhere. Also, it's me. *I'm* a small town girl.)

I'm suddenly not so sure about this stunt stuff.

I look around and everyone in the trailer is smiling at me like I've just won the lottery. I don't get it. I look back to Laura and ask, "Can I think about it?"

One by one the wardrobe people's mouths drop open.

"Sure. Just need to know by the end of the week," she answers me with a shrug.

The second she walks out of the wardrobe trailer I'm instantly bombarded with everyone's (unsolicited) advice.

You have to take this opportunity.

You'll get your SAG card.

And SAG pay!

Some people work fifteen years before they get this chance.

It's hair. It'll grow back!

Don't waste this opportunity, Emma.

I'm naive about this industry. Clueless. All I know is I don't really want to cut my hair off and I don't really want to dye it mousy brown. My hair is dirty blonde and I like it. I'll take dirty over mousy any day.

Am I being vain? Sure. But who *would* want to cut their hair off and dye it an intentionally very unattractive brown?

Exactly.

THE NEXT MORNING AMY, the super famous drop dead gorgeous movie star, comes to see...me. *Me.* She walks into wardrobe while I'm putting on a very basic version of what she will be shooting in today. The entire wardrobe team looks at her expectantly. Okay, so it's clear they won't take no for an answer. Or more like they won't take *Ummm, I'm not sure can I think about it?* for an answer. They obviously told Amy about my hesitation.

"Emma," she says kindly. "Talk to me. What's your holdup about the stunt work?"

I shake my head and let out a sigh. "I don't know that I want to cut my hair and dye it," I blurt out as I slip a black crewneck shirt over my head.

It sounds so silly when I say it out loud. Ridiculous even. Because I mean, *she* cut her hair off and dyed it for this role. Then again *she's* getting millions of dollars for this movie so it's not really a tomato/tomahto type of situation here.

She nods. "Listen, I worked eleven years before I got my SAG card. You've been in this world for two months. This is one of those lucky breaks you hear about. Your hair will grow back. You can dye it back to normal. But you might not get a chance like this again. At least maybe not anytime soon. I think you should do it."

So I do.

And just like that, my status on set is elevated. I am no longer *Emma, the stand-in*. I am *Emma, the stunt double*. I get my own mini trailer. I have wardrobe appointments. Makeup. Hair. I have a stunt coach. I get SAG-AFTRA stunt work rate for each day I work stunts, and I am also still standing-in so on those days I make double.

And it just all feels so surreal because I literally just stumbled into all of this.

Not too shabby for a haircut and bad dye job.

4

EMMA

One month later

I don't want this to end.

Maybe ever.

It's been an exciting few months and if I'm being honest, it seems weird to think of just going back to work F&B like I didn't just have my eyes opened to an entire other world. A world that is refreshing because it's such a 180 from anything I've ever experienced. A world where I can earn money and potentially, maybe, possibly, one day, down the line, years from now, earn *big* money.

We just wrapped our last day of shooting, and I feel equal parts inspired to make a real go of this and defeated because I don't know *how* to make a real go of it. How can I, a small-town-grew-up-in-a-doublewide-then-bounced-around-foster-homes-and-now-a-casino-bartender ever "make it?" I'm just not that girl. That's not my story, and I'm not sure how to write myself into that plot line.

At our wrap party that night, hugs and promises to see each other again flow freely. Everyone is tipsy, everyone is having a great time, and everyone knows this movie will be a success. Everyone also says they'll help me if I decide to move to L.A. and give it a go, but I'm a realist and I know everyone is saying that because it is just one of those things you say to be nice.

Everyone except Dante, our director.

Dante Roedner. The "it" man of the moment. Definitely not Scorcese level or anything—not even close—but he is sought after for sure. He's good at what he does, and he seems to be a genuinely good human. We're friendly. Not like *friendly* friendly. Just friendly. *One word* friendly. For clarification, the stand-in for the male lead actor and I are on more of a two word friendly status. *Friendly* friendly. There's...a difference. You spend so much time together it's bound to happen. I guess that's why actors always end up getting together when they film together— you're just so entrenched in each other.

Dante and I always chatted between scenes while he sat on set waiting for the actors to arrive and I...well, stood there. When he'd introduced himself my first day on set, I'd countered by asking how long he'd been back from the Inferno. He was silent. Dead silent. For a solid twenty seconds. It was one of the most awkward moments of my life. I just stared at him, before scrunching my nose and saying "Alighieri? Dante's *Inferno*? *The Divine Comedy*? Sorry, I've never met anyone with that name before and it was just the first thing that popped into my mind."

He was still shaking my hand except there was no shaking. Just stillness. And silence.

Oh shit I blew it, I'd thought.

He'd looked at me a beat more and said "I've been doing this eighteen years and you're only the second person who has ever made that reference." I couldn't tell if he meant that in a good way or a bad way, but then his lip twitched slightly. "You're well read, Miss Stand In."

The knot in my chest had loosened and I'd sent an avalanche of gratitude out into the universe aimed directly at my AP English teacher.

During some of our earliest small talk time-killing moments, he'd asked me if I wanted to be an actress. I'd been honest and told him I had never considered it but thought I might want to give it a try after this experience.

When I'd walked on set for my first day of stunt work, Dante had asked me if I was going to abandon the acting world for the stunt world. I'd scoffed and replied that you can't abandon something you're not part of in the first place. All he'd said back was, "We'll see."

Tonight, Dante approaches me right after I finish my good-byes with the hair team. Even though they purposely botched the hell out of my hair, they were just doing their job and I still adore them. I cannot say the same for my ratchet lob, but nothing a little biotin and dye can't help remedy.

Dante nods at them and then looks to me. "Emma, may I have a moment?" He gestures to a standing cocktail table off to the side of the bar they'd rented out for the party. I smile and walk over with him.

"Listen," he begins. "I know you stumbled your way into this. And I know being a stand-in doesn't feel like a big deal, but—"

I cut him off, without even meaning to. "I don't feel that way! Well, I do about the stumbling part but not about the stand-in part." I furrow my brows, looking for the words. "Being a stand-in has been like a three month exposé of the inner workings of movies, acting, the shooting process....I mean, I've gotten to see so much. I feel like it was a really big deal."

He chuckles softly, nodding. "This is exactly why I wanted a minute. Emma, you have a spark. A spark I think could be stoked into a wildfire if you give it the chance. You're magnetic, even when you're just standing on your mark doing nothing but looking into the camera for us to place lighting."

I feel my face heat to such a degree that there's no way I'm not visibly blushing.

In general, I have a hard time accepting even the most simple compliment. This? This sounds like he couldn't possibly be talking about me.

"And you're so emotive. You don't even realize how expressive you are when you talk, when you tell a story, or answer a question, when you react to something...You owe it to yourself to try your hand at acting and see what you're capable of."

I'm honestly not sure anyone has ever really believed in me this much. Or at all. I feel my eyes well with tears. How could something I didn't even know I wanted a few months ago be all I want now?

Dante continues, "I don't know your whole story. But I don't think this is a one-off for you. I think you have potential, and I mean potential to go further than being a stunt double. If you decide to try your luck in L.A., I'll do what I can to help you."

And then he asks me to take down his number and email.

I. Am. Gobsmacked.

Shook.

Floored.

How is this esteemed director standing in front of me telling me he thinks *I* should give acting a chance?

Dante's voice breaks into my thoughts. "Hand me your phone." I do and he adds his contact info before handing it back to me. "Good luck, Emma. I'll be rooting for you."

And he turns and walks off to mingle with the rest of the crew and cast.

Color me shocked. Dante Roedner just gave me his number,

with seemingly no ulterior motives. He didn't even hint at sex. He didn't tell me all those absurdly flattering things and then make a move on me. He just told me and walked away. That goes against everything I've ever heard about this industry.

The rest of the night is a blur to me. A happy, loud, and surreal blur. I go home thinking about whether I really could leave the only place I know and try to make something of myself. I suspend reality for a moment and allow myself to dream about what that would feel like. About how it would feel to make enough money to be comfortable. To get a nicer place. I think about not having to sling drinks and deal with being hit on by creeps who don't know when to stop. I think about making friends who don't judge me because I'm the girl who grew up in a mobile home park and played musical foster homes, only to go right back to a trailer once I turned eighteen. But you know what? Mobile homes are underrated. They can be nice. Why is it that tiny homes are all the rage but trailers are considered trashy? Make it make sense.

I let my mind play tricks on me a little longer and imagine meeting someone, because maybe if I "make it" someone will think I'm a catch. For more than a night.

The truth is, I know I can do it. Be an actor, that is. Don't get me wrong, I also know I'm no Meryl Streep. But truth be told, if I've learned anything these past few months, it's that you don't necessarily have to be Streep status to "make it." I was on set with a huge ensemble cast with some of the larger names in the biz and several of them were not obscenely naturally talented. For three months, I saw how many takes they got, how many chances to get their lines right, how much explicit direction they were given on everything from their inflection to how they moved their hands...and, well, I know I can at least do *that*. I can follow directions. Hell, most anyone can.

And more than knowing I *can*, I know I *want* to.

The last few months have been pretty damn mesmerizing. The lives of these stars. Private drivers, homes booked for them, private dinners wherever they want whenever they want, private trainers and nutritionists shadowing their every move...I mean no wonder they all have ridiculous bodies. All the rest of us would, too, if we had nutritionists and personal trainers with us twenty-four seven.

It is just such a different world.

A world I want in.

5

JAKE

This show—*Hierarchy*—is going to be a winner. I can feel it. Everyone involved can feel it. Sometimes you just know. Maybe like how some married people say they knew when they'd found the one. Well, same. This is the one—the *show*—that is going to be huge.

I can't believe I'm attached to something with so much buzz. Hell yes, I signed on. Honestly I tried to play it cool when we got back to L.A. and not immediately sign away the next several years of my life, but I only managed to hold out a couple days after the pitch meetings.

The author of the book series? Brilliant. The production team they've put together? Top-notch. The studio that bought the rights? Heavyweight. The director they lined up for the first six episodes? Visionary.

The book series is a worldwide phenomenon and after reading it through—*four times*—I am an admitted fanboy. It's an incredibly gripping storyline. The female main character is nobility. She's catered to and sheltered, but with a fiery spirit her prestigious family can't seem to rein in. The male lead—my role —is, of course, nowhere near nobility. He's rough around the edges and constantly underestimated because of his lack of wealth and status. He gets captured and forced to join her guard since he's considered disposable. You can imagine how that goes. She doesn't want a protector and he doesn't want to protect her because she drives him absolutely mad.

Until she doesn't.

The whole story takes place in a fantastical version of Earth with mythical beasts and malevolent faeries. Even if I wasn't starring in and producing this show, I'd watch the hell out of it.

We don't even have to shoot a pilot and *hope* to get picked up. We're already green lit. I've never experienced something like this before—being part of something that is considered a sure thing instead of a bet. And they keep telling me I'm in the driver's seat but frankly I'm just thankful to be along for the ride.

I signed a contract for three seasons with executive producer status. To say I'm pumped would be the world's biggest under-statement. Timbo is pumped, too, because my character in *Hier-archy* is described in the books as being basically a god among men so even though I'm "lifeguard shredded" in his words, he says he's got "a lot of work to do."

Thanks man.

There's only one unknown about all of this, and it's a huge one: the female lead. The search for our Annabelle Claiborne has been exhaustive. And unsuccessful.

They've brought in lots of big names to read with me. Huge names. Names I never thought I'd ever be in the same room with, much less decline the opportunity to work with. But the right chemistry just hasn't been there. It has felt forced. And now that we're only six months away from shooting, I'm feeling insecure. I think I have imposter syndrome. They cast me first and I'm signed, sealed, and delivered—so now it feels like all of this rides on me and how well the female lead plays off of *me*. Pressure much?

We're running out of names so the studio is going to take it to the evil yet necessary step all actors have to churn through at some point: auditions. For a show of this stature, they would typically never hold auditions for the female star. For the side parts? Absolutely. But for the lead they'd just contact agents to ask their clients to come in and read. So, still an audition, but more of an invitation-only audition.

But, we've been there done that and still haven't found Annabelle. Since we've had no luck, the author, Lisa, suggested that maybe we need a brand new face. And as part of her contract for rights to adapt her novels, Lisa gets to help cast her characters. And I'm not mad about that because she is apparently the one who brought my name to the table (thank god for that viral TikTok). But for Annabelle Claiborne, the gorgeous and feisty heroine in her series, everyone has come up short. So, the studio obliged and now we're gearing up for days on end of auditions for Annabelle. And the studio wants me there because the chemistry between Daniel (my character) and Annabelle is crucial to making this series work.

I've read the books now and I have to agree. Our chemistry is vital. Think Jamie and Claire on *Outlander*. On steroids. That's what we're shooting for here.

We've just got to find my Claire.

6

EMMA

"I'll take it."

The landlord, Marci, looks almost surprised but she masks it quickly. "Ideally we want someone to start a lease on the first of the month, but that's only two weeks away..." she trails off.

I've been staying at what has to be L.A.'s cheapest motel the past few weeks while I tried to find a place, and this is the first one that is in my budget and not reminiscent of a prison cell. It *could* be cute. It's in a good*ish* spot. I like it and tantamount to that is the fact that I'm ready to get out of that motel because those walls are *thin*. The stuff I've been hearing should *never* be heard.

I smile, "Actually, if it's available now, I can move in as early as today. I would just want the rent prorated for the month."

Now she's definitely surprised. "Oh wow, okay, well I believe we could make today work. It's ready. We just have to work out the details of your security deposit and lease terms. Are you wanting to sign for the year?"

"I would prefer month to month, though I don't plan on going anywhere anytime soon. And I'll pay in cash."

After the film wrapped, I'd gone back to the casino for two weeks to save up enough money to make the move. I'd told my manager to put me on the schedule for as many shifts as possible, so I worked doubles almost every day to save up. No one likes to drop money on drinks quite like big spenders at a casino.

I also sold virtually all of my belongings except the clothes that I could fit in my car, plus I sold my trailer to the owner of the mobile home park.

I'm flush with cash and ready to test the deep waters of Los Angeles.

Actually, it *is* L.A., so maybe they're shallow waters. Only one way to find out.

I know my cash stash won't go far, but it will get me started. I'm here and I'm ready to dive in. Or jump in feet first. Same same.

Marci's voice breaks through my thoughts, "It's yours." She extends her hand to shake mine. I swear I hear bells chiming in celebration.

ONCE I'M SETTLED into my new apartment, I waste no time contacting Dante. And god if that man doesn't hold true to his word and congratulate me for making the move before offering me a role in his newest film. It is a small part, but it's a start. And it's a credited speaking role so that is huge for me.

Less than a week after I filmed that role for Dante, which took all of two days, I got a call from Amy's assistant. She said they needed a stand-in for a makeup commercial Amy would be filming. They could've found anyone to be her stand-in, but they called me simply to throw me a bone. A bone I very happily took. Amy was giving me an *opportunity*.

Her commercial has Peter Stannish at the helm, which is inexplicable seeing as he's literally an Oscar-winning director. And it's co-starring a music superstar named Ray—no last name —again, for who knows what reason. It is literally a mascara commercial. Why you would ever need an Oscar-winning director and rap star for a mascara commercial is lost on me. But they're huge names and I'm no idiot, even if I don't understand it all. I said I'd do it before Amy's assistant even gave me the rest of the details.

PETER, the mascara commercial director, and I hit it off. He's fresh off an Oscar win. His first. I don't have a lot of time with him since it's a short shoot, but we talk off and on all day, and when I tell him I just moved to L.A., he gives me endless recommendations for every type of cuisine you could imagine.

"You're speaking my language," I say with a grin.

With a raised brow, he asks, "Food? Food is your language?"

"Yeah, I think it's my love language," I respond with a laugh.

When we wrap the next day, Peter shares his email and tells me to reach out if he can ever help me.

And it seems like he means it. Like really means it. Just like Dante had. There was no bribe, no strings, nothing. That part kind of shocked me. *Again.* I mean, I wouldn't sleep around to climb up the showbiz ladder. But I guess I halfway expected to be approached that way? Or for these big names to expect something in return for their help. It seems like that's what you always hear about. And here I am with two super famous, highly regarded directors just genuinely offering to help me out if they can.

Maybe L.A. isn't as fake as people make it out to be.

EMMA

One month later

Oh L.A. is fake alright. It's swimming with egos and entitlement and arrogance. I managed to land a serving job at Stella's, the restaurant the biggest stars love to frequent, and wow are so many of them unlikeable. It kind of makes me wish I didn't pick Stella's because so many of the actors who come in are incredibly pompous and it's low-key ruining lots of movies I love. But the money is damn good, which is the reason I gunned for this job so hard. I knew I'd meet people, make great money, hear conversations that could help me, maybe even meet some directors or casting agents and wow them with my unrealistic dream and lack of experience... who knows? The world is my oyster.

I just got home from my brunch shift, which is my favorite shift of all, when my phone rings. I almost let it keep ringing because I'm just walking in the door, but I have no real excuse not to answer it and I'm trying to get out of my comfort zone in every aspect of my life, so I grab it just before it stops.

"Hello?" I say half-expecting a spam call since it's an unknown number. Then again, I only have like three saved numbers, so nearly every call is an unknown number.

"Emma? It's Peter. Stannish. We met on the L. Beauty commercial last month."

Why is he calling me? And how did he get my number?

I need to sit down. But I don't have any furniture yet besides a bed so I just sit on the kitchen floor. "Yes of course I know who you are, Peter. Mr. Stannish. Pete."

I squeeze my eyes shut. *Oh my god, what am I even saying?*

He chuckles. "No one calls me Pete. But I already told you—call me Peter. Listen, I have an in on a new series being developed. It's being adapted from a popular book series and they want a 'new face.' We thought of you."

I would fall down but I'm already on the floor. *We? Who's we?*

I'm quiet. I have zero words. The silence hangs between us and I finally find enough of my voice to ask, *"We?"*

"My partner Dante and I."

I can't help it. I scream. "Ahhhh! Dante? Dante Roedner? *He's* your partner? How did I not know that?" I don't even know if he means *partner* partner or directing partner or writing partner or pickleball partner or what, but it doesn't matter. Anyone who is good with Dante is good with me.

I hear muffled talking and then a familiar voice comes through the line. "Emma, it's Dante. *I* wanted to tell you but Peter has the in on it so he won."

"Are you kidding me? I didn't know you were partners! I'm speechless. About *all* of it." I take a breath but keep right on going. "But not really speechless I guess because I realize words are still coming out of my mouth, but I just...I'm so overwhelmed that you even thought of me. I don't know what to say!" I scream again and they both chuckle.

This time Peter comes through. "We're on speaker, is that okay?"

"Yes, of course. I love Dante."

"I know the feeling," says Peter. And now I'm thinking it's *partner* partner. "So listen, a friend of mine is helping develop it and they already have their male lead. He apparently got cast because the rabid book readers petitioned for him to get it."

I laugh thinking about how people who have read a book don't play games when it comes to film or show adaptations. They always have thoughts and a *lot* of them. "Well that's really cool. Is it a name I know? And what's the series?"

I'm trying to play it cool. But this world is so foreign to me. I've somehow tricked everyone into thinking I belong and just need to catch my "break" but the truth is I don't know what the hell I'm doing and I definitely don't belong. Nor do I deserve to catch a lucky break. I've never been a good catcher anyways. I can throw decently enough, but I can't catch to save my life.

Peter answers. "Yeah, maybe. Jacob Morrow. I didn't know of him. He's big on a show out of Australia."

"Oh shit would I have to do an accent?" I blurt out before I can stop myself. *Shit.* A real actor wouldn't ask that. Or say *shit* to someone like Peter. Or Dante.

Well *shit*.

Peter chuckles. "No, it's a fantasy world but the female character is American. And so is he. Jacob's from the U.S., but he had a role on an Australian soap and he's a whole thing in the Aussie world. And the book series is called *Hierarchy*."

Dante chimes in, "It's a sweeping fantasy with lots of action, lots of drama, and lots of romance."

"Sounds kind of *Outlander*-ish," I say, thinking aloud.

"That's exactly what it is," says Dante. "I've read the books and you'd be great as the female character. When Peter told me about the series and how they've struck out on finding the female lead and want a new face, I just kept thinking how perfect you would be if we could get you in. Turns out I know the right person for that." I can hear the smile in his voice.

"That you do," says Peter. "Emma, you have an audition Thursday at 11:00. I hope you can be there because I won't be able to change it. They say they want a 'new face' but I don't think they are thinking of completely green. It took some convincing."

"Thank you for going out on a limb for me," I say. But what I think is *Thank you for going out on the world's thinnest, most fragile limb of all time for me.*

"Sure thing. The audition is right down from the soundstage we shot the commercial on. Suite 102. Cold read."

"Got it," I try to sound confident and upbeat. I make a mental note to look up "cold read" because, once again, I don't know what the heck that means. "I'll be there." I take a deep breath and then add, "Thank you both so much. I'm still not sure how this happened...it seems like such a long shot, but I'll give it my best. But...I mean, how did my name even come up? And how crazy is it that the only two directors I've ever worked with are actually partners?"

"Crazy." They say in unison. Then Peter continues, "I was just telling Dante offhand about the project and he said he had someone they should see. Someone who would be perfect for the role if they wanted a newbie. I'd heard him talk about you when he was shooting, but we connected the dots when he showed me a photo of you and I told him I'd just had you on my set."

"Kismet," I sigh happily. "Thank you both for throwing my name into the pile. I won't let you down."

Well I guess I'm a stone cold liar now. Because I do believe I will most definitely let them down.

8

JAKE

"Ten more." Timbo gestures to the weights I just set down.

"Dude, are you trying to kill me? This is overkill."

"Twelve more."

"Aren't *I* paying *you*?" I lean against the wall.

"Yes." Timbo stretches his right arm across his chest and hooks his left arm around it to deepen the stretch. "Yes you are." He switches arms. "You're paying me to make sure you have the type of body people literally turn on the TV just to see. And I'm good at my job, which is why you've got twelve more lateral raises."

He grabs his water bottle and chugs some. "Then we'll hit some shrugs. It's shoulder day baby."

"Kill me now," I groan. It's not that I can't do it. That's not the issue. The issue is I'm freaking sore. Timbo has been pushing me hard, and I feel it in every muscle fiber in my body. Maybe even my bones. Is that possible?

I pick back up the weights. "This isn't *Sunset Cove*, man. There's meat in this series."

"Hate to break it to you, bro, but *you're* the meat in this series."

I shoot a deeply annoyed look his way. "You know I don't love all the shirtless shit." And I mean it. I really don't. It makes me feel like that's all I'm there for. All I'm good for. I want to be there because I'm good at *what* I do, not because I look good doing it.

"I know you don't and that's why I still hang out with you. Because you're not obsessed with yourself. But your character is like Jamie Fraser meets Aragorn meets Thor's little brother so I'm just doing my part so you can play your part."

"Thor's little brother?" I question.

"Well, I mean...it's *Thor*. No one is going to be Thor. So we're aiming for the next best thing," Timbo reasons.

"And that would be his little brother?"

"*I* think so." Timbo stops and I can tell he's really thinking about it. "But the Efron brothers make that theory questionable because Zac's little brother is every bit as ripped as he is."

I finish my set and shake my head at the ridiculousness that is this conversation. I put my dumbbells down and reach up to stretch my insanely sore shoulders. Timbo swaps my thirty pound dumbbells for seventies and then instructs me, "Three sets of eight. Rest for ninety seconds in between. Then a drop set with fifties until fail. You're going to be burning."

I pull the bottom of my shirt up to wipe the sweat off my face and neck. "And by the way, the whole Jamie Fraser-Aragorn-Thor's brother thing...those are three very different vibes and I don't even think they go together. It makes no sense."

"It makes total sense," Timbo argues. "Women fawn over all of them. Jamie for the intense love and adoration of Claire, plus the hair and muscles. And accent I guess. Aragorn because he's...I don't know, majestic as fuck? Also the hair and accent don't hurt. And Thor because, well, Chris Hemsworth."

"Dude, you just named three characters you think I should emulate and they all have long hair and accents. You clearly have a type." I take a sip of my water. "And you do know I'm American, right? *And* playing an American character which means no accent. Plus look at me." I gesture to my head. "I don't have long hair and my role doesn't call for it. Your comparisons suck."

Timbo shakes his head, unconvinced. "You have something better than long hair. You, my friend, have natural curl."

I pick up the weights but before I begin I say, "This is the weirdest conversation we've ever had. And we've had some weird ones." I start my first set.

"You know what's not weird? Natural curl. I have it too, man, and it's like kryptonite for women. They love being able to have a little something to grab onto. And it's low maintenance, unlike Thor's locks." He looks me over. "You should probably grow yours out a little to give them something to imagine putting their fingers in."

I let out a huge exhale and keep going, exasperated with Timbo and this entire conversation.

Timbo lifts his phone up and snaps a picture of me mid shrug.

"What are you doing?" I ask on a strained breath.

"A thirst trap for your traps. It's only fitting."

If he wasn't my best friend of like twenty years, I might actually hate him.

9

EMMA

I am so grateful, so in awe, and...so freaking scared because *I don't know how to act.* I've said like eight lines in one movie. That's it. That's all I've ever done. Besides stand there and be a placeholder for the people who *do* know how to do this.

I don't know how to cry on demand. I'm not even sure I know how to *laugh* on demand. Or maybe even *speak.* Oh god, how can I audition when I don't even know how to do what it is that I am supposed to be auditioning for?

I'm not an actor, though I *have* managed to trick some marquee name directors into thinking I am an undiscovered talent. So actually, maybe I *am* better than I think? I fooled them, after all.

My previous confidence about thinking "anyone could do this" is so far gone I think I'll never find it again. There isn't any time to take classes or hire a coach. I really don't have the money for a coach yet anyways, so that's just wishful thinking.

I look up *cold read audition.*

Oh no.

Ohmygod I don't find out what I'm supposed to say until I walk into the room? That's a thing? How is that a thing? No script ahead of time? No sides in advance for the scene I'm supposed to act out? *Sides* are like a miniature script—they're typically half the size of a regular sheet of paper, stapled together like I could've printed them at home, and they have the lines for whatever scene you're shooting. Not that I have much experience, but so far on every production I've been part of, sides are a given. You get sides for each day—and sometimes for each *scene*—so you can memorize your lines and then brush up between takes. And if the writers or director make any changes to the script, you get new sides that reflect the changes. A script and sides are like a belt and suspenders. And I'm used to having both. *In advance.*

So how on earth do I audition without staring down at the sides the whole time because they're lines I've never seen before? Or is it okay to stare down? That seems like it would make for a terrible audition.

My mind is reeling.

I decide to keep the Google train going and search *what do you wear to an acting audition?* I don't even have any friends in the industry to ask. I'm too new. I've only just moved here. I want to ask my agent/landlord but then I feel like she would know that I have no clue what I'm doing. And probably feel duped. Yeah, it turns out my landlord Marci is a talent agent. Actually, it turns out she's *my* new agent. I name-dropped Dante a time or twenty in front of her, because I knew the weight his name carried. And when Dante did indeed give me a speaking role without being signed to an agency, I used that in a big way.

It went like this:

Me: *Hey Marci? Sorry such a random question but who better to*

*ask than my landlord? Do you know where Midas Soundstages is? I'm
totally lost in this town!*

Marci: *Sure! I'll send you the pin. Something going on over there?
I usually hear about the best functions.*

Me: *No, I'm just shooting this week on Dante Roedner's film and
had no idea where that was. Thank you so much!*

Marci: *You've got a role in Dante's new film? That's incredible.
Who is representing you? Why didn't you tell me you were in the
industry when you signed the lease?*

Me: *I'm not signed yet. Just trying to break into it. Hoping to look
into that next week after I wrap on this. But I know Dante.*

Marci: *Emma, I'm an agent.*

Me: *Really? Well you didn't tell me you were an agent! So we're
even.*

Boom. That's how it's done.

At least I think it is.

I FEEL proud and amused and just maybe a little ashamed
remembering how I low-key convinced Marci that I was worth
signing.

And then I shift my attention to the most important thing in
this moment: Googling Jacob Morrow.

It's homework time.

The search populates and I immediately click on "Images."

And holy hotness. *My god.* He is so sexy I actually lift my
finger to the screen to touch his torso. It's just so...*sculpted*. I can't
help but wonder if it looks like that in real life or if this is some
Photoshop magic. I keep scrolling. He keeps getting hotter. He's
got thick, wavy brown hair that my fingers are instantly itching
to grab onto. And his eyes are a rich, deep brown. Dark and soul-
ful. His skin is literally golden, like the perfect skin-colored

crayon you can never find in the box. Basically, he's Goldilocks. Ripped but not body builder ripped. Mussed hair but not disheveled. Tan but not body oil tan. Hot but not...who am I kidding? He's definitely *too* hot. And apparently he really *is* a big deal in Australia. There are countless fan sites about him. But I can tell he's only just now really blowing up in America. Every news article on him in the U.S. is super recent. I bet he wants to pull a Hemsworth brother and make it big in the States....except for the fact that he actually *is* American.

The level of hotness on the man is criminal. I wonder again if he might actually be an AI creation but when I see all the candid paparazzi shots of him I realize that he's even hotter in those. Walking out of the grocery store in a backward hat and sweats. Getting out of his car with coffee and a book in hand. A *book*? Can you fall in love with someone by just looking at photos?

Probably not.

But can you be massively turned on by someone by just looking at photos?

The dippy feeling below my belly button is a resounding *yes*.

I've got to move on from this before I spiral into Jacob Morrow obsession. Next search: the *Hierarchy* book series. I've heard of it, and I know it's popular, but that's the extent of what I know. I don't know the premise or really even the genre, beyond what Dante and Peter told me.

A quick search tells me that the *Hierarchy* series is insanely popular. Like a worldwide phenomenon. I suddenly feel like I've been living under a rock. Not like fully under one, but partially under one for sure. I've definitely heard of the series, but I didn't know it had a cult following (can you still call it a cult following if the following is huge?). And I hadn't heard that they were adapting it for television. And I obviously didn't know about Jacob Morrow.

Apparently the author tweeted that her pick was for Jacob to play Daniel Teller, the male lead character, in the show. Her rabid fandom took it viral and threatened to boycott the show if he wasn't given the part. They were impassioned about the fact that no one knows Daniel like Lisa Giles—the author—and I guess it worked because the studio made it happen. He's on board as Daniel and also has executive producer billing. I don't know the differences between what makes someone an executive producer and just a producer, but I add that to my ongoing "Things to Google" list.

I don't even have anyone to call and tell about the audition. The gravity of an audition like this when I don't have any experience to my name or know what I'm doing is *definitely* something to share, but I don't have anyone to share it with. Yet. There are a couple people at work I like a lot. We're not really friends yet, but I feel like we're *becoming* friends, which is good because "make some friends" is another thing on my "Get Out of my Comfort Zone" list.

Yeah, I have a lot of lists.

But maybe it's okay that I don't have anyone to tell about this. Because right now I just kind of want to keep it to myself and internally grapple with how I ended up here and how the hell to prepare for this Thursday.

10

EMMA

I 'm sitting in my car before my audition and giving myself the universal car pep talk, telling myself it's more about the opportunity and opening of doors rather than the actual role. I know I can't pull off a lead part even if that is technically what they are bringing me in for so I might as well manage my expectations.

I'm honestly just hoping to land *any* speaking role so I can keep trucking along and keep trying to "make it."

I'm wearing jeans and a white tank to the audition. Classic. Can't really mess up with that combo. At least that's what I told myself after trying on what felt like ten different outfits. I'd worn my hair back in a ponytail, then pulled it down, then back up, then down.

I get out and walk into Suite 102. Except it is less suite and more office building. Nothing like the soundstage and sets I've been on. *Weird.* I wonder if this is always how auditions are.

It hits me again that this is my first.

My first audition. And it is a big one. For a role opposite a guy who is so smoking hot I'm actually worried to see him up close in person. But I assume he might also be a total asshole because who can be that hot and that successful and *still* be nice? Thinking about him being a prick calms me down. Also, let's be honest. I don't think I'll actually see him up close in person anyways, so I can't let myself spiral.

The waiting room is warm. And crowded. *So. Many. Beautiful. Girls.*

And they look so "together." Several of them are doing voice exercises. Some are meditating. Some are running lines silently.

What lines? Do they have the lines? Or are they just running random lines?

I check in and sit down. Yep, I'm literally just sitting here. Not because I don't want to prepare. But because I don't know how to. I don't even know *what* to prepare for.

I pull my hair back up (okay it's final now) and wipe my neck off. *Good god, I'm sweating.* I never sweat. I dab my face with the inside of my shirt. Why didn't I bring a tissue? *Rookie.*

I don't know how long I wait. I don't even pull out my phone to distract myself because I feel like I should stay focused. But I get distracted anyways just watching all the women around me.

"Emma Watts!" a short woman with red cat eye glasses calls out.

Shit. That's me.

I raise my hand and answer, "Here."

I raised my hand and said "Here."

Ohmygod I raised my hand and said "Here."

What an idiot. I'm not in homeroom class or something. I internally facepalm. The cat eye lady gives me a quizzical look. I stand up, walk over, and reach out my hand to shake hers. Another weird look from her.

Okay so I guess that's not something we do at auditions. I make yet another mental note.

She leads me into the room. It is extremely basic. I guess I expected something...nicer? With productions like this costing so much money, this whole place seems so...bland. It's kind of shocking actually.

There are six people sitting in folding chairs at the front of the room. Not even nice chairs—just those cheap folding ones. Some have notepads in hand, some have laptops. Only one even looks up when I walk into the room.

Well okay then.

I kind of just stop walking. I'm not sure where exactly to stop. The red glasses woman stopped walking and I'd continued for a few steps before realizing I should probably stop, too.

"Ready?" I hear from my right.

Followed by a deep, "Yes."

My head snaps in that direction.

What the actual hell? So he's *here? Just standing there? And I hadn't even noticed him?*

I turn to fully face him and *good god* he's blinding. So handsome he doesn't even look real. Except he does because he's not polished. He has scruff, his hair is...not unkempt, but not... *kempt?* It's wavy and thick and a little wild and I *love* it. His eyes are deep pools of the darkest brown. And he kind of just glows, with that golden skin that's really tan, but not like a beach tan. I think that's just the color of his skin. His very attractive skin that I suddenly really, really want to touch.

Am I drooling? I might be drooling. Also, how long have I been standing here salivating over this man?

I give my head a little shake to snap me back into reality. "I'm Emma," I say, holding out my hand.

Dammit I forgot I'm not supposed to do that. Old habits die hard.

He looks at my hand. And then up at me. He extends his arm and and I look down at it. Holy forearms. Holy forearm *veins* to be more precise. I don't know why forearm veins are so hot but they *are*. My gaze follows up his arm and over every arm muscle in existence. This guy is like the perfect male specimen or something. I'm having a hard time remembering why I'm even here.

His hand wraps around mine in a firm shake. "I'm Jacob."

I'm so glad he didn't do that flimsy handshake guys often do when they shake a woman's hand. Like the one where they kind of hold your fingers and put their other hand on top and give you a tiny lift up and down.

That's not even a shake. It always drives me nuts.

Jacob just shook mine like I could've been his boss. I *like* that.

I quickly glance down his jean-clad body and back up over his white t-shirt. "We match." I state it like we're seventh grade besties. I mean, I'm in a scoop neck and his is a v-neck, but we are basically twinning.

He breathes out a laugh. "Great minds and all that."

Suddenly a man in sneakers and what can only be described as an old school windbreaker claps his hands together. "Okay let's go."

A different lady stands up and motions for me to come towards the front of the room. She hands me the sides for the scene.

Oh my god what do I do now? I knew it was a cold read and I know what a cold read is thanks to my trusty BFF Google, but I've never done one and suddenly now it seems both impossible and like it makes absolutely zero sense. Like, why wouldn't they *want* to give you the lines ahead of time? To see what you could do with practice? Because if you're hired for a part, you get the lines ahead of time to learn. It's not like shooting a show is going to be a cold read situation. You'll know your lines. All I can think is how backwards this whole situation is.

But that's all I have time to think because suddenly Jacob's voice rings out, "What do you mean you don't know if you want me?"

Um, come again now? I turn back toward him. He's looking at me. Yep, he is looking at me.

And waiting. He is waiting. Ohmygod he is waiting on *me*.

He flashes me the tiniest grin and an exaggeratedly impatient look as if to say *C'mon, you're up.*

"What do you mean you don't know if you want me?" he repeats.

"I-I..." I stammer. How do people do this? Am I supposed to be mad? Sad? Turned on? Scared? How do I know?

I scan the page quickly. A few words stick out to me. *Scared. Unnerved.*

Okay so I'm going with upset. It sounds like she's upset. I feel like Joey and Chandler playing the game to win the girls' apartment.

Monica categories her towels. How many categories are there?

Ughhhh eleven?

Eleven? Unbelievable. Eleven is correct!

I steel myself, gathering all my resolve. *It's worth a shot,* I think to myself.

"Well I know I don't want *this* version of you," I counter, with a touch of anger in my voice.

Okay so I guess *eleven* was right. Because he continues.

"I thought this is who you wanted me to be." He steps closer. "This is the version *you* molded. You're right—it's *not* me. But you made me think it was who you wanted, so it's who I became."

"I think...I think I *did* think that," I respond. "I think I *did* want you to change. You scared me. You were too much for me. Way too much. And your words are so...*sharp*. That unnerves me. I'm not used to people speaking to me like you do."

I swear to god I think I levitate. Yeah, I'm pretty sure I actually lift out of my body and just watch the rest of the audition. If this isn't an out-of-body experience, I'm not sure what is.

"What are you used to people speaking to you like?" he presses, taking another step closer to me.

It takes me a second to snap back into it. I repeat his words in my head so I know where to pick back up since I've completely lost my place. "I don't know. More...respectful. Like being more ginger with my feelings or something," I hear myself saying aloud.

"You don't think I've been...respectful? I've wanted to tear your clothes off since the very first day I met you and I haven't so much as made a single move!" He's basically shouting at me. "I've been nothing if not respectful!"

What. Just. Happened.

I literally feel his words in my stomach. Way below my belly button. Like, I *feel them* feel them.

And I know they aren't real but they sure feel real. Damn, he's good.

I swallow. Hard. So hard I think it may be audible. But no one moves, including Jacob, so maybe it was a normal decibel swallow.

I look down at my sides. And then I shout back, yelling out *my* next lines, too. "God, Daniel! Like I said. You're too much! You're too brazen when I need you to be respectful and too respectful when I want you to be anything but that!"

He challenges, "So sometimes I'm not enough of a gentleman and sometimes I'm too much of one?" He closes the gap between us with that sentence, leaving only about six inches between our faces.

It feels like we're supposed to kiss.

Ohmygod do people kiss during auditions? How do I know when we're done? Are there more words?

I want to glance down at the sides in my hand but I can't seem to break his eye contact. He's unflinching.

I don't know what to do.

The room is so hot. I'm hot. I can feel the sweat beads at the base of my neck. I've noticeably sweated twice today and I normally never break a sweat. Not even a small one. And my hands are getting clammy.

Am I going to pass out?

How long have I been standing here silent? Seconds? Oh god, *minutes?*

I finally look down. I scan for his last words. "...too much of one?" I see my next line.

I decide to just dive in because I'm already so far in over my head. Yep, I'm totally in the deep end. And just treading water to stay afloat. I've just got to keep my head up, right? Isn't that the entire point of treading water?

I drop the sides. Like literally drop them to the ground. I just let them fall out of my hand. And I step forward, though there is hardly anywhere to step because we are already pretty close. So I lift my chin up, bring my lips to about two inches from touching his own, and then whisper, "Yes, that's exactly what I'm saying." I whisper partially because I think it would be weird to speak loudly when I'm *thisclose* to his face, and partially because I don't think I could find my full voice if I tried.

I don't move. I just stay there. Holding it. Because I literally don't know what else to do.

I guess I'm waiting for someone to say "End scene!" or something. Or for him to move. For someone to...well I guess not clap, but just somehow signal that we're done. That had been the last line on the sides. But no one moves. So I stay a beat longer and then, with my eyes still holding his and my lips still essentially *on* his, say "Thank you." Then I turn to the front of the room. "Thank you so much."

The good news is they all have their heads up. So they'd at least watched.

The bad news is the looks on their faces...well they're not smiling.

But they're not...*not* smiling either.

11

JAKE

Well, we found her.

We just found our Annabelle Claiborne.

I'm staring at this girl mere inches away from me who just rocked this entire room with her performance. I can *feel* it. I side eye the front of the room and register the expressions on everyone's faces. Clearly they can feel it, too. Everyone from our producers to the author Lisa to our casting director looks as floored as I am.

What *was* that? What did she even just do? I've never had an audition go quite like that. She just...went for it. She was so *raw*. She yelled at me. She threw her sides on the floor. She almost kissed me. I thought she was going to. *Hoped* she was going to. Not that I want to be making out in front of a room of industry professionals, but I'd be lying if I said I wasn't dying to taste her after having her lips that close to mine.

I'm just standing here, unmoving, staring at her. Everyone is staring at her.

I don't think anyone has said a word.

I clear my throat.

And this girl—*Emma*—turns abruptly and heads to the door.

"Wait!" I hold my hand up as hers closes around the door handle. She turns to look back at me, but I can't find any words. She's just so unnerving. Beautiful. It's hard to look right at her and yet it's impossible to look away. Dark blonde hair in a casual ponytail with pieces floating down around her face. And I don't even think the loose hair framing her face is intentional. It looks like she threw her hair in a ponytail and didn't try to do a perfect one. She's got light brown eyes with flecks of green and gold that seemed to darken and lighten with the spectrum of emotion during her audition. Full lips, but natural. She has on minimal makeup, probably because she just doesn't need it, and is wearing jeans and a white top. Simple and yet a thousand times sexier than the showy outfits most of the other women auditioning today have been wearing. She's probably five foot seven or eight, and I love that she wore sneakers and not heels to try and enhance her height.

I just can't stop staring at her and it's taking all my willpower not to scan my eyes over her entire body. But she's holding eye contact with me and she would absolutely see my eyes divert to take in her full self.

When she realizes I'm not going to say anything, she tilts her head with a smile and walks out.

That *smile*. It's disarming. I think it might be the entire room's undoing.

As the door closes behind her, I look to the row of people sitting in front of me and say simply, "*Her*. It's got to be her."

They nod in unison.

With that assurance, my stomach bottoms out. I'm so relieved, so happy we found Annabelle. But I'm equal parts nervous because how the hell am I supposed to work with that girl every day when running lines with her for five minutes makes me want to succumb to my baser instincts and see if I can make her yell for entirely different reasons?

Casting her will either be the greatest decision or the worst move of my life. I think the show will be a success with her at the helm, *and* I think there's a strong chance that I've just sentenced myself to years of self-inflicted torture.

Only one way to find out, I guess.

12

EMMA

I don't know the protocol for what to do after you finish an audition, and no one said anything to me except for when Jacob asked me to wait but then didn't say a word after that, so I literally just walked out of the room, straight through the holding area, and out to my car.

I climb in and immediately give thanks for the tint on my windows, hoping it will provide at least a shred of privacy. I drop my head to the steering wheel and take a few breaths. Part of me wants to cry but the whole thing was so ridiculous that I can't help but laugh.

I sit in silence while I just try to achieve some type of internal equilibrium which feels impossible at the moment because I am absolutely reeling. This flood of unsettling emotions requires a car sit. There's nothing like a good car sit. I am a master of car sits. My parents used to leave me in the car all the time so I became quite adept at car sits at a very young age. It's when I get some of my best thinking done.

But in this exact moment, thinking about that audition makes me uneasy because I am quite sure I blew it and didn't even do things correctly. I yelled at him, which feels like an obvious bad move. But it felt right in the moment. I moved in like I was going to kiss him, which feels wrong because the script didn't call for it. But that *also* felt right in the moment. I dropped the sides to the ground. Is that even allowed? Was it disrespectful? Or will they know I was just in the moment?

I finally emotionally recalibrate enough to drive, but as I begin to back out my reverse camera alarm starts to sound immediately. I glance in the rearview mirror and oh man—a guy is walking right behind my car—and I'd gotten way too close to him. I roll my window down and shout, "Oh my gosh, I'm so sorry!" and reach to shift my car into park but before I even can he pops his head in the window.

Holy heartthrob. It's Jacob Morrow. With his head almost in my car.

I stare at him and repeat "I. Am. So. Sorry."

"No problem." He laughs it off, shrugging. "But if you kill me there will be no show for you to star in." Then he drums his fingers on the roof of my car and hesitates there like that, like he's about to say something. But when he doesn't immediately speak I panic a bit and barely let my foot off the brake. I start to drift backward and he jumps back, holding his hands up as if in surrender. "Wow, so you've *really* got places to be, huh?"

I squeeze my eyes shut then blink them open. Yep, this is real. "Oh, you know—just trying to get out of here before I add to my track record of almost kissing you, then almost backing into you, then almost driving over your foot."

"Yeah things do seem to be getting progressively worse for me."

I nod.

"But I like the way they started."

Cue the stomach swoop.

I let out an uneasy laugh, then continue to back out. I've *got* to get out of here. I finish backing up, yell "See ya later!" and then immediately feel like a dummy. Like how when the ticket person at the movie theater says "Enjoy the movie" and I always respond "You too!" out of habit. *See ya later?* Not likely. Why didn't I just say "Bye?"

As I shift into drive and start to pull away, Jacob nods and says with a tilt of those full lips, "Yeah I think you will."

13

EMMA

That audition ignited something in me. It was fun and exciting and scary and unnerving and *addictive*. Whereas I didn't care so much before and I was just trying to do this whole acting thing because, well, *why not?*—now I want to do it because I freaking *want* to do it. The whole experience is pretty intoxicating.

I spend the next few days researching acting classes. Coaches. Improv clubs. Working shifts at Stella's.

Marci has been submitting me for things but I haven't gotten any calls yet.

Until today that is. The phone rings and although I have yet to save him to contacts, I immediately recognize the 310 number as Peter's.

"Hey, Emma, they want to see you back. They'll talk to your agent about a call back but I just wanted to congratulate you. Sounds like you made an impression on casting!"

I don't blink, much less speak.

"Emma?"

"Are you for real?"

He laughs. "Yes."

I'm not convinced. "A callback for that role or a callback for a different part?"

"I don't know yet. But a callback is a callback. They wouldn't do it if they didn't like you. Keep me posted."

A half hour later I get a call from Marci relaying the news Peter had already shared with me, and this time I ask some questions. Callback-specific questions. A girl's got to be prepared. And I figure that since I'd secured a callback she'll be less alarmed at all my questions. Basically, she says it'll be very similar to the audition. That they're just trying to narrow it down. Her final advice is to "just do exactly what you did at your audition and you'll be fine because that worked!"

But the problem is that I don't *know* what I did. I just kind of floated outside of my body and then my body did the audition. I was both very unsure and very turned on during the whole thing. How do you repeat that?

Two days later I strip off the midi dress I'd picked for my callback. The dress was easy and casual but I just didn't feel fully confident in it. And I kind of feel like I should wear something a little different but look the same-ish so I'll be recognizable. So I throw on jeans—but different ones—and a black tank (how creative) and this time I decide to wear my hair half up as a compromise.

I make my way back to the nondescript office building, sit down and wait my turn. There are only a handful of us this time. Beautiful girls. Confident girls.

And then there's me.

I sit and wait while the other girls get called in one by one. Each minute that passes makes me more anxious. I wish I'd been first so my nerves wouldn't have a chance to get the best of me.

After the last girl before me walks out of the audition room, I stand up to get ready but the red cat glasses lady pops out to tell me they need a moment and aren't ready for me yet.

Another round of anxiety tops me off. I'm overflowing with it at this point.

I wait.

And wait.

Until finally the door opens and the windbreaker guy from the first audition says, "Come on in, Emma." He's not wearing a windbreaker today, but he is wearing a full on sweatsuit.

He knows my name.

I'm briefly flattered until I realize he'd read it off the list on his clipboard. *Oh.*

"Good to see you again." I nod with a smile as I stride through the door. This time there are eleven chairs up front. A few new faces. Some familiar ones. One *really* familiar one.

Jacob Morrow is sitting up there.

So he'll be watching today? Oh. My heart sinks a little. It makes me nervous to think of him watching me. Plus, I liked reading with him.

The windbreaker sweatsuit guy sits down and gestures to a lady a few seats down from him. "Miriam will be your counterpart." He holds out the sides to me. I walk up and take them, quickly scanning them as fast as I can.

"Ready when you are, Emma."

I take a few steps back and nod.

A woman sitting third from the left shifts in her seat before reading the lines. "Can you believe we got away? I bet we couldn't do it again if we tried a million times." Her voice is robotic.

Ohhhhhh. So *that's* what sweatsuit guy meant. Miriam is being Jacob's role. Well that's quite a curve ball. How on earth am I supposed to show the same emotions with her? She doesn't turn me on and she sounds slightly dead inside.

I give it my best shot. "Tell me about it. I've never moved that fast in my life. Or stayed that quiet. Well, I might've stayed that quiet once or twice under...different circumstances..." I trail off and then smirk at her like the scene calls for.

Okay so this is weird.

"Very different circumstances," she deadpans. She was supposed to emphasize *very* but she didn't.

Cool.

"Do you think they'll come back for us?" I ask in a slightly quieter voice.

"Yes. They'll be back."

Could they have picked a more boring person to run lines with? She's not even trying.

"When?" I whisper.

"At first light," she responds at normal volume.

But the sides indicate that we're both supposed to be hushed. She's not playing the part at all. I can feel frustration start to creep in.

"Well what should we do?" I continue to whisper, because even if I can't act I *can* freaking follow directions, unlike ole Miriam up there.

I see a quick movement up front and then hear a quiet "Make tonight count," in a deep voice that sends an immediate wave of heat through my body.

It's Jacob.

It takes me just a second to regain my composure before I

continue, "We're basically experts at that by now. We've thought we were going to die so many times before that we..."

"...know how to make it count?" I can hear the grin in his voice.

"Yes." I feel like I'm floating again. "But I'm always down to practice, you know, just to make sure."

"Practice does make perfect." Jacob is still sitting up there sandwiched between everyone and their mom, but he's making me feel like I'm the only other person in the room.

I quirk a brow at him. "That's awfully temp—"

Sneaker guy claps his hands together, cutting me off, and says simply, "Thank you, Emma."

Yet again, I don't know what to do. I'm standing there alone this time and I swear I almost bow. *Almost.* Thank god I catch myself and spare everyone that humiliation. Instead I once again thank the room and close with a wave as I leave the room.

Yep, I wave goodbye. Like I'm a little kid leaving the playground or something.

But just as I turn my back, I catch Jacob's wave back.

THREE DAYS later I'm in the shower when I hear my phone ring. It stops then starts again. Then *again.* I panic thinking there must be some type of emergency with someone or something. But I also am fully aware that I am nobody's emergency contact. I mean, who would I even be an emergency contact for? I lean out of the shower, soaking wet, and grab my phone. It's Marci. "Hello?" I shout, worry consuming me.

"Emma, it's Marci. Are you sitting down?"

"No, I'm standing up and soaking wet from the shower. But I'm listening. What's up? You scared me to death. Did I get an audition?"

"No" she says.

My heart sinks.

"You got a *part*. You got THE part."

My phone starts vibrating in my hand. It's Dante.

"What do you mean?" I ask Marci, not believing what I'm hearing. Not even for a second.

"You got the role of Annabelle Claiborne in *Hierarchy*."

Crickets.

"Emma are you there?"

More crickets.

"Emma?"

"Yeah." I swallow. "I'm here...I'm here."

"Congratulations! This is HUGE! Your first lead role! This series has been on the best seller lists forever! It could be huge. It could be *Game of Thrones* big. *Bridgerton* big. *The Summer I Turned Pretty* big."

Marci is going absolutely postal in the best way.

But I can't even take her words in. *How?* is all I can think. *How* did this happen? *How* did I do it? *How* is this my life?

Marci hasn't stopped jabbering in excitement. "You start pre-production in three months. Enjoy your time before you begin. Series like this can be grueling to film. We're waiting on the full contract terms, but I'm so happy for you."

"Thank you so much, Marci. Thank you so, so much."

I hang up and sit down, dripping wet, on my bed. I have a new voicemail. It's from Dante.

You did it, kid. You blew them away. I knew you had it in you. This thing might be huge. Congrats. I'm happy for you. And then I hear another voice follow Dante's. *We're so happy for you!* It's Peter, absolutely yelling into the phone. *Hope you're ready to be famous, Emma Watts.*

How did I do this? How did I fake everyone out? How did I

convince people that I could actually be good at this? I start to panic. I feel like a farce. A phony. A liar.

I turn the shower back on. And cry my eyes out. I feel so confused. Complete ecstasy mixed with crippling doubt. I stay in the shower until the water washes it all away, which never happens so I stay in until the water gets cold.

And I guess now I know why people love cold plunges so much. Because by the time I finally get out of the shower, I'm freezing but weirdly refreshed and with a much clearer mind.

So I guess I'm an actress now.

14

EMMA

It's been two months since I got the phone call telling me I got the part of Annabelle Claiborne.

The studio wanted to keep my casting a secret until pre-production when we do all the promo shots and the glamour begins (or so I'm told). My agent Marci actually agreed with the decision because she was afraid the book's rabid fan base would dissect me and start an online petition like book purists tend to do...and possibly sway the studio and cost me the role in the process.

Yes, I do have a contract. But according to Marci, studios have extremely deep pockets and contracts get broken all the time.

The news that they'd cast a newcomer for the role of Annabelle leaked immediately. And of course the speculation ever since has been endless, with the casting mystery "solved" every week with a new actress's name attached. It's been a whole thing.

But since I'm not even in pre-production yet and my casting has somehow remained a secret, it's been...not really a thing at all. My life is unchanged.

Like I said before, this industry is so weird.

Marci says the studio will shoot tons of promotional material and do a big reveal. Like an *Introducing Emma Watts, our Annabelle Claiborne* type of thing to make me look like I'm the perfect fit for the part. I guess they don't think grainy paparazzi pics of me heading into my server job or bebopping around L.A. in yoga pants and a ponytail will seal the deal with the fans. They're probably not wrong.

So basically no one knows.

Well except for everyone involved in the deal, everyone at the studio, and of course Jacob Morrow, plus whoever he told and swore to secrecy.

But that's all.

Wellll, except my friends Mandy and Sal. But I swore them to secrecy, too. The studio made everyone involved sign NDAs, so they are definitely not telling anyone because it would be very serious for me to break that contract. Which I obviously did in telling them. But they won't mess up—because we're friends. Yep, that's the one thing in my life that actually *has* changed. I have friends now. Real life friends.

dusts off shoulders

I've never really had solid friends. It's hard to form connections with people when you're constantly jumping school districts and never stay at a school for even a full semester. I've had casual friends, sure, but none of those lifelong friendships I see others carry with them through each phase of their life.

But I'm low-key hoping that will change with Mandy and Sal. My *friends.* Two drop dead gorgeous beings also trying to "make it" in this business. Mandy, with her dark red hair and a light smattering of freckles across her nose and upper cheeks.

Very Taylor Swift glitter freckle vibes, but Mandy's are real. And Sal with his six foot four self, dark blonde hair and piercing blue eyes. He looks like a giant surfer boy. They're amazing. And they're pretty much doing exactly what I've been doing: serving at a restaurant (literally the same restaurant), taking acting classes (literally the same acting classes), and living in shoeboxes. And not like those big knee high boot boxes—more like a super thin flip flop box.

It's refreshing though because they "get it." They get *it*. This whole weird lifestyle. I had to tell them I'd been cast in *Hierarchy* because I suddenly stopped going to auditions. Because I didn't *need* to anymore. And they demanded an explanation. They thought I was giving up on my (very short-lived) dream. They three-way called me because they were too nervous to discuss it in person, and I finally broke and told them why I never needed them to cover my shifts anymore and why I had stopped auditioning. They absolutely freaked out. Mandy actually fainted. I heard the thud through the phone. Then I cried and panicked because she wouldn't answer us. It was a whole thing. She has apparently read the series three times through, so it hit her hard. And she swears she "can see it"—me playing Annabelle, that is. I'm glad someone can, because I sure as hell can't see it yet.

Since they know all about *Hierarchy* and how big of a production it's going to be, they keep telling me they'll drop me like I'm hot the second I act un-relatable.

They can't believe I've kept my job working at Stella's, but I'm not about to give the cash up. I live in a shoebox, and I'd like to upgrade to something more like a stove box at some point. Or hell, even a refrigerator box. I make great money at Stella's, for serving anyways. It's the "it" restaurant and it was hard to land a job here. I don't want to give it up yet. Because I mean, nothing is guaranteed, right? The studio could change its mind about me, and then where would I be? I don't think I'll believe it's a real thing until we actually shoot the first scene.

So I've had two months to live it up, make money, and enjoy a pretty free schedule. And I've got one month to go until I start my "real" job. Which kind of seems like a fake job if I'm being honest. Because I'll basically just be playing make believe. Day after day. But it's oh so real, because I will be making *real* money. Life-changing money. *<insert emoji praise hands here>* But also, I'm not mad about the wad of cash in my pocket after every shift at Stella's. It's the best part of serving and bartending. IYKYK.

Still, I can't wait to start making *grown up* money. Like the kind of money that takes you off the day-by-day track. I was born on that track and have never found my way off of it. To be honest, I wasn't sure I ever would.

I'm utterly shook by how much money is in this industry. It's ridiculous how much they pay you to pretend. My contract is money I never dreamed of, and yet I know it still doesn't even touch what Jacob is getting paid for this series.

Yeah, I like to think of myself as a super strong female thanks to a lifetime of having to prove that I could in fact do it—whatever that *it* may be. And I'd love to say I demanded equal pay to my male counterpart, but let's be real: I'm just happy to be out on the field. It wouldn't be wise for me—with barely two credits to my name (and minor ones at that)—to come in guns blazing demanding pay equity with the hottest thing to come out of Australia since Thor. That would've been delusional.

I know equal pay is a hot button topic right now, but the bottom line is that I'm super happy to just be part of this whole thing. I signed a three year contract and if I blow them away with my previously untested acting skills, I can always negotiate a higher pay if the series gets renewed. Honestly, I'm thrilled to be locked into a three year contract. I hope it makes it hard for them to fire me when they find out I'm a phony.

And in the meantime before we start shooting, I'd rather be making *something*. Plus, I have all this free time now that I don't need to go to auditions. And I *like* working at the restaurant. Mandy, Sal and I work together. It's fun. And with any extra time I have, I go to yoga (because in the books, Annabelle shows some skin) and acting classes and improv nights because I still feel like the world's biggest impostor. I mean, I'm honestly still not sure I even know how to act. I keep feeling like I've fooled everyone.

So while a lot has changed, kind of nothing has.

Yet.

I still work at the restaurant. I still live in my tiny but cute apartment. I still drive the same car.

I still do the same things I did before I was cast. Sure, some of the big agencies started calling and trying to poach me when I was cast opposite "Hollywood's newest heartthrob" because though my casting is a secret to the bigger world, the rumblings get around in the surprisingly very small L.A. world. But my loyalty lies with Marci because she believed in me—or more accurately—she *believed me* when I acted like I knew what I was doing. Foolish woman but God bless her.

I've got another month of my normal life and then we'll see if my life *actually* changes. It's so weird constantly being told I'm on the cusp of huge change. Weird and *familiar*. I can't count the number of times I've been told my life was about to change.

Spoiler alert: it never did.

15

JAKE

T minus twenty-seven days until I get to see her again.

Actually, let me reframe that.

T minus twenty-seven days until we begin preproduction for *Hierarchy*. Not that I've been counting down.

Okay, I've been keeping a caveman-style tally mark countdown on my wall.

Wall. Dry erase board. Basically the same.

I'm revved up to start shooting. This experience has already been worlds apart from *Sunset Cove*. It feels good to be a boss. Not even going to act like it's no big deal. It's a huge fucking deal. I love having some control over things.

I can't wait to get things moving. We have a killer team in place for the show, from the ground up to the top. And the top? God, she's perfect. She's going to be the key to this whole thing. I'd like to think *I* am, but I know she will be the one who elevates the entire series.

Emma Watts.

I haven't seen her since her callback. We already knew we were going to cast her, but that second audition sealed the deal. I haven't spoken to her since she walked out that day. I could've. I probably *should've*. I don't have her number, but let's be honest —I could've easily gotten it through my agent, the studio, basically anyone. I don't have it because I didn't ask for it. And I didn't ask for it because I couldn't figure out how to just casually text her. I mean, what do I say?

Hey this is Jake, the guy from the new show you're going to be shooting. Want to grab a bite to eat and get to know each other?

Actually, that would've been perfect. Dammit. I'm an idiot.

And Timbo has given me hell for the past couple months because I've complained about not having her number but yet wouldn't ask for it. He said I was being immature. Actually, I think his exact words were, "Grow the fuck up and stop acting like a scared teenager."

I did try to find her on Instagram, but she's nowhere to be found. I searched every combo of her first and last name and initials possible, and nothing came up. Nothing that was her anyways.

But I'll see her soon enough, because the countdown is on. We've been prepping. The script is fantastic. Emma's agent, Marci, has communicated that Emma is working with an acting coach to ensure she'll be ready. I kind of wish she wasn't though, because I don't want her to change anything about the way she acts. She's so authentic. *Real.* I don't want a coach to coach that out of her.

Timbo has been punishing me in the gym almost daily. I despise him for it, but love him for the results because damn the regimen he wrote for me has worked and then some. Daniel Teller is keeping it tight, that's for sure.

I'm thinking about whether my current fitness level is sustainable once we start shooting when my phone rings. It's my sister, Lilah.

"Hey sis. What's up?"

"I need you to quit your job."

"What?"

"Jake, I love you and you're talented, but I cannot have you play Daniel Teller."

I chuckle. "Wait so did you finally read it?"

"Yep. Finished the whole series."

"Oh you did? Man that was quick. What'd you think?"

"Well I'm obsessed. I didn't know I was a fantasy girl but turns out I am."

"*Roman*tasy," I say, emphasizing the beginning of the word.

"Ohhhh, well excuse me. Is that what they call it? *Romantasy*?"

"Yep. I mean, I didn't know that before, but now I consider myself well-versed in the romantasy world. So you liked it?"

"Yeah, so much so that I'm calling to ask you to bow out of the project."

I laugh again. "Why?"

"Because Daniel Teller is a desirable stud and I just swooned for him through six books. And you didn't tell me this series was so sexy. But it is. And I just can't have my brother ruining this whole series for me. It will be too weird to have you play a character that I am attracted to. I don't think I'll even be able to watch the show."

"Oh come on, you've got to watch it. That's a copout. You watched every episode of *Sunset Cove* and I wasn't winning any awards for my acting in that."

"Yeah, but I didn't fall in love with your character on *Sunset Cove* before you started shooting. I think anyone who has ever read the *Hierarchy* series has a mad crush on Daniel. And Annabelle, for that matter. Because damn, she sounds incredible."

"I know."

Lilah lets out a sigh. "Okay okay, you'll be amazing at this part. I mean, I think you were made for it. Sucks for me, but I'm really excited for you."

"Thanks sis. I'm going to try to do him justice. Timbo at least has me looking the part, that's for sure."

"I bet," Lilah says. "And for the record, your Annabelle better be a gorgeous badass. I mean, I've seen her in the snapshot you sent and she's definitely stunning, but she better be a badass woman, too. Or at least play the part that way."

"Oh I think you'll be happy with her as Annabelle," I say, knowing the girl will deliver. It's only a matter of time before the world is obsessed with Emma Watts. Including my sister. I'm not sure anyone will be immune to her.

"TBD. I'll let you know after I see more of her. But you two better have chemistry. Like sizzling chemistry. Otherwise the book readers will hate you. Including me."

"I'll keep that in mind." I say, rolling my eyes. But I know she's right. And I also know we *do* have that chemistry. Maybe even too much chemistry. That's the real TBD.

"Any chance you can have your double shoot the sexy scenes so I can still watch them with heart-shaped eyes?" I can tell by her voice that she's completely serious.

I scoff. "Not a chance. Besides, there's no nudity or anything. You don't have to worry," I assure her, knowing full well there is no way I'm going to give up my chance to be close with Emma like that.

"Okay but you will be making sexy sounds and I absolutely do not need to hear that from my brother. Gross."

"Grow up, Lilah."

"I *am* grown, which is why I love the steamy tension in this book, you big dummy."

"If the series goes like I think it will, you'll love the show, too. I've gotta run. Talk soon?"

"Sounds good. Love you."

"Love you, too," I say as I push *end*.

16

EMMA

Twenty-two days to go before my life is supposed to change forever. Until then, I'm working as many shifts as I can.

I clock in, get my tables ready, and then chat with Mandy and Sal until we open for lunch. I worked brunch yesterday and raked it in. I don't resent working here. I have fun. It's one of the prominent "it" places in town—like The Ivy hot spot I used to always hear about. *(Is that place still a thing?)*

Stars come here often. Usually they sit out on the patio so they can be seen and then feign annoyance at being seen....*out front on the patio.* I mean, come on. And if someone famous wants to *act* like they want privacy, they'll sit inside in the dining room but get that coveted paparazzi shot on the way through the front entrance.

And if someone famous wants to come eat to well, actually *eat* (because our food is banging), they'll sit in the back courtyard and enter through the back entrance. Those are my favorite ones. Because they actually don't want the press. They really do want the privacy. And we provide that for them.

Which is exactly what happens today when the FOH (front of house) manager Deb briefs us that we have four VIPs coming in during lunch. She never tells us the names. I have no idea why not. I think because it makes her feel powerful to be the only one who knows. I personally think it'd be good for us to be prepared for who's coming, but Deb's the boss.

"Sal and Seth, you're out front today. Mandy and Tarot, you're inside. Emma and Ashley, you're out back."

Dammit. Ashley is not my cup of tea. She is such a kiss ass. To any and everyone whose ass she thinks needs to be kissed. And a flirt. A huge one. With any and everyone she thinks can help her. Yes, she wants to be an actress, too. And yeah, Tarot wants to be an actor, too. And obviously Mandy and Sal do, too. It's kind of a thing. We're in L.A. after all. But Seth? Seth is just here because the money is really, really good. For serving.

Anyways, I don't love working with Ashley. We just don't really gel.

Deb continues, "Two VIPs in the back, one inside and one out front. Emma, Ashley, Seth and Tarot. Tables 9, 14, 5 and 3."

The front courtyard is the only place we never sit more than one VIP. Because in the front, they go there to be seen. Not to share the attention. When their handlers make their reservations, they make sure of that.

We'll seat more than one VIP inside, but we'll stagger their reservations so their arrivals don't overlap and they each get the shots they want.

We almost always have multiple VIPs in the back courtyard at a time because none of them care about the attention, or lack thereof. The courtyard is for the people who truly don't give a shit about being seen. They come to Stella's for the discretion (the courtyard might as well be a separate restaurant) and the food (it is genuinely delicious).

Which is why I love working the back patio. I get put back there a lot. Because I'm...how do I put it? *Chill*, I guess. Calm. I don't twirl my hair at the George Clooneys or stare with thinly veiled jealousy at the Sydney Sweeneys.

I leave that to Ashley. Which is why I'm so shocked she's out there with me today. She is the exact opposite of chill. She's hot. Wait, that's not what I'm trying to say. I mean she *is* hot, but I don't want to give her that because she's just honestly such an insincere human. *Okay think, Emma, think*—opposite of chill, opposite of chill...She's....smoking? Dammit. On fire?

This game sucks.

She's just *not* chill.

And to prove it as if on cue, approximately thirteen seconds later she spots "her" VIP being seated at Table 14 and squeals.

"OH. MY. GOD. Oh my god! You won't believe who just sat at my table!"

Is she talking to me? I look around me. Seems like it.

I shrug. "Matt Damon?" It's a worthy guess. He comes in often with his beautiful wife and I love them both. And not just because she used to be a server and he fell in love with her and gave hope to all us lowly servers with their whole happily ever after situation...that has absolutely *nothing* to do with it. I swear.

"*Lame*," She says with an exaggerated eye roll. "I'd rather have Ben."

Of course she would. I, on the other hand, would not. We're very different, Ashley and me.

I humor her and ask, "Who then?"

"JACOB FREAKING MORROW."

A plate crashes to the floor and shatters.

WAS IT ME? Did I drop it?

No, it was Sal. And it wasn't *a* plate. It was a *stack* of plates. His eyes catch mine. Wide as saucers. "Holy shit," he mouths.

I'm just a few weeks away from the news coming out.

Long story short: Ashley has no idea. No idea that I'm about to star in a show with Jacob.

And I don't know whether to be mortified and hide from this man I'm about to costar with so he doesn't see that I'm working at a restaurant and realize how unqualified I really am...or to just own it and wave hi. Or maybe even pretend I don't recognize him. Or I could also pretend I'm *not* me if he recognizes me.

Or maybe I should just quit my job here right this second.

The latter option might win. I could quit today and make it a month. They gave me an advance when I signed my contract, but I was saving that. Trying to be all adult and shit and not quit this job the day I got the call about *Hierarchy*. Because what if it all falls through and I've already given up this source of income which pays my rent a few times over?

I make my decision. Yep, I have enough saved to float me. I'm out.

"Ohhhh no you don't."

It's Mandy. Flanked by Sal.

"We know what you're thinking." Mandy places her hands on her hips. The universal *I mean business* signal.

"And *how* do you know what I'm thinking?" I counter.

"Because you're literally untying your apron right now." Sal looks down at my waist and back up at me.

I look down at where my hands have loosened my server apron strings.

"And you're not going to do that. We're not going to let you,"

Mandy says in a strong but quiet voice, so no one overhears. She ties my apron back. "Let me see if Deb will let me switch with you."

"Ha, you think you're going to be the one server she's ever let switch...*ever*? She didn't even let Mark switch when the guy who sued his entire family and basically stole their family empire got sat in his section." (By the way, that was WILD. Needless to say, Mark no longer works here and isn't allowed within 100 feet of the restaurant. Also, I'm totally Team Mark.)

Mandy's eyes harden. "I think I can convince her." Oh sweet, delusional Mandy.

Then Sal speaks up, trying to whisper but it turns out he's not great at it. "Okay, shut the hell up. Both of you. Emma—you stay right where you are. I vote that you walk right out there and say a casual hi on the way to your tables."

"And then what?" I ask incredulously. "TTFN?" I shake my head. "That's ridiculous."

Sal furrows his brows. "What the hell is *TTFN?*"

"Tata for now!" Mandy and I both say in unison. Yeah, we're the same age and it shows.

Deb pops her head around the drink station and whisper yells, "Emma! Get out there. 9 just sat down."

I peek through the window out to the courtyard. Allison Jones? OMG. I love her. Like *love* her. She and Kristen Bell are top tier for me.

"Screw it. I'm going out."

"That's my girl!" I hear Sal loud whisper behind me.

I go out, walk straight to my table, greet Allison and her friends, take their drink orders, turn around and...

He is staring at me. *Hard.* So hard I feel like he can see through my clothes which is impossible because my black jumper is thick and totally opaque. I've been out here two minutes and my back was to him for 100 of those 120 seconds.

How could he be that quick? Maybe he doesn't *recognize* me. Maybe he just thinks I look familiar and he's trying to place me.

His nose scrunches and his left eyebrow lifts.

Oh he recognizes me all right. I can read it all over his face. Well here goes nothing.

I walk straight up to him, do an arguably awkward lean against his table and say casually, "What's up Jacob? Long time no see."

He raises both eyebrows now and starts to open his mouth and I panic about what he might say so before he can say anything I blurt out, "See ya soon! In just a few weeks, huh? *Crazy.*" And then for reasons absolutely inexplicable to me, I give him two thumbs up. Not even one. *Two.*

Like I'm freaking Siskel and Ebert or something.

I walk back in, ring in Allison's order and feel someone too close behind me.

"What...*WAS*...that?" I turn to look at Sal, who looks utterly mortified on my behalf.

I let out a groan.

"Thanks, Sal. You're the one who encouraged me, ya big jerk."

"I didn't encourage you to do *that.*"

Deb's voice cuts in sharply. "EMMA! You know we do not talk to other VIP tables. Ever. That's VIP 101. And Ashley said you just talked to 14."

Of course she did.

But *talked* is putting it loosely. Because I don't know what the heck that was but it sure wasn't talking.

I nod. "I did. I...know him. It would've been rude."

"*You* know Jacob Morrow? HA. I'd like to see *that.*" Ugh. *Ashley.*

"I mean, you just did. You literally saw it," I say with a shrug.

Sal and Mandy chuckle and then quickly straighten when

Deb side eyes them. She turns her glare back to me, "I better not see that again, Emma. I'm serious. You'll be out the door without another word."

I don't say anything. Because what can I say? *I'm about to shoot an epic series with him that will propel me to stardom?*

Because that's believable.

I clear my throat. "Actually, can I switch with Mandy? It might be better...for the customers, that is."

"Nope."

Cool cool.

Deb dismisses me with a wave and I grab my drinks and head out to the courtyard. I drop them at Allison's table and am relieved she has a big party. It takes a little time to get their orders, so it's not obvious that I'm avoiding Table 14 or the absurdly handsome human sitting at it.

I swear I can *feel* his eyes on me, but I keep doing what I do. I ring in more orders, grab the apps that just popped up for one of my tables, and when I turn to head back out I see Deb at Table 14. Talking to *him*.

Damn. It.

He wouldn't get me in trouble, right? Maybe he actually *didn't* recognize me. We haven't talked since I was cast. Not even once, which I have to admit I find so odd. But all my shiny new "industry contacts" tell me that's how it goes. You don't just suddenly become BFFs when you get cast to work with some-one. Yet another thing that validates how weird this whole industry is.

Deb walks back in. "Mandy, grab those apps from Emma. You're taking her tables since your big party doesn't come for another hour. Emma, Table 14 wants you. You're done with your shift."

My eyes widen in surprise.

Well holy curveball.

17

JAKE

This girl. What is it about this girl?

I'd been prepared to lobby hard to get her cast opposite me in *Hierarchy*, but I didn't have to. Her talent spoke for itself. Well, that and our searing chemistry. I've had a *lot* of love interest co-stars and I've never felt the fire like I did with her. And those were just the auditions. Add wardrobe and setting and production and even though we will be surrounded by cameras, once we get in that zone I think we will burn a hole in the set.

I've thought about her a lot over the past couple months. Wondering about her. About her personality. Whether she is as nice as she seemed. As *real* as she seemed.

Turns out she's definitely as hot as she seemed.

And if I'd had any doubt about that (which I definitely didn't), when that girl in a black jumpsuit walked out with her little notepad I couldn't help but stare. Just at her shape and the way she carried herself. But then when I panned up to her face and saw that it was *her*, I stiffened because apparently she just has that effect on me. And I'm not talking about my posture.

It's like my body just instantly remembers how she made me feel the last time I saw her.

And the time before that.

Only two times. That's it. But that's all it took.

Not good. This isn't good. Sure I've had crushes on costars before. But have I ever *acted* on those crushes?

Okay, yes. Yes I have.

But this—this is different. I've hooked up with plenty of costars—even while we're filming. But it's always been with guest stars or day players...or me as the day player and them as the lead. Basically, there's always been an endpoint. Which has worked. I've never gotten with someone I shoot with daily for an extended period of time. I've never crossed that line with another lead.

Okay that's not completely true. I *have* crossed that line, but only after filming wrapped. Never during.

Okay that's not totally true either. I did cross that line during filming but just *once*—and only because I thought we were done shooting with Claudia. I had no idea they were bringing her back the next season.

I know how badly things can go and how hooking up with a costar can absolutely wreck a set, which then impacts so many people. It's just never worth the risk.

Which is partly why I'm frustrated that I have such an unexpected crush on this girl. I mean, I don't even know her. We do have amazing chemistry and I think that's a big part of why she got cast—I could *feel* the sparks with her and I swear I think they might have been physically visible to everyone watching us. Like tiny fireworks shooting off of us.

And that's good. You *want* organic chemistry with your costar. Especially one who's supposed to be your all-consuming love interest. You just don't want *so* much chemistry that every day you have to tuck yourself up into the waistband of your briefs, which is exactly what I foresee happening.

We start prep in a few weeks and then we will basically live and breathe each other. For *years* if our show is a success. Preproduction is grueling and I normally dread it. The days are long, there are so many exhausting details to figure out, but you're not actually shooting yet and you definitely don't get that same high when you nail the dialogue at a table read. The promo photography is exhausting, too. I usually hate all those things, but I've actually been looking forward to them because I want to get to know this girl. And I mean on a purely platonic level.

Right.

It's just that seeing her see me and hop over to my table with no hesitation and speak to me with all the confidence in the world....damn I want to *know* her. I'm excited about working with her. She's different. I mean, she gave me two thumbs up. Who does that? It was adorable. And who works as a server when they've already been cast in a starring role on a huge new show? I have to admit that I don't really get that, but I respect that she isn't too prideful to do that. Such a change of pace from the people I'm usually around.

And, I just can't take it. I mean, she's *right there.*

And Timbo is running late anyways. It's too perfect. I never flex my "next Brad Pitt" status—and I do mean *never*—but damn if I'm not about to.

I tell my server, who is so not the kind of girl I'm into but is so obviously into me with her not even remotely veiled flirtation, that I need the manager. A couple minutes later this small, incredibly put together woman walks out and it's clear she's the manager. I see her face visibly shift from a *because-I-said-so* look to a *how-can-I-help-you-sir* look as she walks toward me.

"Hi," I look at her name tag. "Deb is it? Listen, I hate to do this to you..."

Her eyes widen into huge saucers. Like I am about to fire her or something. Like I even could.

I continue. "But, Emma is a friend of mine and I'd really love to have her join us for lunch. Can you have someone cover her shift?"

I know I'm not a douche but I'm low-key worried this is the first step to douchedom.

The smile Deb gives me is saccharine sweet. She's definitely the right person for her job. "Oh absolutely. You know Emma? She's my best. Consider it done. I'll let her know." She nods at me and heads back inside.

And that's how it's done folks. What good is being famous if you never take advantage of any of the perks?

While I wait for Emma to come out, I get more nervous by the second. I don't want to seem entitled. Was this going to come off that way? That's not me. Oh shit. She might read this wrong. She might be disgusted with—

"Well my day just took quite the turn." Emma is standing at my table staring down at me.

Okay. She seems okay. The bullets I've been sweating start to evaporate.

I shift in my seat, trying to gather my confidence back up. "Well seeing as we are about to work together for some of our best years according to what people say about their thirties, I can't believe you were literally just going to say hi to me and that's it."

She leans down and puts both palms flat on the table. "Okay first, I'm twenty-eight. But I get your point. Second, I honestly was debating between dodging you completely or saying hi, so be glad I went with the latter."

"Why would you have dodged me?"

She thinks for a second. "Mainly just because this is kind of an unusual way to see you again when my life is supposedly about to change in huge ways really soon. I mean, I said *hi* but what I really wanted to do was hug you and thank you because I heard you went to bat for me and tell you how excited I am and how crazy this is...But that's a lot for someone I don't really know, so I just settled on *Hi*."

"Well can you do the other thing instead?"

She cocks an eyebrow. "Dodge you?"

I let out a laugh. "No. I mean all that other stuff about how excited you are and how I went to bat for you... And I mean, I wouldn't turn down the hug."

She laughs. A real laugh. Then she pauses. "Listen, I'm not going to interrupt your lunch." She smiles reassuringly, like it's no big deal for her to not join me.

"There is no lunch. *Yet*. We can order."

"What about the person you're meeting?" She gestures to the place setting for two.

"He won't mind. He'll be happy actually. He's heard about you."

She looks at me and raises an eyebrow without raising an eyebrow. Not sure how that's a thing, but she just made it one. Then she turns around and leaves. It kind of stuns me if I'm being honest. I'm not used to people turning me down.

As I'm sitting here deciding if I should slip out from embarrassment or hold the line and act unbothered, she returns with a chair, sets it down, and then scoots the other one over just enough so there's room for her.

She sits down and within a millisecond says, "Okay, so what's up guy I'm about to spend nearly every day with? Let's play the Question Game to get to know each other."

"The Question Game? Is that a thing?"

She shrugs. "Yeah, sure it is. We each get five questions. I'll go first."

Damn.

This girl.

18

JAKE

She gives me an indiscernible look, clearly deciding on her first question. "What's your favorite food?"

"Pizza."

She laughs. "Simple man...I respect it." She takes a drink of the iced water in front of Timbo's seat. "With toppings I'm guessing though..."

"Yeah, pepperoni and mushroom."

"Yum. Okay, your turn."

"Well, what's *your* favorite food?"

"Chips and queso. No question."

I scoff. "Chips and queso isn't a meal."

"False. It depends on the quantity." She takes another sip of water before continuing, "Anything can be a meal if you eat enough of it." She smirks. "Plus, you said favorite *food*—not favorite *meal*. Though my answer would be the same. I definitely eat enough chips and queso to qualify as a meal."

I'm curious now. "Just queso or salsa, too?"

"I mean, don't get me wrong—I love salsa, too. But nothing compares to queso." She narrows her eyes at me. "That was your second question, by the way. You've got to play smarter."

But my next question is already spilling out when she says that. "What about guac? People either really love it or really hate it."

She barks out a laugh. "Is that another question?" She shakes her head like she feels sorry for me. "I love guac when it's good and hate it when it's not good."

"What makes it good or not good?"

"Okay, you're *terrible* at this game. Possibly the worst ever. You've wasted four questions on food. And I felt bad for you so I was gonna throw you a bone and tell you what makes guac good or not good but before I could elaborate you asked me another question." She laughs and puts her head in her hands.

"Well dammit." I breathe out a sigh.

She holds her hand up for me to be quiet, I'm guessing so I don't ask another question before I realize that's what I've done. "Okay..." she smiles at me. "*Okay.* I love like chunky fresh guac that is really green and not too mushy. I like it with a lot of lime, too. My fave is when they make it at the table because that's just a level of extra that I happen to appreciate in the guac world. And one time I had it with candied pepitas on top and I went to that restaurant daily for a solid couple of weeks. But if it's just kind of a bowl of mush or has even the slightest brown tint, it's a no go for me. Like I won't even want to try it if it looks weird— even if it tastes good. Otherwise I'm all about a triple dipper with queso, salsa, and guac. But I always order an extra queso, too. And *that* one's my meal." She winks as she says that last line.

And now *I'm* the one laughing. "Noted." I take a sip of my water before adding, "Well if nothing else, I have a keen understanding of your Mexican food preferences." I hold my water glass up like I'm about to toast her. "And I'll make that count." I do a solo air clink with my glass.

She nods. "Good. Because you're fully loaded on those details now. And you still have one more question and I'm not an expert at this game or anything, but I'm clearly not the novice you are so I feel like I should advise you to make it good. Like a question with some meat to it or something. But maybe not a question *about* meat because you've run the food theme hard already."

"Do you have a boyfriend?" I blurt it out before I can check myself. And I immediately want to bury myself under our table and never come back up. Why did I ask such a personal question? Such a *desperate* question?

"Jacob, you're killing me. Such a rookie mistake." She shakes her head like she's ashamed of my misstep.

"Why? You can't ask about stuff like that?"

"No, you definitely *can* and *should*. That's prime info. But it was technically my turn. And also, you never, *ever* ask a "yes or no" question. That's like Question Game 101. You've got to ask open-ended questions. Because then I can't just answer you like I'm about to."

"Like how?"

"Ask me the same question again." She raises her eyebrows to prompt me when I don't immediately speak.

"Do you have a boyfriend?"

"Nope."

I wait for her to say more. To elaborate. But she's silent.

"Wait, that's it?" I ask. "Just *nope?*"

"Yep. And *that's* why you don't ask yes or no questions."

I put my head in my hands. "Damn, you're ruthless. Lesson learned."

"Yeah you disregarded some cardinal rules of the game for sure. But hey, now you'll be ready next time you want to get to know someone via the question game." She gives me a pity smile before bursting out into laughter.

Oh I like her alright. She is funny and fun and just seems totally at ease being herself. Not many women are like this around me. They are never this easy to just talk with. I'd started to think girls like her might not exist.

"Okay but hold on, *you* asked *me* a very basic question first. I mean, asking my favorite food isn't exactly bringing out the big guns," I state confidently, knowing I busted her.

"You're totally right. *But* knowing someone's favorite food is pretty important. Like a key to their soul. Like, if you're having a great day, I'm going to suggest we order pizza to celebrate. If you're having a rough day, I'll have your favorite pepperoni and mushroom pizza delivered to set. Stuff like that."

Okay, I am a dude. I might even consider myself to be a dude's dude whatever that actually means. And I didn't really realize a dude's dude could feel butterflies but apparently it's possible, because when she said "we order pizza" like it's something we'd do together to celebrate something happy, my stomach bottomed out. No girl has ever, ever given me that feeling. Plenty of girls have given me lots of other feelings, and Emma is giving me all those, too, because man is she a smoke show. But no girl has made my stomach do that. Like a little flip. *Shit.* What is going on here?

Just then our server Ashley comes back to the table. She had tried to come over about twenty times before but I just kept waving her away. But now she sees an opening and goes for it.

"Would you like anything to drink besides water?" She asks with a smile, looking at me and me alone. "I wanted to ask earlier but you seemed like you didn't want to be...disturbed."

"I didn't. Thank you for noticing that. I'd love a session IPA." I look at Emma, "What about you?"

"Hmmmm," she closes her eyes and tilts her head to each

side like she's weighing her options. "I'll have our frozen G & T. The 6oz. Thanks."

Ashley gives her a curt nod and walks away. I furrow my brow and barely swing my head in her direction as if to say *What's up with her?* but Emma just smirks and shakes her head dismissively.

"Ahem," Emma says dramatically. "My turn. *Finally*," she says on a very fake eye roll. I can't help but laugh. "What did you study in college and if you didn't go, why not?"

I blink. Twice. Three times. "Oh okay, *wow*. You're asking some...real stuff. Well, I went to—wait! That was two questions!"

"No, that was a compound question and frankly a much smarter tactic."

"Compound questions are allowed?"

"Oh absolutely. One hundred percent. Proceed," she says with a big grin as she gestures for me to continue.

I look at her suspiciously but answer, "I wanted to get out of my hometown just so I could have some new experiences, so I went out of state and ended up at UGA. University of Georgia," I clarify. "I didn't know what I wanted to do but I thought I might want to do broadcasting or something because I love sports but I knew I wasn't good enough or big enough to play after college." The same cannot be said for my older brother.

She breaks in, "You look big enough to me."

Wait, is she flirting with me? Is that a flirty look or a look meant to console me because I wasn't good enough to play after college? "Thanks. I played baseball at Georgia and I was good, but I was never a great. You have to be a great." Gray was a great.

She nods like she understands, and I keep going. "So I majored in broadcast journalism. Georgia has a great program. And then on one of my internships I got to be on-air for some sports coverage and an agent out of Atlanta happened to see me and she thought I seemed natural on air so she got in touch with me, and that's really how it all began for me."

"Wow. Talk about a lucky break, huh? That's awesome."

"Yeah, it was a total lucky break. I've thought so many times about what I'd be doing now if she hadn't seen that first spot she saw me in. Would I be a sports broadcaster? Or a commentator? Would I have made it that far? Or would I be working a desk job at a random company I don't care about?"

"I mean, I think you made it. Maybe not in the way you initially thought, but you've definitely made it." She holds her water glass up to clink.

"Thanks." I think about that for a second. Then I clink my glass to hers and say, "I think you've made it now, too."

She takes a sip and then shrugs her shoulders as if to say *we'll see*. Then she asks, "Can you tell me about your family?

My eyebrows raise in surprise. "*Such* an open-ended question. Damn, you're good."

"Why thank you, sir," she says with a mini bow at the table.

"I mean, you've absolutely schooled me."

"Facts," she nods in agreement. "Go on..."

"I have a great family. I miss them. I have an older brother named Gray. He still lives in my hometown—"

She cuts in. "And your hometown is..."

"Gainesville, Florida."

She nods.

"Anyways, Gray still lives in my hometown and I don't think he'll ever leave. He played baseball at the University of Florida and is a trainer there now. He's a big shot name around town. He's not married and I know he dates but he never, ever brings a girl around so he's a pretty big mystery. Gray's just really like...set in his ways or something. He's a big softie with a very gruff outside. And I'm thankful for him because he's the one who looks out for our parents. They live just a few minutes apart and he's the one all that kind of stuff falls on, since he's there."

"He sounds like a great son."

"He is. A good brother, too. And then my sister Lilah is just a couple years older than me and we've always been super close. She's married to Aaron, our hometown golden boy, and is head of marketing for a huge hotel conglomerate out of Chicago. She's the quintessential"—I throw out some air quotes—"*badass boss girl.*" I take a sip of my beer.

"Okay first, that doesn't warrant air quotes. Badass boss girls are a real thing. And second—I would have assumed that *you're* the hometown golden boy."

I laugh. "Hard no."

"But you *are* the baby in the family."

"Yeah. Gray is thirty-seven and Lilah is thirty-four. I—" My mouth drops. "*Oh.* You're just asking questions in statement form."

The corners of her mouth slowly tick up. "Yep. And it's working. I mean, now I know you're early thirties and you're a Florida boy." She raises her eyebrows and shrugs. "But you haven't told me about your parents yet."

"Yeah, well, you're going to have to ask and"—I hold up air quotes—"*use a question* for that info."

"Nuh-uh. I don't have to ask about them. Your parents *are* your family, so for a complete answer you've got to include your parents. You can't give an incomplete answer."

I squint at her. "You really are ruthless. But fine—my mom is a saint and my dad has an incredible sense of humor. And while we're at it, my best friend Timbo is a brother to me. My brother from another mother."

She raises her brows. "Timbo, huh? *Timbo?* He sounds... interesting."

"That's one word for him," I laugh.

Ashley comes back with our drinks and sets Emma's in front of her a little harder than is necessary causing some to slush over the side. She puts mine down gingerly on a cocktail napkin she'd laid down first. Then she looks at me, "Would you like to order something to eat?" Her voice is candy sweet.

"Yes, I think *we* would like to order something. Emma, what would you like?"

"Shouldn't you wait on your friend to order?" Emma asks.

"No—it's actually Timbo, and he won't care. He probably won't even eat anyways." I gesture to Emma to order.

She faces Ashley. "I'd love the fried green tomato chicken sandwich with a side salad and extra bacon jam on the side please. Thanks, Ashley."

Ashley doesn't even look at her. "And you, Mr. Morrow?"

"I'll have the mushroom flatbread. But can I have a side of bacon jam, too, please? That sounds good."

Emma silently mouths *so good* and I feel a pulse between my legs, a response that seems ridiculous considering she is literally talking about bacon jam.

"Of course," Ashley holds her hand out to take my menu and then snatches Emma's without even looking at her.

"So she's a treat."

Emma chuckles. "That's one word for her." She winks again, and it hits me that this is probably the first person who has ever winked at me that made it seem endearing and not creepy. Is she just really good at winking? Or is she just really good at being herself?

I take a sip of my beer. "Okay next question. What you got?"

"It's intermission." She smiles. "I need to run to the restroom. I'll be right back."

The second she walks away I grab my phone and pull up my messages with Timbo:

Me: Lunch is off. Don't meet at Stella's. I'll
explain later.

Timbo: ... ...

The three little dots are still there and I know he's responding as Emma walks back to the table. I click the screen off, hold up my phone up and say, as casually as possible, "Timbo can't come. Looks like it's just us."

"Well I look forward to meeting him in the future. He's got me pretty intrigued with a name like Timbo."

"He's something, that's for sure. Okay, next question." Could I be more eager? I know I must sound like a little kid asking *Are we there yet?* on repeat. And yet, I can't stop myself.

"So, how are you feeling about this show? You must've really wanted to do it to sign on with a total nobody as your costar."

"*Our* show, not just *this* show." I shake my head. "And I feel good about it. I'm actually really pumped about it. We get to premiere with a built-in audience. That's pretty rare. The books are awesome and they have such a large cult following that I feel like as long as we do a good job, we can't help but make it a successful series. I love the team working on it, the author seems like she really wants to work with us to keep the scripts in line with the books and keep the fans happy, and it's a badass fantasy-adventure-romance-action series so to me...I hit the jackpot."

She is absolutely beaming with a smile that takes up her entire face.

"The only thing that had me nervous was the costar role," I say, gauging her reaction as the words leave my mouth.

Her face falls for a split-second and I can tell she doesn't want me to notice, but I can't help but notice because it was such an abrupt change from her glowing smile a moment before.

I continue, knowing she'll like where I'm going with this. "The producers kept floating names—really famous names— and I kept vetoing them. I know they got frustrated with me, but those actresses just weren't it. They were amazingly famous and talented actresses and yeah I'm sure they would've been good for publicity for the show, but they weren't Annabelle Claiborne. So Lisa, the author, requested we hold auditions and try to find a diamond in the rough...someone who hadn't been found yet, and then you walked into the first round of auditions and stole the whole show right out from under us." I smile. "So, yeah, I feel pretty fucking good about things, especially now that we found a *nobody*"—I bring back the air quotes for emphasis— "who has so much talent that she's about to be the biggest *some-body* ever."

She doesn't move, doesn't say a word. She has tears in her eyes and I can tell she's fighting hard to keep them there and not let them fall.

Ashley brings out a bread basket and sets it on the table between us. She lingers for a moment but when neither of us speaks, she sighs dramatically and leaves.

Emma's eyes bore into me. She quickly grabs the damp cock-tail napkin out from under my beer and then leans her head down over the napkin and blinks her eyes repeatedly, letting the tears fall straight onto the napkin. She keeps her head leaned down like that for a moment, completely horizontal. Then when it seems like she's sure no more tears are coming she looks back up at me, lashes wet and stuck together, eyes glistening.

"Thank you, that was...really, really sweet. And I don't know what to say except thank you. And plus if I say more I am defi-nitely going to start really crying. Like full-on ugly crying."

"I'll believe that when I see it," I joke. As if she could ever look ugly. "But, I meant it," I say. And then I pick up my beer to cheers and she grabs her glass and we clink them together.

We sit there in silence for a few long seconds just looking at each other. Then she breaks the silence. "Alright, I have my final question," she declares.

"Shoot," I say.

Just as she opens her mouth Ashley walks out with our food. We're quiet while she sets it down and I don't push for conversation because I can tell Emma doesn't speak openly in front of her.

When she leaves, Emma leans in close and gestures for me to do the same. "Okay, so this...*industry*. I guess my question is, is it as sleazy as you hear it is? Because my extremely limited experience has been...kind of golden. Like so good and above board that none of it seems real. The casting director didn't ask me to sleep with him, my agent didn't tell me she could help me if I help her....stuff like that. So is that like just sensationalized stuff or can it really be like that and I've just gotten lucky?"

She leans back and I can tell she genuinely wants my answer. But man is that a loaded question.

I think for a moment before I answer her. "Well, I think you may have gotten lucky. There is a lot of that kind of trashy stuff in this business. I scratch your back you scratch mine kind of stuff. And even things not on that level, but there's also a lot of cheapening yourself to please the studio or director or whoever. I mean, I'm a guy and even *I* felt too sexualized on the soap I was on. And some of the people working with me definitely made me feel...like a commodity. Like a commodity *they* were in charge of. So yeah, there is a lot of that. That's why I'm so invested in this show and to have an executive producer role... that's huge for me. Because I don't want to be in that position again, where I don't feel like I belong to myself."

She reaches her hand across the table and puts it on my arm. "Thank you," she says softly. Thank you for telling the truth. I appreciate it."

"You're welcome. And listen—you just so happened to land on a great show, with great people. I hear your costar is awesome and the producing team is top tier." Now a huge smile spreads across *my* face.

She laughs—like really laughs—and says, "I think I can vouch for both," as she grabs her sandwich and takes an enormous bite.

"I promise I'll have your back." I mean it.

We spend the rest of the lunch talking about the show and how the press shoots are about to start. I explain how all of that works and what the timeline typically looks like. I ask if she's ready to quit working here at Stella's and she hesitates before explaining that she is *and* she isn't—that she's ready for this big new adventure but that it feels very not real to her while serving feels very real.

"Plus, I get to work with people I really love here so that makes it more fun than you'd think," she says matter-of-factly.

"Who, Ashley?" I ask, my tone laced with sarcasm.

She levels me with one look. "No, with my friends Sal and Mandy."

"They work here?"

She nods.

"Are they here today?"

She nods again and looks over to the glass doors off the back patio. "Yeah, they're in there, probably losing their shit." She laughs and then leans in close again. "I'm going to level with you. They know about the show. They know that I had to sign an NDA and how bad it would be if the studio knew I broke that. I trust them. They're chill about it and won't breathe a word. But Mandy's a superfan of the series and is most decidedly *not* chill about you."

I chuckle, flattered. "Tell them to come out. I want to meet them."

She glances at our plates and since we've all but scraped up every last crumb, she clears the plates. "Okay I'll be right back."

"You don't need to clear our—" I start to say, but she's already gone.

A few minutes later she comes out with two insanely attractive people flanking her. I briefly feel like I might be on an episode of *Punkd!* or something.

"Sorry it took a minute, I had to convince our manager that you did in fact request to meet them." She shakes her head in exasperation. "Jacob, this is Mandy," she says as she gestures to the beautiful girl beside her. "And this is Sal," she says as she looks up at her tall and extremely handsome friend. *Male* friend. And my first thought when I see him is that I hope he's gay. Because otherwise I'm not sure I can ever compete with him. Not that I want to compete with him. But just, you know...just like maybe one day in the future or something.

I stand and shake their hands and they are very obviously flipping out internally. I'm about to ask them if they want to sit but then Emma speaks up, "Okay, well this was awesome. I actually am so glad I bumped into you, as weird of a setting as this was." She laughs. "Lunch was comped so the bill is taken care of. And don't worry, yes I still tipped Ashley even though she hates me." Sal and Mandy chuckle quietly.

Wait, *what?* We're done? I didn't expect her to just up and call it a day. "So wait, I'm leaving this lunch feeling like you know almost everything about me and I know really nothing about you except that you really love Mexican food. That doesn't seem fair."

Sal and Mandy hoot with laughter and then Sal elbows Emma. "Yeah that tracks," he says. Then he looks at me. "I don't know man, I'd say you might know her better than you think," he adds, still laughing.

Emma nods in agreement. "I mean it's really *not* fair but you kind of did it to yourself. But we're about to work together all day every day so I think we'll be just fine in the getting-to-know-each-other department. I just got a head start."

She holds out her arms to hug me. "Thanks, Jacob." I stand and hug her back, using every ounce of my willpower to not smell her hair. As closely as her friends are watching me, they would spot it. She breaks the hug first and waves as the three of them turn to walk back inside.

And then she's gone.

And I?

I'm gone, too.

For her.

A total fucking goner.

19

JAKE

Timbo throws his keys down as he walks in the door. "So what the hell was so important that you canceled lunch and then didn't respond to any of my texts?"

I'm just going to say it. Timbo is a really good-looking guy. Girls lose their minds over him. He's an inch taller than me at six foot three, his body doesn't look real, he has jet black hair that he doesn't do shit to but it always looks good. It's not curly, it's not straight, it's just...really good hair. But what kills people are his eyes. They're blue, but not just regular blue eyes—they're *dark* blue. Navy eyes. One look from Timbo and panties just fall off. Seriously. I've witnessed it happen for years.

And he's funny as hell. We've been best friends since we were eleven. We played on a rec league junior basketball team together and have been inseparable ever since. We went to UGA together and he came with me to Los Angeles because I asked him to, and because he didn't have anything keeping him...well anywhere. He has no siblings and his parents are the least parent-y parents I've ever seen. My family kind of took him in when we were growing up because his parents just didn't really seem to want to be parents. I mean, they provided for him and stuff, but they were always, *always* out partying. Or traveling for big blocks of time. He had to grow up fast at a really young age. He'd always come home with me after practices and join our family dinners. He'd spend a weekend night here and there. And then that morphed into full weekends. And it gradually evolved into him all but living with us every summer, and for months at a time during the year when his parents were gone.

He's like a brother to me. And much less grumpy than Gray.

I "hired" him as my personal trainer years ago because the dude knows what to do and the studios pay for me to have one so it's a win win. Other actors have tried to poach him because if I can be honest without sounding like a douche—my body is one of the reasons I'm popular. One of the reasons I get book-ings. One of the reasons every part I book always has shirtless scenes. I look like a less huge version of Chris Hemsworth's body and Timbo is the reason for that. Several years back I complained about how I couldn't get where I wanted to in the gym and he said if I'd come work out with him he'd get me there. He was working as a trainer at a local gym at the time. I didn't really believe him but I went to his gym anyway and he proved me wrong. Completely transformed me.

He's taken on several high profile clients over the years, but only after he swore to me he'd always prioritize me first. I helped him get noticed in the first place so I joke that he owes me that loyalty. But that dude is loyal as hell anyways. When I booked *Sunset Cove*, he didn't hesitate to move down under with me. He's not tethered to anyone, anything, or anywhere and though I know he feels the effects of that sometimes, he makes the best of it and then some. The dude has fun.

So, we work together, we play together, and we live together.

Technically he has his own place but I think he just keeps it for hooking up. Which he does a *lot* of. I really never bring girls here either. I prefer to go to their place mainly so no one finds out where I live and tracks me down here. My place is pretty much a dude zone and we like it that way.

"I ran into my new costar—she works there. And I had lunch with her instead."

"Cool, cool. So you ditched me for her?" he jokes.

"Absolutely."

He laughs. "So tell me about her. You like her? Is she gonna be good? You make the right choice?"

"Yeah she's amazing. Like perfect." I correct myself. "For the part, I mean."

"Oh man, glad to hear it. I know casting that part was a *struggle*. So glad you found her man."

"Yeah no kidding, me too." I say. "Me too."

"Tell me about her. You've hardly told me anything. Where's she from? How long has she been acting? What's her story?"

I think for a second. *Shit.* I can't answer any of those questions. I still don't know much about her. Or anything really. "She's...she's just really cool and sweet and funny." It's all I can think to say.

"Yeah, you basically already said that. What else?"

"She really likes queso. Like she *loves* it." I nod my head. "Yeah. Yeah, she loves queso."

Timbo looks at me like I am a nut job. "Does Stella's have queso now? Did you two eat a lot of queso for lunch or something?"

"No, they don't have queso there."

"So why are you talking so much about how this girl loves queso?"

"I don't know man, it's hard to explain. She just really likes it."

"So you had lunch with this girl—your future costar on a huge new show that you're also producing—and all you can tell me about her is that she likes queso?"

"Pretty much."

"Why are you being so weird? What's up with you?"

"I—I didn't really get to know much more about her."

Timbo lets out a breath and grimaces. "I'm sorry to say it, but honestly she doesn't sound great. You eat lunch with this girl and all she talks about is queso? I don't know man, I hope she's smarter than you're making her sound."

I feel my face heat with aggravation. "Dude. You don't know her. She is. She's super smart. And the queso thing was my fault. I just kept asking her about queso and I couldn't stop."

He looks appalled. *"Why?"*

"Because I couldn't think straight. She's really hot."

"Well why didn't you start with that, dumbass? Now it makes more sense."

He opens the brown paper bag he walked in with and pulls out Chinese takeout boxes. "I got Huang's for dinner."

"Awesome, thanks man."

He rounds the couch with our food. "So does she like salsa too or is it just queso?"

I sigh with relief, knowing I can finally answer a question about her. "She likes salsa, too."

"Guac?"

"Sometimes. Depends on if it's chunky or not."

"I get that," he says while shoveling lo mein in his mouth.

I take a bite of my moo goo gai pan, a dish we always ordered growing up but that no one else seems to know exists. But Huang's will make it for me because we order from there all the time and because one time Timbo told them I'm super famous and I would give them a shout out on Instagram just so they would make it for me. I did and now they do.

"So you obviously like her. Is that gonna be a problem?" He shakes his head in disapproval. "That never seems to work out."

"I don't like her." I look at him like he's an idiot.

"Dude." He doesn't even look up from his forkful of noodles.

"I mean, yeah I like her but not like that. We're going to be working together. It's not like that."

"I *know* you're going to be working together, which is *why* I'm asking if it's gonna be a problem. Because costars fooling around rarely works out."

"I told you—it's not like that. It can't be. And we don't even know each other really. We just hung out today for a couple hours, but I'm happy because I can tell it'll be fun to work with her."

"Uh huh. How hot is she?"

So hot. Unreal hot. Smoking hot. Smart hot. Cute hot. Sweet hot. Funny hot. Hot hot.

But I want to downplay things so I just say "She's pretty."

"Okay. You said she was hot earlier, but okay." He raises an eyebrow knowingly. "I guess I'll just have to see for myself."

"Yeah, I'm sure you'll meet soon." *Shit.* I'll be busted. Not like I can hide her. Or her hotness.

"Are you gonna see her again?"

"What kind of question is that? Of course I am. I'm about to see her every day, man."

He flips on the TV. "No I mean like before you start shooting. You have a few more weeks before the show ramps up."

"Yeah. And no I don't think so. Probably just when pre-production kicks off." I take another bite. "I mean, I don't even have her number remember?"

That's right. I still don't have her number. Why did I not get it today so we could be in touch if we needed to be? Why didn't she want mine? In case she had more questions or something. I'm tempted to go back to her restaurant tomorrow to get it but that just seems stalkerish. And a stalker, I am not. At least not an in-person one. I've been trying to stalk the hell out of her online.

"Don't even have her number..." Timbo chuckles and then looks over at me. "Honestly man, I can't wait to see how this plays out."

I roll my eyes and jerk the remote away from him. I punch in O-Z-A and tap *Ozark* when it auto-populates. I lean back on the couch and look over at Timbo. He smirks at me and I punch his arm. "Shut the hell up."

"Didn't say anything."

"You were thinking it."

20

EMMA

I wake up not knowing what the heck to expect. We're supposed to shoot all the promo images today. These are the ones they'll use to promote the show and also announce me as Annabelle Claiborne. No pressure, right?

So much pressure. All the pressure. *All* of it.

I've never done this before. And my fellow aspiring actor friends are even more clueless than me if that's even possible. Because none of us have ever landed a real role like this. Sal and Mandy are zero help other than just being the ultimate hype squad. And they've done a *lah-hot* of Googling and briefed me as much as they could. I really, really wanted to ask Marci more of what to expect, but I was scared to divulge how much I really don't know what I'm doing because I don't want her to get nervous or the studio to get nervous. Even though I know she's in my corner. But still...I'm trying to keep up the facade that I've got this.

It hit me the day after my impromptu lunch with Jacob that I didn't get his number. And I should have, because I really think he *would* have my back and I'd feel comfortable asking him questions like *How long will today take? Will there be a lot of wardrobe changes or are we just doing one look? Do you intensely regret picking me for Annabelle?* To name a few.

I arrive at the soundstage that Marci told me we won't be shooting on for the series even though it has been made to look exactly like the set we *will* be shooting on in a mere week's time. I have so many questions, starting with *Why all the extra work? Why wouldn't they set all this up where we'll actually be shooting starting next week? Do they really have to break all this down and move it to a different location?* It just seems so wasteful and inefficient. So much extra work. I add those thoughts to my ever-growing list of things to ask Jacob about.

The moment I walk in I am immediately whisked away to hair and makeup. I don't even know who takes me there, because he leaves before I ever get his name. There are three women in the room and they are chatty and fun and I'm instantly grateful for them. I want to scream out *I don't know what the hell I'm doing!* and get their advice because they seem like they have a lot of thoughts about a lot of stuff, and maybe they could help me. But I don't want them to know I'm clueless, either, so I just keep faking it. Fake it til you make it, right? I'm becoming an expert at that.

I've been in the chair now for forty minutes. They can't decide whether they want to cut my hair or not. I do not want to cut my hair again. It's finally grown out some. We never discussed cutting my hair—not my agent, not the production office, not Jacob. I'm scared to speak up because what if I'm supposed to have it cut and I just didn't realize? I hate not knowing all the things I feel like I should. I find myself internally chanting *I need Jacob, I need Jacob, I need Jacob* simply because I know he'll know what to do.

I silently wonder when I'll get to see him. Will he come say hi? When will *he* get all made up? I'm kind of surprised he hasn't been by to like, oh I don't know, welcome me or something? Like doesn't someone want to make sure I'm here *and* confirm I'm the right girl for the job? Who is in charge around here?

Just then a woman walks in and it's obvious that at least in this room—*she's* in charge. And cool. Or at least she *looks* cool, and I find myself hoping she actually *is* cool.

"Hi, I'm Willa. I'm the first assistant director." She's wearing ripped jeans and a faded Zeppelin shirt with the coolest denim jacket with leather and stud detailing. I like her already. She extends her hand out to shake mine. "And you look like a nervous mess."

"I think you're spot on," I give a half-hearted laugh. "I'm Emma."

"Emma, what do you need before we get this thing going? We've only got six hours in this space and need to make it count so we can get everything we need."

Six *hours*? And she said it like that's not that long. We're going to take pictures for six *hours*? Sweet Jesus. "I need Jacob," I hear myself say out loud.

"Got it." Willa grabs her walkie talkie and says, "Jake, we need you in hair and makeup. Emma wants you."

Well that's one way to say it.

Not even three minutes later, he walks in and I feel the entire room go limp in his presence. He really is devastating. He has a smile on his face when he simply says, "Emma."

I nervously smile back and hop out of the hair chair. I walk to a corner of the room and he follows me over and then whispers, "What's up?"

"First of all, hi," I say. "And second of all, I need your help."

"Okay, tell me."

"They are considering cutting my hair and I didn't know we

were going to do that. And I know it's just hair and not a big deal, and I'll totally do it, but...but is that something I'm *supposed* to do? Like do I get a say or do I just need to follow along? I don't know the protocol." I feel my eyes pool. "I also had no idea we'd be taking pictures for six *hours*." I pull him closer and whisper, "I feel like I don't know anything about anything."

"How much?" he asks.

"This much." I hold my hands up to indicate a space of about three inches.

"And you don't want to?"

"Not especially." I sigh. "I've been growing it back out and it's finally long enough for a solid ponytail again."

His Adam's apple bobs and I can't help but watch. How can a throat lump be sexy? I force my eyes back up to his face.

"Okay, well for the record you would look beautiful with shorter hair. Or a bob. Or super long hair. Or...no hair. But it's perfect like it is and I don't think you should change a thing. She has medium length hair in the books, right? You have medium length now. Medium is a range. They don't need to do anything."

My stomach somersaults at his response. "Thank you." I breathe a sigh of relief. "How do I tell them that?"

"I will."

"No!" I whisper shout, grabbing his arm to keep him there. "You can't! Then they'll know I told you."

He looks at me and then over at the group of three women who are staring right at us. "Okay two things," he says, holding two fingers up like a peace sign. "One, they already know." He nods his head in their direction and I look over to see six eyes taking in our hushed conversation. Yep, yep...they definitely know. "Two, it's my job. I'm an EP on this so I can have some creative control among other things. So, it actually *is* my job. And frankly, it's their job to listen."

I swallow, replaying his words. Not going to lie, his assertiveness is extremely attractive. I've only witnessed him be sweet and mild, maybe even a bit meek. I haven't seen this side of him. I honestly didn't know he had it in him. Turns out I like this side a *lot*.

"And third—"

"Wait, there's a third?" I furrow my brows.

"Yeah. I'm adding a third. I told you I would have your back, didn't I?"

I nod.

"So let me." And with that Jacob walks toward the door but before leaving he says, "Don't cut Emma's hair. I like it like it is." And then he's through the door.

And that, ladies and gentlemen, is how you make a girl swoon.

THE HAIR and makeup ladies know how to work some serious magic. I'm terrible at names but I added them to my notes when they weren't looking. I have no idea if they're just my team for today's shoot or if they're going to be the team for the entire show, so I jot their names down just in case. Angela, Blair, and Lin. Three wizards who made me look like an absolute siren from the neck up before a wardrobe assistant grabbed me to go put my costume on. Do they call it a costume? I don't think so. I think they just call it wardrobe. Another question for Jacob. The wardrobe assistant's name is DJ and he's amazing. I want him to stay with me the entire day because he is warm and immediately puts me at ease. Plus he's so complimentary. When he saw me in hair and makeup he gasped. Like an actual, out loud gasp. I'm a ball of nerves and happily welcome any and all flattering gasps.

Keep the gasps coming, people. I need them.

DJ leads me to a large room and tells me Diana will be here

in a minute to "work her magic." Not gonna lie, pretty excited about said magic.

She walks in, asks me to strip down to my bra and panties (goodbye last shred of modesty), and then has me climb into a dress that she holds in the back so it's cinched in. She looks me over *hard* and then calls for DJ to grab the "push up corset, but not the full corset." He brings it over and she hands it to me. I walk behind the little makeshift curtain and change out of my sporty bralette to the corset-y one and when I look down I'm shocked at my own self. My tits look—*spectacular*. Yay for Diana! I pull the dress back up and hold it in place with one hand as I walk back out from behind the curtain.

"Yes," is all Diana says. DJ is smiling huge and gives me a reassuring wink. Big fan of DJ.

Then, Diana turns me around and sews up the back. Yes, *sews*. She doesn't button it up, even though it has buttons. She folds the button side in and then literally sews it *onto* my body. What is this world? Who does that?

I want to ask her why but she is a lady of few words so I make a mental note to ask DJ later.

She whips me around to face a full length mirror and then gets on her knees and grabs the skirt of the dress, holds her hand toward DJ who immediately places a pair of scissors in her outstretched hand, and then makes the tiniest cut in the bottom hem. From there she literally rips the dress open up to my thigh. She does the same thing several more times in different sections of the skirt. She rips some parts just a little but rips other parts so high they almost expose my panties. She crouches down and pulls loose string after string out of the open slits to fray the edges and I'm a bit mesmerized just watching her work.

After what feels like several minutes, she gets up, stands back and turns to beckon DJ over. He comes and stands next to her and then they both just stand there silently taking me in.

Diana finally speaks. "You look incredible."

Wow, so she *is* nice?

"Off the charts," chimes in DJ.

"Like a badass who is also unbearably sexy," Diana nods.

"Um, can I keep you guys forever?" I ask, fully meaning it.

"You look like that because that's what you are," Diana says as if she is stating something as factual as a math equation.

Suddenly, I love her. I love DJ. I love Willa. I love the entire hair and makeup team. I love how Jacob stood up for me. I love how they've all made me feel. I love this job and it hasn't really even started yet.

And for decidedly the first time ever, I love my life.

21

JAKE

Holy shit. Diana must be fired immediately, because I know I won't be able to deal with this on a daily basis. And the entire hair and makeup team. They've got to go, too. This is just...this is just more than any man can handle.

Every time I've seen Emma I've thought she was stunning, but this is a lot to take in. I just saw her forty-five minutes ago and she looked gorgeous. But this—well *this* is testing the strength of the zipper on the pants I'm wearing.

She's in a raggedly sexy dress. A dress that was clearly once pristine but supposedly worn out by adventure. Actually, seeing as this show is going to be quite steamy, I'm imagining it's been worn out by adventure *and* by the hands of one rugged and studly Daniel Teller.

Please let her think I look rugged and studly.

The hem of the dress is ripped in several spots and it's the first time I've seen Emma's legs. I guess she's always had on pants when I've been around her. Her legs are...*good*. God, her legs are good. Damn why do her legs have to be *so* good? They're toned and smooth and—*ouch*. Is that a real bruise? It can't be, right? They would've covered it up. It must be part of her *look*. She has her hair half up, half down with loose messy waves. Nothing perfect, just kind of lived in. A bit matted even. It looks super hot. And then it hits me why.

It's bed head. She has sex hair.

I feel my pants tighten even more at that realization.

And I know she must have on makeup and probably lots of it so the camera doesn't wash her out and hell, even *I* have a lot of makeup on. But you can't tell she has on much—they've let her natural beauty show through. I freaking love what they're going for here and the angle we're taking with these promo shots.

Note to self: Diana and the rest of the team are most definitely not fired. They can stay. And do this every day.

Sure, it'll be utter torture for me, but the world is going to fall head over heels in love with this woman. She's going to steal the entire show. Guys will be lining up for her. They will be— *wait*.

I don't want guys lining up for her. The firing is back on. Diana and Angela and the team can get to packing. I don't want guys lining up for this perfect girl we've found.

It's like I want to share her with the world and no one at the same time.

"Jacob? Jacobbbb? Earth to Jacob, are you in there?" Emma's voice brings her back into focus. "Woah, you just really zoned out there. You alright?"

I nod.

"What on earth were you thinking about?"

You. Your legs. Wrapped around me. How easily I could pull that dress up. My hand in your hair. How good it would feel to pull it just a little bit. Your neck. Your lips. On me. What you taste like...every-

where. I don't tell her all that, but I also don't lie. "You took my breath away."

"Really?" She asks, clearly unsure. "You like..." She gestures up and down herself. "*This?*"

I clear my throat but my voice still comes out choked. "Very much."

"Well, I like..." She gestures up and down me. "*That.*" She smiles and nods approvingly, but *casually.* Like I'm not undoing her the same way she is undoing me. Like I look good but she could take it or leave it.

Meanwhile it's all I can do not to take it right here. Take *her* right here.

We spend the rest of the day posing for what can only be described as the world's sexiest engagement-style shoot. We're constantly touching, pressing into each other, holding hands, cupping cheeks, gazing into each other's eyes, and brushing lips.

During a quick break while production looks at some of the images, Emma leans into me. "Can we go out to get a drink or ten after this?"

Ummm god yes is what I think, but "Yeah sure, I don't think I have plans" is what I say.

"You don't *think* so? How do you not *know* so?"

I chuckle. This girl. Calling me out every chance she gets. "I know I don't."

"Okay phew." She mimes wiping sweat off her brow like she's relieved. "And also food. Somewhere easy. I need to feel normal after a day like this." She shakes her head in disbelief. "Because this has been the least normal day of my life."

"Done."

She turns back to face me. "And also, just in case I need help curbing the impending existential crisis stemming from impostor syndrome at any point in the future, I'm going to need your number."

"Thought you might never ask," I say with a smirk. She hits my arm and then Willa yells at us to take our spots.

I'M PUTTING back on the clothes I wore to set this morning when my phone chirps.

> Timbo: You done yet? Wanna hit Dap's tonight for some burgers?

> Me: Yeah, but not with you. Emma asked if we could go out tonight. So no.

> Timbo: Dude.

> Me: Not like that. To talk about the show and stuff.

> Timbo: Oh, then can I third wheel it? I want to meet this chick who has you losing it.

> Me: I'm not losing anything you dumbass.

Except maybe the blood to my head, I think. Because when I'm around her all the blood in my body is most definitely not flowing to my head. Or actually, it's just flowing to a *different* head. A *lower* head.

> Timbo: So is that a yes?

> Me: It's a hard no.

Timbo: Come on man. I'm craving Dap's and you're about to start shooting and I need to meet this person you're gonna be spending all your time with.

Timbo: I'm feeling needy.

Timbo: Placate me.

Me: Fine. But I want to have drinks with her first. Without you. So meet us at 8:00. If you get there before that I will tell her about that time you botched your threesome.

Timbo: 8:00 it is.

I WAIT for Emma while she "transforms back into herself" as she put it. There's nowhere to sit and I don't want to stay in my tiny dressing room, but I also don't want to lurk right outside her door, so I'm just standing randomly in the hallway a few doors down from her room.

She makes me uneasy. Not in a bad way. More in a doofus way, if that's a thing. It's like I can be Mr. Confident in front of everyone but her—and she's the one person I actually *want* to be confident in front of—but she makes me feel like a sixteen year old with a raging crush that he doesn't know what to do with.

I hear her talking from inside her dressing room but can't make out what she's saying or if she's talking to wardrobe or on the phone or what. Then I hear her door open so I turn toward her, but not too eagerly because I've apparently devolved into a teenager trying to look cool and not the self-assured successful actor I am and...*oh.*

Oh. So this is what she looks like dressed down ready to hang. Jeans, a white sleeveless top tied up just a little in the front, showing a few inches of her stomach. Her insanely sexy stomach. Neon sneakers. Hair loose just like it was all day, but down. She's stunning. Natural. *Perfect.*

Emma walks toward me. "Ready?"

You know how cartoon characters get those heart eyes that bug out of their head? I have to think I look like that right about now. But I try not to let on. "Yeah."

"Where are we headed?" She asks as she slings her duffel over her shoulder. It looks heavy so I take it from her without even thinking about it. She looks at me in surprise. "Thank you. That's sweet."

I nod. "Well, my friend Timbo wants to meet us out if that's okay with you. But I thought we could go have drinks before we meet him so we can catch up."

"Sounds good. So where to?"

"Have you been to Dap's?"

"Ooh no! But it's on my list of places to try. I've heard they have amazing burgers and truffle fries."

"They do." I look at her with an apologetic look. "But no queso, I'm afraid."

She bursts out laughing. "I think I can handle it."

22

EMMA

"There he is." Jacob holds a hand up signaling Timbo to our table.

Timbo walks towards us and my mouth drops. I can't even help it. *"What?"* I say to no one in particular, and more to myself than anyone else.

"What?" asks Jacob, eyeing me quizzically.

"I mean, I don't know what I expected, but that is not it," I say tilting my head in Timbo's direction.

"What's not it?" he asks, glancing back and forth between me and Timbo.

I continue my Timbo-induced stream of consciousness. "Okay, well I actually *do* know what I expected and yeah, he's definitely not it."

"I'm lost." Jacob shakes his head and shrugs at Timbo, who has just reached our table.

Timbo shrugs back and extends his hand to me. "I'm Timbo,

and it's really good to meet you because I've heard a *lot* about you." He smirks at Jacob.

I glance over at Jacob and catch him side eye Timbo, but Timbo hasn't moved his eyes from mine.

I take his hand and shake it. "I'm Emma." I smile. And then because I decide to just lay it all out there, I say "Timbo, I don't know you so don't think I'm this forward all the time, and I might have a tiny bit of liquid courage already on board, but the name Timbo doesn't necessarily scream"— I gesture up and down him—"*this*, so I'm a little taken aback."

He laughs. A real, deep laugh way down in his belly. "Well, what did you expect?"

"Well, when Jacob kept talking about Timbo, I just...I envisioned something...*someone*...else."

Jacob chuckles. "Who did you envision?"

I pause, wondering if I'm digging myself into a hole. But screw it. Might as well be honest. "I don't know, like smarmy or something. Like a greasy wheeler dealer type of guy who makes underhanded deals and promises he doesn't intend to keep."

"Okay first of all, what does it say about how you think of me if you thought I would be best friends with a dude like that?" Jacob asks, jokingly offended. "I mean, you do know this is real life, right? We're not in *The Godfather* or *Pulp Fiction*." He barely holds back a laugh.

"So Emma, let me just get this straight," Timbo puts both hands on the table and levels me with his eyes. "You thought Jake was meeting a mafia kingpin for lunch that day?"

We all three burst out laughing. "No no no," I can't stop laughing. "The name Timbo just conjured up something different for me I guess." I give them both an apologetic shrug. "No offense Timbo."

"Only a little bit taken," he responds.

Jacob kicks out a chair toward him. "Sit down man. We clearly need to prove to Emma that you're not a sleazy creep."

"Okay well in my defense..." I start to clarify, "I've never heard the name Timbo, but I've heard the name Jimbo. And Jimbo is typically not—okay Jimbo *never* is—a good-looking regular guy. Jimbos are usually pretty slimy. And so in this world, I thought that a Timbo might be kind of like that."

"Slimy?" Jake asks.

"Hold on hold on," Timbo pipes up. "Can we circle back to the good-looking part?"

I throw a half-hearted eye roll his way.

"I just gotta say that wow, Emma, Jake told me a lot but he neglected to tell me about your extensive knowledge of slimy mafiosos."

I cover my face with my hands and shake my head. Then I look up and say, "And *I* gotta say that Jake didn't tell me about your un-Timbo slash Jimbo-ness either."

Jacob waves his napkin in surrender. "That's true. I didn't. It didn't dawn on me to clarify that my friend Timbo was in fact a regular guy and not a mobster who looks like an overinflated Snape. My bad."

I lose it, keeling over the table in laughter.

A server comes over to take our drink order and he's—in a word—hot. Jacob gestures for me to order first and I order another Moscow Mule. My go-to safe drink that tastes delicious and doesn't get me housed. I am not cut out for martinis or old-fashioneds or any of those strong drinks. And I've never been a big beer fan. The guys order a couple beers and our server leaves.

"Well he was super obvious," Timbo says casually.

Jacob just nods in agreement.

"About what?" I ask.

The guys look at each other and then back at me. "About *you*," answers Jacob.

"Oh, because of the Mule? Is this more of a beer place?" I shrug and don't even give them a chance to answer. "C'mon though. A Mule is an easy one. I was a bartender and Mules have like three ingredients and you really can't mess them up. I mean, I *could've* ordered a mojito. Those are my *favorite*, but bartenders hate when people order them." I should know, since slinging drinks was my former life. I hated making them but man do I love drinking them. I continue, "I am saving them for pools and resorts and places where it's basically a rule that you *must* order a mojito."

I've never been to a pool like that, but when I do—I'm going to order the hell out of some mojitos.

They both laugh. "No, not about your order, which by the way, if you want a mojito I'm going to get you a mojito," Jacob says.

"He thinks you're hot." Timbo says bluntly.

I panic for a brief moment. *Who* thinks I'm hot? Jacob? Is he talking about Jacob? What do I even say to that? That I think he's hot, too? I mean, he obviously is. So is Timbo. Hell even the server is hot. I'm surrounded by hotness in this moment. Like drowning in hotness. Smothered by it.

I haven't said a word but they can see me running through things in my mind.

Jacob speaks up, looking over at Timbo. "I think she's one of those girls who doesn't realize. She's oblivious to it."

Timbo nods in agreement and chimes in, "You're right. Probably why you think she's cool."

I pipe up. "Okay, first—I'm literally right here. Don't talk about me like I'm not. Second—I'm not oblivious. I'm incredibly *blivious*. And third—if you think I'm cool it's because I am."

Both guys crack a smile. Our server returns with our drinks

and we all shut up awkwardly while he sets them down. Yes, I notice his eyes lingering on me a little longer than need be. And the way he brushes his hand against my arm when he asks if we need anything else. The second he leaves, both guys look at me with raised eyebrows that simply say *See?*

I raise my eyebrows right back at them. "Just because I choose not to *acknowledge* stuff doesn't mean I'm oblivious to it."

"Oh *damn*." Timbo does a mini bow to me.

"So not oblivious, just *unphased*..." Jacob is looking at me with an expression I can't quite read. "Yeah, I see that now." And then he adds, "I like it."

"Of course you do," Timbo ribs him.

I ignore both of them and take a sip of my Mule. "Okay so can we circle back to the incredibly unique Timbo name and then I swear I'll never ask it about it again? I'm just so curious because I've never heard that name before. Is it a family name or a nickname or..."

Timbo drops his head and runs his hand down his jaw. "My name is Beau."

"Beau?" I ask incredulously. "*Beau?* Like *B-e-a-u* Beau or *B-o* Bo?"

"B-e-a-u."

"Wow. A little bit fancy..." I trail off. "So it's actually Tim*beau*? Man I had it so wrong."

Timbo gives a little smile. "Nah, it's Timbo—with an *o* at the end."

"So how did you get Tim*bo* from *Beau* then?"

Timbo drops his head back and then looks right at Jacob. They stare at each other for a moment and neither one speaks.

I can take a hint. "Okay so it's a top secret thing. Roger that. Timbo it is and I'll accept it with zero explanation even though I want *all* the explanation." I do a little salute and take a sip of my drink.

Jacob shifts in his seat.

"It's fine," Timbo says. "Go ahead, tell her."

Jacob doesn't say anything for a few seconds and then says, "Well, Timbo is one of the greatest guys you'll ever meet..."

I can't help the *Awww* that escapes from my lips.

"But he's also....how do I put this?" He takes a sip from his beer and looks up at the ceiling like the answer's up there. "A man whore."

I burst out laughing. "Okay that is *not* where I saw this going." Through laughter I say, "Please continue."

"It started back in high school—"

I turn to look at Timbo. "Your man whore-ness?"

He just nods.

Jacob continues. "So in high school he got around. And he's never really stopped getting around. We started jokingly saying he was a bimbo. A *him*bo if you will. And since his name is Beau, it just...fit."

I nod, listening. "If the shoe fits..."

"Exactly. So his name's Beau but his first name is Timothy. So it just kind of morphed from Himbo to Timbo and that was like...seventeen years ago."

"Wow. *Wow*. Crazy to go from a pretty regal-sounding name like Timothy Beau to...*Timbo*." I take a sip and then turn to Timbo. "Do you *like* being called Timbo?"

He's quiet for a minute. "No one's ever asked me that." He pulls at his beer. "I mean, at first it was funny. I was an idiot when I was younger so I wore it like a badge of honor because I was getting laid like crazy and I thought I was the man. But now...I mean I'd like to think I'm no longer an idiot or a whore so it doesn't feel like the whole origin of the name fits me anymore, but I've been Timbo for so long I hardly remember what it's like to be *Beau*. Only a few people call me Beau." He chuckles and shrugs his shoulders.

I look at Jacob who clearly has no poker face. I nudge him, "What? What's that look?"

He turns to Timbo and says with a muted laugh, "Dude, the origin of the name is still fitting. I mean, just saying..."

My eyes dart between them and now I *have* to hear Timbo's response.

"I will neither confirm nor deny," he says and takes a big swig of beer.

I laugh. "Well, tonight has been...enlightening. I just have a couple more questions."

Both guys raise their brows.

I look at Jacob. "Should I call you Jacob or Jake? Because you introduced yourself to me as Jacob, but I hear everyone call you Jake."

"Either one. Both. I mean, Timbo and my brother Gray always call me Jake and most of my buddies do, too, but my sister and parents use them interchangeably."

"Okay, *Jake*." I smile. "I'll try them both out." I turn to face Timbo. "And my final question is for *you*."

He holds his hands up. "Me?"

I nod. "Do you want me to call you Timbo or Beau?"

Jacob and I both stare him down before he says, "Let's try... Beau."

"Nice to meet you, Beau." I hold up my glass and we all three clink our drinks together.

23

JAKE

"Dude, I love her," Timbo says, not even two seconds after he shuts the Uber door. Emma insisted on taking her own Uber home, even though I didn't like the idea of sending her off alone with some rando who could follow her inside her place or do something to her in the car. She assured me she takes solo Ubers all the time and her friends can track her location on their phones, but I still don't love it.

"I know," I reply. "She's great."

"You like her?"

"Yeah, of course. What's not to like?"

"No I mean do you *like her* like her?"

"Oh. No. It's not like that man. We're about to work together. I just think she's cool." And that, ladies and gentlemen, is what a blatant lie sounds like.

"Okay then can I ask her out?" Timbo asks nonchalantly, like he didn't just break bro code.

"What the hell man? No. What's wrong with you?"

"What's wrong with me? Why wouldn't I want to ask out a gorgeous, sweet, funny, smart girl? She was amazing. Something would be wrong with me if I *didn't* want to ask her out."

"Well you can't."

"I *can't?*"

"That's what I said. You can't." I take a deep breath. "She's off limits."

"If you want her then just go for it. But you can't make her off limits and *not* go for it."

"The hell I can. Listen man, we're about to work together for —honest to god if all goes well—hopefully the next six or so years. That's a long ass time and I need us to be good. I can't have you coming in screwing things up before we even get started."

"Who says I would screw things up?" He asks, feigning offense. "Maybe I would just screw things...*good*."

I know he's just messing with me to make me admit I like her, but it still pisses me off. I turn to him and punch him in the chest. Hard. "I swear dude, don't you dare touch her. Or even joke about her like that. She's off limits to you. To your jokes, to your looks, and definitely to your dick. *Off. Limits.* Treat her like she's my sister."

Timbo's face falls at that last sentence. He quickly shakes it off, but I catch it before he does. I've always suspected he might have had a thing for Lilah back in the day, but naturally I made her off limits, too, because she actually *is* my sister.

"Are *you* going to treat her like she's your sister?" He asks defiantly.

I drop back against the seat with a dramatic thud. "I fucking should," is all I can manage to say. I glance over at him and he looks back at me knowingly.

"You're toast." Timbo shakes his head.

"You think?" I ask, half sarcastically and half genuinely.

"Yes," answers a third voice that startles us both. It's our Uber driver, weighing in on the mess that has quickly become my life.

24

Wednesday

Jake: Okay, now that I have your number I thought we could keep the question game going via text so we could keep getting to know each other.

Emma: I like it. Hit me.

Jake: What is your favorite breakfast food and how do you like it cooked?

Emma: Pancakes. Ooh or a ham and cheese omelet. I like my pancakes thick and my omelets thin.

Emma: Also, way to step up your question technique! Well done.

Jake: Thank you. I learned from the master. Your turn.

Emma: Hmm, I wasn't prepared. Let me think.

Emma: . . .

Emma: . . .

Emma: What's a movie that you'll stop and watch anytime it comes on TV?

Jake: Legally Blonde.

Emma: Did we just become best friends?

Saturday

Emma: Who are your top three closest friends?

Jake: Timbo, Timbo, Gray

Emma: Gray's your brother right?

Jake: Yeah.

Jake: They both are.

Emma: awwww

Monday

Jake: What's your favorite genre of book to read?

Emma: Spicy romance.

Jake: Is that a thing?

Emma: It's not A thing, it's THE thing.

Jake: Like porn?

Emma: No not like porn you imbecile. Spicy romance books are romantic in an all-consuming way. Sweet epic love stories. With lots of sexual tension and yes hopefully lots of sex.

Jake: Sounds like porn.

Jake: And also like I read the wrong kind of books.

Emma: You probably do.

Emma: But also, Hierarchy qualifies as spicy romance.

Jake: No, Hierarchy is romantic fantasy. Romantasy. Check yourself.

Emma: Yeah, with some spice. SPICY romantic fantasy.

Jake: Point taken.

Tuesday

Lilah: Hey bro. I'd say "good morning" but…

Jake: Wait, what's up?

Lilah: The secrecy, that's what.

Jake: Lilah it's 6:00 in the morning. Stop being human click-bait. I'm asleep over here. I only answered because your cryptic text woke me up and made me worry.

Lilah: Have you seen any news today?

Jake: No. I'm sleeping. You shouldn't call people before 8 btw. Don't you remember anything mom taught us?

Lilah: I didn't call, I texted. Bye.

Jake: Ugh okay I'll bite. What is it?

Lilah: Pics of you with your new costar are all over the place. No one's calling her your costar so that's safe, but they are calling her your new girlfriend.

Lilah: Also, IS she your new girlfriend?

Jake: Shit.

Tuesday, 20 Seconds Later

Jake: Are you awake?

Emma: Yes. And I've seen it.

Jake: Are you okay?

Emma: Is this the question game or a real question?

Jake: 1) The question game IS real. You taught it to me. 2) Real question.

Emma: Ummmm. It's wild. I don't think I was... prepared?

Jake: For the attention?

Emma: Yeah. All of it. The attention. The speculation. The criticism. The praise.

Emma: It's a lot. We haven't even started shooting yet.

Jake: It is a lot. Especially for you right now because you've been such a mystery. I'm already out there but this is everyone's first dose of you. It's a frenzy out there.

Emma: Will they get over it?

Jake: You?

Emma: Yeah.

Jake: No chance.

25

JAKE

The last few days have been a blur. I've slept in, gone to bed early and generally tried to get as much rest as possible before our demanding shooting schedule starts. I've been working out extra with Timbo because I have the time and because, if I'm being honest, I'm motivated to get in even better shape so my smoke show of a costar can't be *unphased* by me. Like a few days can really even make a difference, but still. I'm going to try.

The images came back from the press shoot and they were... hot as hell. The studio was right to wait and announce Emma as Annabelle Claiborne this way. The response online and in the press has been overwhelmingly positive. Emma's face is plastered all over the internet and based on the insane amount of social media posts about her in the past seventy-two hours, the world is clamoring to know who on earth this girl is.

Before the casting news was released, a few pics of us hanging out at Dap's the night of the promo shoot got out and naturally all the gossip outlets were speculating as to who my "girlfriend" could be. Of course they'd cropped Timbo out of every shot because they have to sensationalize everything and make it look like it was just the two of us. I told my rep not to comment or even say "no comment." Told her I wanted crickets.

But the second the press releases rolled out and the promo images were released, people quickly made the connection that she was the girl in those bar pictures, and it turned into a whole *are they or aren't they thing?* which I was afraid might really bother Emma or even piss off the studio heads. But my manager said the studio is thrilled with the added mystique around the whole thing.

I, for one, am partly thrilled and partly annoyed by it all. I don't want it to freak Emma out and turn her off, but I'm also a little flattered by it because holy hell she is a catch and I *wish* the headlines were true. But I guess that's a take-it-to-the-grave thought because I know we can't jeopardize the lightning in a bottle we've captured with Emma.

And I don't fully know how she feels about all of it yet. I texted her when the news first went wild, and then I checked in again and she sounded okay. She was all, "I guess this just comes with the territory, right?" I couldn't get much out of her. So I'm just waiting until I see her. Tomorrow. At our table read. We start filming the following day.

And I'm mildly panicking because we got the script for the first episode and there's a love scene. And apparently we're shooting that *first*. Like our first scene we'll ever shoot together. Why do they do that? Why do they make actors shoot intimate scenes right out of the gate like that? This isn't the first time it has happened to me either. It's a legit thing. Directors swear by throwing actors in the deep end on stuff like this. And usually I'm not nervous, but with Emma as my costar? My boots are basically shaking.

Am I nervous to see her and what she thinks about all this insanity? *Yes.*

Am I going to get off tonight to calm my nerves? *Also yes.*

Will I be staring at the pictures of her from our press shoot when I do? *One hundred percent yes.*

Is that a bad idea? *The worst.*

26

EMMA

Everyone is sitting around the table chatting on our break and they all seem so comfortable. Confident. Literally every single person in this room looks completely relaxed, including Jacob.

Starting with Jacob.

But me? I feel out of place. Like an outsider among the innermost of insiders. This whole table read feels a tad awkward to me. I understand why it's important. At least I think I do. But reading love scenes out loud in front of everyone? Not my favorite thing. I know that's weird because we are about to *film* those scenes together, but that feels very different. We'll be in character, on a set, in costume. Not two people sitting beside each other at a crowded table.

Plus, I'm still not convinced I know what I'm doing. I keep waiting for everyone to realize they've made a huge mistake in taking a chance on me.

I'm sitting next to Jacob, and when there's a lull in the

conversation he's been in, I lean in close and ask quietly, "Can you hang back with me for a few minutes after we wrap up today?"

He cocks an eyebrow. "Sure. Is everything okay?"

I say in the most chipper voice I can manage, "Yeah, of course!" It comes out a bit manic. Definitely a little *too* chipper.

His eyes widen in mock fright. "Alright, what's going on? You seem a little...off."

I give a subtle, reassuring shake of my head. "Nothing's wrong. I just...need your help with something. It's kind of private."

"Well, I'm a vault. And I've got no plans." His lips tug up just a bit, reassuring me.

I ignore the fact that I'm relieved he has no plans and whisper, "Thanks," just as Alex, our director, clears his throat and I can tell that must mean it's time to start back up.

For the rest of the read, Jacob seems slightly distracted, and I know it's because he's wondering what on earth I want to talk about. What I need his help with. I can tell he has a million questions running through his mind. But I guarantee they've got nothing on the one in mine.

WHILE EVERYONE else gathers their things and talks eagerly about filming the next day, Jacob and I wait. Wait for them to pack up. Wait for them to clear out. But everyone is too amped up about how well the read-through went and they won't stop talking.

Jacob already let Willa, our first assistant director, know that we're going to stick around to work on some things on our own. So now we're just waiting, standing around like a couple of awkward teenagers at a party who don't really feel comfortable enough to talk in front of others yet, but still keep stealing glances at each other.

Finally, Jacob can't stand it anymore. He sidles up right beside me and says out of the corner of his mouth, "Tell me."

I snap my head to him. "What? No way. Not until everyone leaves." I shake my head and Jacob groans just loudly enough for me to hear.

Then he pipes up over all the remaining voices in the room, "Great job, everyone. Now clear out so we will all be ready for tomorrow." It's the second time he's tried to poke everyone to get a move on.

But these people just won't leave.

I watch Jacob walk over to Willa but they're across the room and I can't make out what they're saying. He comes walking toward me and stops at the table to grab his things and slip them into his backpack. He gestures for me to come over, so I do.

"Grab your things," he says. "There's a vacant room down the hall we can use."

I look around at the lingering cast and crew in this room and it's clear no one is in a rush. So I gather my things up and follow him out, awkwardly waving to the room as we walk out so as not to officially ghost exit.

I follow him down the hall and he turns left a few doors down.

The second I walk in after him, he shuts the door and turns to face me, exclaiming, "For the love of God woman what is it? You've had me wondering all damn day."

I roll my eyes. "It's been like an hour."

"Longest hour of my life," he jokes. "Now please tell me what's going on."

I look down at my feet, rolling each one from side to side. Watching them. Stalling. I really, *really* need his help but it's just so hard to say it out loud.

He takes a step toward me. "Emma? Are you alright?" His voice is gentle, tinged with worry.

I nod and look up. "I'm...I'm just nervous."

"About tomorrow?"

"Yes." I take a breath, steeling myself to voice the world's most ridiculous worry. "Okay, so you know how acting is a really odd world, right?" I ask it like it's simply a fact.

He just looks at me, clearly puzzled. I don't wait for him to answer.

"And this is super weird for me to talk about, but you're the only person I can really ask about it."

"Okay..." His brows are furrowed so deeply I wonder if there will be lines there forever.

I keep going. "So you obviously have substantially more acting experience than me. I mean, I've been in some scenes, but they were small and I can count them on one hand." I think about it for a split second. "I can count them on two fingers actually."

I am rambling. Full of words. *All* the words, maybe. I'm needlessly verbose, talking my way in circles around the one thing I can't seem to voice.

He is quiet.

"Okay, so I've never done a romantic scene. And seeing as this entire series is basically a live-action rendering of a sexy romance novel, I need to make sure I know how to do it."

He finally speaks. "Do what, exactly?"

"Well, specifically..." *Geez how do I say this without sounding like a complete amateur and making him regret I was cast as his lead?*

"Specifically *what*?" Jacob presses me, taking another step closer.

Okay, out with it. Just say it.

"Specifically I need to know about kissing on camera." The

words tumble out. I wait for him to respond, and when he doesn't I add, "And maybe touching, too. But mainly kissing."

Jacob is quiet, just staring at me. Why does he have to look so torturously hot, standing there with his full attention on me? It's making me more nervous. But now that I've cracked open the gates, might as well fling them all the way open and let the flood rage on.

"Okay, so I'm confused because I've read magazine articles and seen interviews over the years about how intimate scenes are the least sexy thing to shoot and kissing scenes are every bit as technical and un-romantic. But my main question is...do we actually kiss? Like *kiss* kiss. Because I've also read that actors don't actually use tongue. They go open mouth but no tongue. And that seems weird to me because I can't possibly imagine that could look real. But I guess it does?"

I pause long enough to see if he will answer, but he's staring at me with the most intense look and I see no signs of response, so I push on. "And then there's the fact that I *know* I've seen Jamie's tongue go into Claire's mouth on *Outlander*. And that show does romance and spice right. Like, I love seeing the slip of his tongue. It's *hot*. And our show is supposed to be hotter than even that. Our love is supposed to be intense and raw and I just don't know what to do tomorrow because we are shooting that scene and I don't know whether we're supposed to really kiss or just fake kiss and it's not something I want to learn the answer to with an audience and cameras on me."

Wow. That was an incredibly long-winded diatribe. I could't stop talking. But damn it feels good to finally say it out loud.

Jacob blinks. Slowly. He stares at me for several long beats and then swallows.

But he doesn't answer.

I pull at his shirt sleeve. "Jake, I'm serious." He tilts his head slightly to the side and I move my head to mirror his, making him look right at me. "Do we real kiss or fake kiss on these scenes? I need to know." I take a breath. "I mean I know we have an 'intimacy coach' or whatever they're calling her, and I could just ask her, but I don't want to look that clueless if I'm being honest. And I'm only asking you because I feel like you won't judge me and you'll just answer me. But you're not answering me and I—I really, really need you to."

"Both," he says instantly.

"Both?" I ask, confused.

"Both," he answers again. "I've done it both ways. It's up to the actors. Sometimes we talk about it before hand—"

"Like we are now?" I interrupt him.

His lips twitch. "No, not quite like this." He chuckles. "But yeah, sometimes we discuss it and honestly I usually do whatever my costar wants to do. Sometimes we don't use tongue because it's more respectful of our spouses if we're in a relationship or something...because it can make partners too uncomfortable. Or jealous." He winces. "And then sometimes we do use tongue because it does look more real and for whatever reason we aren't worried about anyone getting upset and we're both comfortable with it. It just depends I guess."

I feel a small sense of relief wash over me, just thankful he's even having this discussion with me. And his explanation makes sense. I get that.

"Okay, so follow up question." I cock my head and study him. "What do *you* want to do?" He drops his eyes for the briefest second before looking back at me. "Or I guess—what were you *planning* to do is the better question. We shoot tomorrow, so what were you *planning* to do?"

27

JAKE

W hat do I *want* to do?

What am I *planning* to do?

I swallow. Those are two very different questions. What do I *want* to do? I want to kiss the hell out of her and use the fact that we're shooting a romantic scene as justification for getting to taste her.

But what was I *planning* to do? I was planning to "fake kiss" her (in her words) because I'm not sure I can handle *actually* kissing her. Even on camera, which is the least sexy setting ever, I think there's a strong chance it might rock me too hard. And make me rock hard. So yeah, it would definitely be safer to not give myself permission to make out with my irresistible costar under the guise of shooting a scene.

Emma's voice breaks through my thoughts. "Oh, or have you not even thought about it because it's just not a big deal to you and I'm making it a much bigger deal than it is?"

Oh I've thought about it. A *lot*. I've asked for a completely closed set tomorrow—and for all intimate scenes—to help her feel more comfortable. But *I* feel the furthest thing from that right now. I feel exceedingly *uncomfortable*. Starting with my pants which are currently pulled so tight across my crotch that I think the fly might bust open.

But why am *I* nervous? It makes sense for *her* to be nervous. This is all new to her. But I've done this countless times before.

I finally answer her. "I guess I thought we'd use no tongue since this is your first scene like this. I felt like you might be more comfortable with that."

"Well I'm not!" She nearly shouts, panic written all over her face. "I don't know *how* to do it that way. I don't know how to do a fake kiss and make it look real!"

She's rocking side to side, back and forth, like she has something else to say. So I wait. I haven't seen her like this. She's so adorably worked up, and I kind of love it. But I can tell she is genuinely anxious and I want to alleviate that for her. When she still doesn't speak, I jump in.

"There's really nothing to it, you just kind of open—" I start to explain, but she cuts me off.

"I need to ask you something else now."

"Okay, go for it."

"I realize I don't fully know what your dating status is..." she trails off.

My heart drops to my feet and my dick perks up even more, if that is possible.

"So this might be totally out of line and disrespectful to your girlfriend in which case I just want you to give it to me straight..."

Give it to her? Oh my god how I want to give it to her. Straight. Below. Behind. Sideways. All the ways.

"But if you want to fake kiss for that scene, can we...?" She lets out a frustrated groan that has every part of my body responding. "Can I practice that with you?"

She looks half sheepish and half confident and I have no idea how someone can look like both those things at once, but she does.

"Practice kissing?" I blink, not fully believing what I'm hearing.

"God no, silly."

"Okay because I was gonna—"

She cuts me off again. "Not practice *kissing*." She shakes her head like that's a ridiculous notion. "Practice *fake* kissing. I know how to kiss. I don't know how to *fake* kiss. I need you to show me."

I blink again. She does not.

Oh boy. Am I on candid camera? Is this some type of a test? Because I feel like I'm *thisclose* to failing it miserably. I remind myself to breathe. "Emma, if you know how to kiss you know how to fake kiss. I don't think we need to practice. It'll be fine. *You'll* be fine."

I should win a freaking award for not jumping at the opportunity she just laid before me. Gentleman much?

She's shaking her head. "Okay first of all, I don't want to be *fine*. I want to be *amazing*." She throws her hands up. "A *fine* kiss? That sucks. Blows. The worst. We can't do that."

For the love of God does she hear the words coming out of her mouth right now? *Sucks? Blows?* What is she doing to me?

"I want to knock their socks off," she says looking straight into my face.

"Whose socks?" I ask, trying to follow her line of thought.

"*Everyone's*. The viewers. Casting. Our director. You. Or—you know what I mean. I want Annabelle to knock Daniel's socks off."

And now she's tugging the hem of my shirt. "So I *do*. I do

need to practice. Just once so I can see what it feels like. And imagine what it looks like. But only if it won't get you in trouble."

"In trouble?" The confusion on my face must show.

"Yeah. Like if it'd get you in trouble with someone you're with. Because obviously it's kind of weird. I get that. We're not being filmed right now, so it's...it's like behind the scenes kissing practice. It's not sanctioned."

"No," I reply simply.

"I don't want to land you in hot water. Or worse—on the couch." She grimaces in mock terror.

"That's not an issue."

She has no idea just how not an issue it is. How my only issue in the chick department is that I am already obsessed with her and starting tomorrow I will have to spend nearly every day with her pretending I just enjoy working together. Pretending I don't obsess about what she'd taste like, how she'd fit in my arms, what she'd feel like clenching around me.

She lets out a sigh of relief and jokingly wipes the nonexistent sweat off her head. "Okay, for me neither. So let's do this," she commands, closing the distance between us. "Jacob, can you fake kiss me please?"

What is my life right now?

First—I can't believe how relieved I am to hear that it isn't an issue for her either. Does that mean she isn't seeing someone? Or at least not seriously? And second—*holy shit I am a nervous wreck.* Which makes no sense because I've done this hundreds of times before. Probably more like thousands if I count all the different takes we've done for each scene. I mean, I was on an Australian soap opera—scenes like this were approximately ninety-five percent of my job.

So why am I internally freaking out? This is my chance to put my lips to hers, even if it is "fake." And I'm a great kisser. I need to seize this chance before she takes it back. Yeah, I know I'll be kissing her tomorrow and the day after and the day after that, but that's different because we'll be on set with a camera tracking our every move.

Right now it's just us.

I try to play it cool, like I'm not burning from the inside out. "Okay, sure. It's literally just an open mouth kiss with no tongue. But you move like there's tongue. That's it."

"Yeah, that sounds weird to me, not going to lie." She straightens her shirt like she's readying herself. "Okay, show me how it's done."

I lean in and put my lips to hers. I'm so tense and stiff—and not just below my belt. My entire body is rigid and the kiss is just as rigid. But I keep going. I open my mouth and she mirrors me, and then we are full-on fake kissing. I tilt my head a bit and she continues to match what I do, moving our mouths together until she abruptly pulls back—

"I hate it."

My heart sinks to my feet. But I try to play it off. "Geez, tell me what you really think why don't you?" I say on a laugh.

"I'm sorry." She twists her mouth to the side and looks at me worriedly. "But it's...it's...it's not good," she says while shaking her head in what looks like...oh god, is that disgust? "Like not good at all. You can't possibly tell me you think that is a sexy kiss."

I feel my defenses flare up. "I mean, I don't know if I'd call it *unsexy* though."

She barks out a laugh. "Oh I would. I would definitely call it that." She shakes her head like she never wants to do that again. "Is that what it normally feels like? Or are we just bad at it together?"

Those words hang heavy in the air as she waits for me to answer. When I don't, she continues, "I mean, it must *look* a heck of a lot better on camera than it feels or something, because otherwise I don't think any actors would ever agree to do it."

"It *does* look better than it feels in the moment," I counter. "I've shot a lot of kissing scenes like this, and...people have always found them to be hot scenes." I shrug and offer up a half-smile. I wasn't trying to toot my own horn, but the truth is there was a reason everyone was obsessed with my character on that soap. My scenes were hot. Facts are facts.

But here's another fact and it's one I can't shake: *holy shit did I just screw up.* I gave her the worst kiss—probably of her life—and now she'll never like me. I feel like I'm thirteen again, trying to kiss the girl I like and absolutely floundering.

"I believe you," she says softly, reassuring me. "I do. But we are Annabelle and Daniel. We're the new Jamie and Claire. We're supposed to have the can't-stay-away-from-each-other-can't-stay-off-each-other kind of love." Her lips curve up, just a hair. "We need the people watching our show to feel that just *watching* us. And a kiss like what we just did isn't going to cut it."

"You really love *Outlander*, huh?" I ask, latching onto that in hopes of shifting the conversation away from how disappointing that fake kiss was.

"*Yes.*" Her answer is guttural. "Well the early seasons anyways. They are so good together in those first few seasons. And the reason I feel that way—along with *millions* of viewers by the way—is because their chemistry is off the charts and their scenes are both tender *and* scorching. At the same time."

"So what do you want to do?" I ask, shrugging. I feel like a total chump. And I can honestly say I haven't felt like a chump in years at this point. I've had a solid chump-free decade. She is unraveling my confidence by the second without even meaning to.

"I want us to kiss for real. Like there's no tomorrow. Or at least make it *look* that way."

"Okay then let's do that." I say, trying to subdue the desire for her that's running furiously through my veins.

"Is that okay with you though? Because I know you were planning to not really go for it."

I smile. "Well, that was more for you. Out of respect for *you*."

"Thank you, that's sweet." Her voice is cordial, if a bit flat.

I raise an eyebrow. "Sweet but not good?"

She crinkles her nose. "Yeah, sweet but not good. Not good *enough* anyways. Maybe respect me like sixty percent less this time," she says with a laugh. "A little disrespect in this setting can go a long way."

My dick twitches in agreement and I just hope she doesn't see that twitch through my pants, because there's no way what's going on down there isn't visible if she were to glance down.

"Emma, sometimes scenes like this can cause a lot of tension," I warn. "Just giving you a heads up since you said you've never really done scenes like this before. Especially if we *really* do them, like you want to."

"Thanks, I appreciate that," she says like she doesn't have a care in the world. Where is that nervous girl from a few minutes ago? "I mean, I think we'll be fine. We're professional. I think a lot of you, I respect you. You respect me. We're friends. We'll be good."

"Famous last words," I retort with a soft smile. "But no, I don't just mean between *us*. But yeah that, too. I meant more for relationships that you or I might be in at some point. Things can get...*tense* sometimes when you're shooting lots of intimate scenes."

"Oh I'm sure."

"Especially if we're *real* kissing—as you put it."

She places her hands on her hips. "Is it a problem for you?"

"Nope."

"Then it's not a problem for me. I know the line. And based

on the mildly robotic kiss you just gave me, you know the line, too. But..." She bites her bottom lip and god does it make me want to bite it, too. "But, if that kiss was knowing the line then I think we've got to *unknow* the line just a little bit."

"Blur the line?" I ask.

"Damn Robin Thicke for ruining that phrase for me when he cheated on his super hot wife." She shakes her head in disappointment. "But yeah, we need to blur the line just a little in these moments I think. Like a smudge. *Smudge* the line."

I laugh. "Okay then. We will smudge the lines."

"Perfect. It's settled. Let's make people root for Annabelle and Daniel."

I cock a brow at her. "By having really hot kisses?"

This time she cocks a brow. "Among other things."

"Do you want to practice a real one since that's what we're going with now?" I blurt it out before I can stop myself, and I immediately regret it.

"Practice a real kiss?" She asks like that's something she hadn't even considered.

"Yeah," I say on a shrug, feigning nonchalance instead of showing my embarrassment at the rejection I can already see on her face.

She shakes her head. "Nah. I don't think we need to."

Dammit. I need a chance to redeem myself. "No we don't *need* to, but I just want you to feel comfortable." I'm trying to save face and not appear desperate but I'm not sure it's working.

"I do now, but thanks. It was the fake kissing that was throwing me. *Real* kissing? *Pshhh.* We got this." She smiles and it hurts a little bit. She's so beautiful it really does hurt.

I cannot let that kiss be it. We can't end today this way. We just can't. She wants our chemistry to knock people's socks off. And I just did the opposite of knocking her socks off. I...I put her socks *on*. Like big socks. Knee socks. God, maybe even compression socks. Yeah, I just put the least sexy socks ever on her and pulled them all the way up and now they might be impossible to knock off.

She nods her head toward the door. "Shall we?" she asks with a relaxed smile.

I grab her arm. "Emma, if you want this giant love you're talking about to translate on screen, I think we should practice. Even just once. To make sure we're...in sync."

She studies my face hard. "You know what? Maybe you're right." She smirks. "Let's make it so good that it's worth abandoning my noble status for."

I'm hit with instant nerves. I feel like I might throw up. That would be terrible. She would think she repulsed me. She just gave me the green light to kiss her and I'm...hesitating? And thinking about vomiting? What is happening to me?

She clears her throat and lifts her eyebrows to signal that she's ready.

I lean in and press my lips to hers again. We stay like that for just a beat, and then I try to turn it on. But I can't. Somehow this practice kiss is way more difficult than kissing on camera. It's the opposite of what I expected. I'd thought it'd be easy. *Hot*. But on camera, I'm in my zone. In my element. In full wardrobe, on a set built to transport viewers—and *me*—into a different world. And even though it's not sexy to shoot those types of scenes, I'm at least in character and just playing a part. Which, by the way, I'm really good at doing.

But this? This is different. This is just the two of us in our regular clothes, in a dull, empty room. There was no build up, no need to act convincingly so the director heaps praise on me, no pressure to perform or impress. Except the pressure to impress *her*, which for some reason is crippling me instead of igniting me like I expected.

She pulls away a second time. I realize I must have been

kissing her during all those thoughts. And I realize that it must not have been good. Because she literally pulls back from me with the tiniest cringe expression on her face.

A cringe look.

In response to my kiss.

Kill me now.

She covers her face with her hands and then looks back up at me. "So I know I poked fun at having an intimacy coach for all these spicy scenes we'll be shooting, but now I get it."

"What do you mean?"

"Well I guess I thought doing this stuff would come more naturally because we seem to have good chemistry...like in the auditions, and just our rapport in general. I thought it'd be kind of organic to do these types of scenes together. We get along, we're friends, and I guess I just thought it'd be easier? But I'm new to this and now I see why the studio brings in people to help coach us on how to make the love scenes hot. Or at least make them *look* hot." She laughs and shrugs. "I just didn't realize *you and I* would actually need help, but now I get that maybe it's just kind of part of the deal. No matter how hot your costar is."

She winks and I realize she's trying to throw me a bone but it's not nearly a big enough bone to wash away the insecurity I'm currently drowning in.

"Sure, I guess I get it, too." Lies. Complete lies.

"It just feels...forced." She says it slowly, like something has just dawned on her. "Oh my god, which I guess it *was*..." Then she bursts out laughing and drops her head into her hands. "Jacob, I'm an idiot. I'm sorry. I *did* force you. I have just been so nervous about this aspect of shooting and now I've made it so weird. I'm sorry. Can we delete the last twenty minutes? *Please?*" Her head is still in her hands.

It wasn't her fault, it was mine. I'd been way too tense. Too nervous to let myself go and really kiss her how I would if we were together or even if we were on set. I want her so badly and I know I can't have her so I was holding back with everything I had to keep her from knowing it. And as a result she thinks I am a terrible kisser and that we have no chemistry.

Fuck. Fuckkkkkk.

She drops her purse strap over her head and under one arm. I love that she wears it across her body like that. A lot of women I've dated had these absurdly tiny purses or giant purses—both of which I think are completely impractical. Emma has a normal-sized purse, kind of like a purse/backpack hybrid. It's such a silly thing but I love it about her.

She pulls her hair out from underneath the strap. "Jacob, seriously thank you. I know I put you on the spot and I'm sorry about that. I was just so nervous. But I feel better now because at least I know what to expect and what we need to do."

"What do we need to do?" I dare to ask. I'm not even sure I want to hear her answer.

She holds up a finger. "Work with the intimacy coach." She holds up a second finger. "Rehearse." She adds a third finger. "And maybe have a drink before we shoot. I don't take shots but if I did, I'd say we need to do that." She throws her head back on a laugh.

I laugh with her, but it's not genuine. I feel my chance to fix this slipping away with every minute that goes by. She is shutting down and about to walk out the door. Yeah sure I'll see her tomorrow, but we'll be with some of the crew and they'll be telling us how to kiss and where to put our hands and when to stop.

This is it.

"Emma." My voice comes out hoarse. Strained.

I reach out and grab her arm. Desperately. Too desperately probably. She looks down at where my hand is wrapped around her wrist and then up at me, confusion all over her face.

I pull her toward me. Slowly at first, but then I yank her into me so her body's flush against mine. She softens instantly. "You're right. That wasn't good." I lightly brush my lips across hers. "I can do better." I place a hand on either side of her head. "If you'll let me."

She nods.

I seal my lips to hers, and this kiss is immediately different. It's more raw. More real. It's *delicious*.

I pull back just enough to ask, "More like that?"

"Oh. *Oh*." Her eyes widen in understanding and she nods excitedly. "Yes. Yeah, more like that. *Exactly* like that."

Then I drop my lips back to hers without another word. Her lips are so soft and plush, something I hadn't even registered on those first two kisses. I'd known they would be, because I stare at them constantly and have imagined them on my lips, my neck, my cock...but when we'd kissed earlier I was so distracted that I hadn't even fully appreciated them. I'm not making that same mistake now.

I tease her lips apart with my tongue and deepen the kiss. She reciprocates without an ounce of hesitation.

If I was sixteen I would've already blown.

But I'm thirty-two. And no way in hell am I about to ruin this moment.

The awkwardness of a moment ago is long gone, but now there is a different problem: we can't seem to stop. We are barreling forward and it feels so fucking good. So fucking *right*. I continue to kiss her with abandon. She tastes like cinnamon gum and coffee. My new favorite flavor, I think. I feel like I can't kiss her deeply enough. And as long as she'll let me, I'll keep going. I snake my right hand around the back of her neck, wrapping it in her hair. Then I tug her head back so I can kiss her exposed neck. She lets out a little moan and it *undoes* me. I can feel my restraint ebb. Feel myself starting to lose it. I kiss her neck over and over, further and further down.

"Yes, like that." Her words are gasoline on the fire currently burning me from the inside out. Her hand barely twitches on my chest, where her palms are still flattened against me. I move back to her lips and she trails her hand down my body, lightly brushing against the front of my pants. My cock jumps. *Oh.* She must've felt me pressed against her. And now she's checking, confirming that she felt what she thought she did. I wonder if she's surprised to feel a rock. Her fingers drift over me. It's a light touch. A *curious* touch, and I feel it in the marrow of my bones. It makes me want to ravage her.

We're way beyond what we set out to do and I wonder if I should stop things before I lose the willpower to. But that thought vanishes the moment she reaches around and grabs my ass. I groan, shifting over to lick her collarbone before brushing my lips over the spot I'd just licked. *God, the taste of her skin.* The *smell* of her skin.

This must be what the whole pheromones thing is about. Like she's emitting a chemical that I am at once addicted to and in danger of overdosing on.

My control is powerless to stop. I have one hand around her back and one still in her hair. I move my free hand up her back, and just as I move it around to the front of her body, she grabs my chin and guides my head up from her collarbone. *Up, up, up.* Until we're face to face.

Eyes locked, neither of us says a word nor moves a muscle. Well, except the one muscle that clearly didn't get the memo and is currently out of my control, pulsing so wildly that I know the movement must be visible through my jeans.

"Um, so I think we're good on *that*." Her voice isn't even a voice. It's just a breath. "That was..." She exhales as if she'd been holding her breath. "Yeah, that was more like it," she says, nodding happily, if a bit dazed. "I stand corrected. I don't think we need help after all."

I'm reeling. I can't think straight. This girl just unhinged me with a *kiss*.

"Let's lock up," she says, like she didn't just rock my entire world to pieces and leave them scattered all over the floor.

I'm a zombie. I throw on my backpack, grab my jacket, and follow her. I still haven't spoken. Not sure I even can.

We walk out together and I punch in the lock code Willa gave me, finally finding my voice. "Are you headed home?"

"No, my call time is super early and I'm so nervous I don't think I'll sleep much anyway, so I think it makes sense just to stay in my trailer. Plus I think it will kind of keep me in the zone. What about you?"

"Yeah, me too." Another lie. I hadn't been planning to. I've never slept in my trailers. Not once. But I'm not sure I can be further than a few feet from her right now.

We walk toward the trailers.

I feel so unsteady. Do I walk her to her door? It's not like I have to make sure she gets home safely. Her trailer is only about fifty feet away from mine. I can see her door from my own. But still, I'm a gentleman. Even if I didn't act like one a few minutes ago.

We get to her little steps and she breaks the silence. "Hey Jacob, seriously, thank you so much for tonight. I know it was weird and I really put you on the spot, but it was really helpful, at least for me." She gives my arm a little punch. Like we're buddies. Like we're bros. Then she turns to walk in her door.

I turn to walk toward my own trailer and shout back to her, "No prob, it helped me, too."

Helped me fall into a raging obsession with my costar and develop a severe case of blue balls, that is.

28

JAKE

I barely slept last night. I mostly laid in bed dreaming about how I wanted to keep going with my gorgeous costar who I'm supposed to be nothing but professional with. I couldn't stop thinking about how her body felt pressed against mine, how her lips felt, how she tasted, how she rubbed her hand against my crotch so she could feel me. Okay, it was definitely more of a brush than a rub, but still.

All night long I tried to convince myself that I just got caught up in the moment. And that I haven't been obsessed with her since I saw her at that very first audition.

I tried giving myself a pep talk about how I *can* handle being completely professional with her and how I should be relieved we have chemistry like that. It bodes well for the show.

None of it worked.

At 3:30 a.m. I finally call it and just get up. My call time is at 5:30 a.m. anyways, so there's no use laying here for another hour or two just torturing myself. I shower and head to set, a full hour and a half early. We're shooting on the sound stages today so I just have to walk over.

But of course, because the universe has a truly wicked sense of humor, the second I walk out of my trailer I see Emma walking out of hers. She's juggling what looks like four different drinks and trying not to drop them as she attempts to pull the door closed with her foot. It's still dark out but I can see she's struggling.

I jog over to help her, grabbing three cups from her hands.

"Hey! What are you doing up? I thought your call time wasn't for a couple of hours?" She whispers, like she's going to wake someone up.

"It's not, but I couldn't sleep."

"Oh. I'm sorry. That sucks. Well, I definitely *could've* slept but being a girl comes with some extra stuff...like a lot of time in hair and makeup, so here I am." She's bright eyed and smiling. Probably so excited for the first day of shooting.

"Yes, here you are...and with four different cups no less," I say with a laugh.

"A girl's gotta hydrate. Or more like dehydrate with copious amounts of coffee and then rehydrate back up."

"Clearly." I hold up the giant travel cups in my hand. "But you know there is always coffee and every other drink you can imagine on set, right? You don't have to bring your own."

"I did *not* know that. Thank you for enlightening me. Tomorrow I won't look like a cup saleswoman."

We walk a few steps in silence, and I know I should probably just let the silence be, but I feel a little insecure around her now, so I force conversation. "How do you like your trailer? Are you settled?"

She abruptly stops walking and glances back at her trailer before turning to face me. "I grew up in a trailer park and am well-versed in all types of trailers," she begins, her eyes instantly glistening. "And that, my friend, is no trailer." She shakes her head in disbelief. "I mean, why do they even call it that? That thing is like a luxury hotel-room-motor-coach-airstream-hybrid and it is spectacular." Her face barely contains her smile. "Is it pathetic that I'm so excited about it? I mean, can I just move in there permanently? My apartment is okay, I've definitely made it look good...but it's economy." She tilts her head, chuckling. "And not even comfort economy. Or exit row. It's *last-row-so-the-seats-don't-recline* economy."

She gestures to her trailer. "But this? This is a different animal. This is *luxe*."

She starts walking again and there's so much I want to ask her. So much I want to know about her. About her life. The little bit she just shared pulls at my heart, but she's also so damn cute, completely fangirling over her trailer. Calling a forty foot basic rectangle things like *luxe* and *spectacular*. "I'm glad you like it. I hoped you would."

"Did you have something to do with it?"

I shrug dismissively. "Not really." I don't dare tell her.

"Well I love it. *Clearly*."

She suddenly stops walking and turns to fully face me again, her expression growing serious. "Jacob, I'm sorry about last night. Kind of all of it. But especially my hand. I totally Ricky Bobbied it."

"You *what?*"

"I was like Ricky Bobby *'I don't know what to do with my hands,'*" she says as she mimics Will Ferrell holding his hands up awkwardly because he didn't know what to do with them. "When I touched you. I got caught up. It was over the line, and I'm sorry."

I laugh out loud. Geez, this girl.

"I get it. Same for me."

"Except not your hands," she points out.

"True." This time *I* mimic Ricky Bobby but say, "I didn't know what to do with my mouth."

We laugh together but then she shrugs and shoots back, "It sure seemed like you did."

Record. Scratch.

A beat passes. Then she laughs. So I laugh.

We both laugh.

Hers is genuine. Mine is not.

She's laughing because she thinks it's funny. And I'm laughing to keep from crying because it's day one and I already want her so badly it's actually painful.

29

EMMA

They keep me in hair and makeup forever. Once again, they can't decide. This time they can't decide whether they want my hair to start half up/half down and get mussed by Jake or whether they wanted it to start all the way up and then get mussed so badly by Jake that it ends up halfway down. I swear they've gone back and forth four times already and still can't decide. It's such a petty thing and I cannot believe how much brainpower they're devoting to this decision.

Angela is messing with it when Jacob pops in to see what's taking so long because he's basically a god on this set and can do whatever he wants. (There's also the minor fact that he's an executive producer so that may play a *little* part in his omnipotence on set.) I've legitimately been in hair and makeup so long that he came to check on me. And when he walks in to make sure I'm okay, I swear there is a unified *awww* from everyone in the trailer.

Except me. I don't fawn over him. After last night, I beat

myself up for crossing the line—actually it was more like just *erasing* the entire damn line—and pledged to myself that I would be immune to...*him*. All of him. We're coworkers and our job has hardly begun. I will not allow myself to become the pathetic physical manifestation of the "falling for your costar" stigma.

I beckon Jake over and then whisper in his ear "Can you please for the love of God help them decide on a hairstyle so we can do this thing?" I lean back and smile sweetly. But I know it doesn't reach my eyes.

He knows it, too. He squeezes my shoulder and asks the team if they need a fifth opinion. There are only three of them so everyone looks around at each other, looking for the fourth. Then Jacob points to me, sitting in the chair with what I'm sure is a look of total exasperation.

"Oh, well, we didn't ask Emma," said Lin, one of the hair wizards. She didn't mean it in a rude way. It's not my place to make decisions like that. It's theirs. I was reluctant to weigh in anyways because two of them wanted it up and one wanted it half-down. It didn't seem smart to try and interject myself into a face-off like that, so I stayed quiet.

"Wait wait wait, you haven't been able to decide and you didn't think to ask the star of the show?" Jake's deep voice has a bit of an edge to it. Not a mean edge, but just ever so slightly authoritative.

It's hot.

"Well, that's what we're doing now," says Blair, with a smile directed only at him.

Okay so clearly she has a thing for him.

Jake doesn't let on that he caught that flirtation at all. "The *other* star." He gestures toward me. "Emma, what do *you* think?"

I shift in my chair and sit up straighter. *Way to put me on the spot.* "Okay, let me preface this by saying I am an absolute girl power female and believe women run the world..." I look at Jake. "No offense, Jake." He nods with a smirk and gestures for me to continue. "But I think in this case the reason no one has been able to decide is we're all women. In this one *singular and very isolated* instance, we need a man to decide." I wince. "I know, I know, I can't believe I said it either," I say with such exaggeration it makes the entire room laugh.

I continue, "But seriously. They can't decide if they want me more polished to start and then as you grope me my hair becomes wild and loose or if they want me to start out more natural and less polished, and you make my hair not just wild but more like...*untamed*."

Jake's brows are gently furrowed and I can tell he is listening intently and trying to make sense of this absurdity.

I go on. "So basically, the reason I think *you*—the lone male in here—should make the call is because we need to do whatever is going to make guys watching this show think I'm irresistible. So as a dude, which way is hotter? You pick."

Jake draws a deep breath and then says with zero hesitation, "Start more natural, less polished, and have faith I can do a damn good job taking it to *untamed* status once the cameras are rolling."

I swear there is a collective gasp in the room. It's like I can *feel* all three of them swoon.

But not me. I'm immune to the swoon. Last night I gave myself a Jake vaccination, veiled as an intense self-help internal pep talk, so that this man cannot affect me. My cells are now impervious to him, equipped to reject any and all Jakeness.

It's just...there seems to be a slight delay in the Jake vaccine taking effect, because I *did* feel an inkling of a swoon. More of a giant ink splotch if I'm being honest. But I don't let on that I felt his words below my belly button. That the way he said that with such confidence made my stomach flutter, among other things.

Instead of acknowledging the steam he just laid on the room, I say simply, "Okay ladies, decision made. Take it down and let's get this show on the road."

And with that, Jake nods at me and walks out. I melt just a little bit inside. Okay a lot bit. Like molten lava is trickling through me and endangering one organ at a time.

So much for that immunity.

ALEX, our director, calmly orders, "Push her up against the wall a bit harder after she pulls away."

Jake nods at him.

Alex turns his focus to me. "And Emma, when you put your arms around his neck, bring one down to just above his butt."

I give a thumbs up. Because how do you really respond to that?

Alex claps his hands together. "Okay, let's try it again."

Jake brushes his thumb over my lips back and forth and stares into my eyes. "If I don't have you I might die right here. Right now." His voice is barely a whisper.

"Well take me," I breathe out. "I can't let you die on my watch."

And he does. He kisses me.

With passion.

With urgency.

And with *tongue*. Just like we'd practiced.

I pull away as if I'm having second thoughts and Jake pushes me back into the wall. Then I wrap my arms up around his neck before dragging one hand down toward his ass. It's a hot scene, and I can tell that we are doing it justice.

"Cut!" Alex yells out and he and Willa crowd around video village—which is what everyone calls the digitally overloaded area off to the side of the set where all the monitors are—to watch the playback.

Jake and I stay put, just watching them watch us on the screens.

Alex is nodding. Then he looks up to us. "That was great. Emma, this time—little moan when he pushes you to the wall. And then keep going. We'll roll through shirts off, okay? Just go until I call it."

Jake had demanded we have a closed set for any intimate scenes so it is quite literally just a handful of us. Not even one production assistant. I am so thankful that he was adamant about keeping things private and locked down on set for scenes like this. It's already weird enough to shoot something like this, and it would be so much weirder if the room was full like it usually is. It's just me, Jake, our director Alex, first AD Willa, the cinematographer Tommy and the lighting lead Raphael. And thank gosh for that because shirts are about to come off. I have on a little camisole underneath my loose tunic so it isn't anything showy, but it's thin and there are sure to be some head-lights on display. And Jake—well, I'm about to see him shirtless. And not just *see* him shirtless, but rub my hands all over his *shirtlessness.*

I feel my sleeve being pulled and turn to look at Jake, who has apparently been trying to get my attention. "You okay?" he asks quietly.

"Yeah. Yeah." I nod, half convincing him and half convincing myself. "But how weird is this, huh? Like, this is crazy that this is a real job."

He laughs. "Yeah it's super weird. But also, I can think of worse ways to spend a day." His smile is coy and yet reassuring.

He knows how to put me at ease.

I throw another thumbs up toward Alex, a gesture that is apparently my new go-to move.

"We're ready," Jake states cooly.

"Okay, and three...two...one...*Action*."

And we proceed to make out and do what can only be described as dry hump against a wall.

Repeatedly.

I guess Jake was right. There are worse ways to spend a day.

JAKE

The show is going to be a hit. I know it. Everyone knows it. It's one of those things that you can just feel. Sometimes you get lightning in a bottle and that's what we have with *Hierarchy*.

And I can say with full certainty that a lot of that has to do with one Emma Watts. She is a star. A humble, unknown, absolutely blinding star. You know that old saying about how some people just have "it?" She doesn't just *have* it, she *is* it.

She'll mesmerize the world the second they see her on screen, or in an interview, or hell—at a coffee shop. Or in my case—at an audition, in a parking lot, at a restaurant...

The past several weeks of shooting have gone great. We've had fun—learning together, testing boundaries together (which has been both sexy and unnerving), crying together (as part of a scene, not real life). We eat lunch together every day we're on set together which is most days right now because Daniel and Annabelle are very much a package deal. We run lines, we share ideas, give each other constructive criticism without getting defensive, and generally have each other's backs.

Basically life is perfect, Emma is perfect, the show is perfect, everything is perfect. My world is perfect except for the fact that I feel things for her I don't think I've ever felt for another human being. And I can't help but feel like I'm not allowed to feel those things for her since we work together on the type of show we do. I'm forced to chalk my spark for her up to the bond you sometimes develop with a costar when you basically live and breathe each other all day every day.

But it's a lie.

My spark with her isn't because of that. It's because she ignites something—*everything?*—within me. Our chemistry is combustive. When we have any type of intimate scene, I swear everyone in the room has to excuse themselves afterwards because the heat that rolls off us is so consuming. So consuming that even I have a hard time breaking out of it when the cameras stop rolling.

I'm lounging on my couch on a day off. My *couch* couch, not my trailer couch. I'm home because we're off from shooting for the rest of the week while they move us to an on-location spot a few hours away. We'll be shooting in San Luis Obispo, California, for several weeks, primarily at Hearst Castle and a vineyard just outside of town. I'm excited to be in my house for a few days before a hotel becomes my home, even if it is a really unique hotel. I used to love being put up in hotels. But after being in hotels off and on for years, I crave being home. Yeah, I could rent a house on location for those weeks, but it's honestly more hassle than it's worth for such a short period of time. The hotel is just easier. We're staying at the Madonna Inn in San Luis Obispo, which I've been to once before and have always wanted to go back to because it's kind of a wild experience. Kitschy and funky and just generally a fun place.

I'm looking forward to driving down and seeing the new set. The studio offered to send a driver, but I want to drive myself. Driving around Los Angeles is crowded and pushy. I hate it. But Highway 1? It's a gorgeous route to drive. The Pacific Highway has so many beautiful spots and the stretches between cities isn't nearly as crowded. I would never pass up a chance to take any kind of drive like that.

And as good as it has felt to be at home, I miss her. I miss being part of her daily routine. I miss carrying her absurd amount of cups back and forth. Yeah, she still insists on bringing her own. I miss her asking what I'm craving for lunch from craft services, or telling me she's packing her own lunch that day and asking if I want a "lunch from home" too.

The door slams shut and I'm shaken from my Emma-induced stupor. Keys drop on the counter and I hear shoes being kicked off. "Still in love with your costar?" Timbo asks, barely glancing over at me.

I scoff, sitting up on the couch. "Dude, I'm not in love with her."

"You probably don't even know what it feels like to be in love, so you wouldn't know if you were," he retorts.

What a cocky bastard. "You're one to talk. Like *you've* ever been in love."

"I think I have actually." His voice is calm. Casual. And he sounds sincere, not like he's joking.

I hop off the couch to face him, demanding, "What? *Who*? When? Are you being serious right now?"

"Yeah, a long time ago. I think I was." He shrugs like he didn't just tell me one of the most shocking things I've ever heard. I mean, this is *Timbo* we're talking about. I thought he was incapable of being in love. He washes his hands, drying them off before adding, "And it felt a lot like what I see going on with you."

I'm incredulous. "Okay first—what the hell, man? You never told me that before. And second—nothing's going on with me. I'm good. I'm normal. I'm...*regular*." I blow out a deep breath.

Timbo throws his head back, cracking up. When his laughing finally subsides he asks, "Regular? Really man? You're *regular*?"

I walk over and sit at the counter. "You know what I mean."

"Do I though?" Timbo asks.

"Well I'm not in love that's for damn sure."

"You might as well be twirling your hair the way you were sitting there daydreaming about her."

"I wasn't even thinking about her."

"Bullshit. Bullshiiiiiit."

Timbo starts mixing a protein shake and grabs two thermoses. I eye him quizzically.

He simply says, "We're going to the gym."

I nod, but then he adds "To whoop your pansy ass into gear before you head out."

"Pretty sure I'm already in gear. I'm good with idling where I'm at."

"Too bad. I've got something new I want to try with you. You'll be able to run through it even at a sparse hotel gym.

"Sure you can't come? It's such a cool spot."

"I wish, but I have too many clients right now. I can't be gone like that anymore." He starts to walk out the door but circles back in for his keys. I follow him like a lost dog. He elbows me on the way out. "This new program is intense. I think it's going to make you more shredded if that's even possible, pretty boy."

I roll my eyes and punch his arm before closing the door behind us. "You're a dick."

"No I *have* a dick—a good one—but I'm not one."

"Only a guy with a subpar dick has to say he has a good one." I reply, knowing full well that's a lie because Timbo does not have a bad dick. That's a concrete piece of knowledge—unwanted or not—that growing up in locker rooms together gives you.

But it's still fun to rib him.

"In that case, do *you* have a subpar dick?" he challenges. He knows I don't either. It's just things you know. You grow up seeing a million dudes change in locker rooms and in the showers, you quickly learn where yours fits on the spectrum, and where everyone else's ranks, too.

"Nope."

"Ah ha! According to your theory, you *must* because you just denied having a subpar one."

"You're impossible."

"Look, just don't do anything with your stack of dimes that you'll regret while I'm not there to talk some sense into you. Don't blow it with her, man. You don't just *want* her. You *like* her whether you want to admit it or not. And you said it yourself—you two are going to work together for a really long time. Don't screw it all up."

We hop in the car to head to the gym. I don't say anything for a few minutes and then I finally admit, "You're right."

"About what?"

I breathe out a huge sigh. "Everything."

31

Emma: What's your favorite kind of shoe to wear?

Jake: Umm, what?

Emma: Like which type? Sneakers? Sandals? Boots? Dress shoes?

Jake: Tennis shoes.

Emma: Is that the same as sneakers? Or are those specifically for playing tennis?

Jake: I don't play tennis.

Emma: Hmmm.

Jake: Same as sneakers I guess. Like Nikes. Adidas. New Balance. Do those count as sneakers?

Emma:

Jake: Do you like heels or flats better?

Emma: Heels for going out, flats for the rest of the time. But always a thicker heel, not a pencil heel.

Jake: Is a pencil heel like a stiletto?

Emma: Yes and I'm impressed you know what a stiletto is.

Jake: I'm not dumb.

Jake: Also I have a sister.

Jake: And I've had girlfriends. Who liked stilettos.

Emma: I like the way they look but they're just not practical.

Jake: Yeah, well, they weren't practical.

32

EMMA

"Are you sure you can't come with me?" I give Mandy the saddest puppy eyes ever.

"You know I can't. I want to! But I can't. I can't miss even one audition and honestly I need the money from the restaurant. I wish I could. But I have to stay."

We went to our favorite yoga class this morning and now we're at our favorite coffee spot. I turn to Sal and try to make my eyes even more puppy-ish.

He shakes his head. "Same. You know what this hustle is like. We're just trying to recreate what you made happen for yourself. And that shit takes time and us being available at the drop of a hat." Sal is always the level head in the group. "We'll be right here when you get back."

"Ughhhh." I let out an exaggerated groan. "I know, I know. But I'm just gonna miss you guys so much. How am I going to be away from you for that long? It sucks."

"Yeah, it totally sucks that you're getting paid a lot of money to go to a cool place and get put up in a nice hotel and shoot a guaranteed hit series," Sal groans.

"You know what I mean," I say, feeling a little guilty because, well, he's not wrong.

Mandy claps her hands together. "Oooh I want to play!"

"Please no."

But she ignores me. "So I guess you're just going to be sequestered with your ridiculously sexy costar who is like the perfect male specimen and who seems to be insanely sweet to you," she says in mock sympathy.

"Okay okay. Enough." I roll my eyes in fake annoyance.

"And I guess you should pack extra panties because I have a feeling you'll need them." Mandy takes an exaggerated bow before registering our faces.

Sal and I stare blankly back at her.

She clarifies, "Because yours won't stay dry?" She looks at us for reassurance that we *got* it, but gets no such thing from either of us, so she starts to explain. "Because you will—"

"Oh we got it," Sal says, rolling his eyes.

"Oh. Too much?" Mandy asks, squinting.

"Yes." Sal and I say in unison.

But she's probably not wrong. Geez I'm going to miss those two.

I PULL up to my trailer to find no trailer. Nothing but a blank lot. In a space that had been riddled with what must have been fifteen trailers over the past couple months, there isn't a single thing. No trailers, no cars, no tents. Nothing.

I feel the panic creep in. I hadn't told Jake yet, but I'd sublet my apartment. Why? For a myriad of reasons. My trailer is nicer.

My trailer is more convenient. My trailer makes me happy. My trailer is free.

I guess somewhere along the way I forgot the most important thing about my trailer. My trailer isn't actually *mine*.

Small oversight. But it seemed pointless to keep a separate place when I was never there, or when I would have to combat forty-five minutes of traffic minimum every day just to get to set. Sure I could've stayed at my apartment on the weekends, but I can't overstate this enough: I really love that trailer. And there was no sublet stipulation in my contract for my apartment, so a few weeks ago I rented it out to one of Mandy and Sal's new coworkers at Stella's. I just did a six month sublet, so it's not like I locked myself out of my own place indefinitely. It seemed smart at the time. Responsible even.

Now it seems idiotic.

Idiotic because my trailer that I love and that has all of my belongings in it is not here. Idiotic because I have no clue where it is. Idiotic because it has all the stuff I need, right down to my toothbrush.

I take a few deep breaths and then make the call I'm dreading to make. He answers on the first ring.

"I believe this is the first time we've ever talked on the phone." Jacob's voice sounds bright, and I can tell he's smiling.

"First time for everything..." I wonder if he can hear the worry in my voice.

"What's up, Emma?" I love when he says my name. I don't even really know why. Maybe because he has to call me Annabelle so much that when he says Emma it just hits different.

"So um...I just came by the lot to grab something from my trailer, and...it's not here."

"What's not there?"

"My trailer."

"Oh yeah, they're moving everything to San Luis Obispo to ready the set."

"Already?" I can feel the hysteria start to creep in and my voice is definitely a few pitches higher than usual.

"Yeah. I mean it takes a lot to get everything set up and in place. On location sets take a ton of work."

"Oh." It's all I can manage to say.

He'd been moving all around during our conversation, but I hear him stop. I know he did, because it's suddenly silent, no more footsteps, no more cabinets shutting. Just silence. "Is everything okay? Did you leave something in there you need?"

Only a bed. My computer. Food. My face wash. Deodorant. My clothes. My life. But I hear myself saying, "Nope, all good. Just my book. I was just surprised when I pulled up to a vacant lot."

I try to "think good thoughts" to reassure myself. *It's okay. It's okay. I can stay with Mandy. She has a couch. And face wash. And clothes. It'll be fun. Like a mini girls' staycation.*

"I meant to ask you—do you want to drive down together? I'm looking forward to driving there and you're welcome to ride with me. You can use my car whenever you need it while we're there."

"Hmmm." I think about it for a split second. It would be more fun than driving alone, plus I hate navigating interstate traffic. And the idea of having a driver for a longer distance like that just felt too out of my realm of existence to get on board with. "That depends. Are you a windows-down-music-blasting type of guy or a windows-up-podcast-at-a-reasonable-volume type of guy?"

He says on a laugh, "Does it matter?"

I answer with zero hesitation. "It's make or break."

The line is silent and I know he's pondering the answer,

wondering if he should cheekily evade answering or tell me the truth and risk being wrong. I clear my throat, prompting him.

"The former."

"My type of guy." I say I before I can catch myself. I don't mean it in the literal sense. Though if I'm being honest with myself, maybe I do.

"So is that a yes?"

"Yeah, that'll be fun. Let's do it."

"Okay shoot me your address and I'll pick you up around 9:00 that morning, okay?"

I hesitate, knowing that I currently have no address to send him since I apparently do not make well-informed decisions. "I'll come to you."

"I can come pick you up, Emma. It's no problem."

Ugh. Why does he have to be so thoughtful. "No, it'll be easier for me to come to you."

"How so?"

I know he's not trying to push me, that he's just trying to be nice, but I close the door on this conversation before he can ask me any more questions. "It just will be. For *me*. Can you shoot me *your* address?"

33

EMMA

I pull up to Jake's house and holy Australian yet American soap opera star. His place is insane. It has that reddish Spanish style roof that I've always thought looked so cool. The kind with the curved clay tiles. I love it. He's putting his bags in his sports car and though I'm more of an SUV girl myself, I can't help but think to myself how fun it'll be to ride in his car.

Jake's head pops up from the trunk just as I shut my own car door. "I'll grab your bags," he says walking over to me. I hardly have anything because all my stuff is in my trailer, but Mandy let me borrow some things and I picked up the other necessities from the drugstore. "Wow, you travel light," he says, eyebrows raised in surprise.

"Just the necessities," I say casually, like it was intentional and not because I currently have zero access to all my things. "Beautiful car." I run my hand along it. It's a matte black Audi S7 and it looks very 007. I open the passenger door and lean in to check it out.

Jake comes up right beside me and leans in next to me. He's entirely too close for comfort and yet comfort is all I feel. Not quite sure what to make of that.

Ahem. He clears his throat dramatically. "You'll notice that all cupholders except the one in my door are empty for you. Every single one is yours." My stomach does a little dip. *Please tell me that's not a pang of desire and the way to my heart is not as easy as simply giving me all the cupholders.*

"Thank you. That's crazy thoughtful."

The front door slams and I look up to find Beau standing at the top of the stairs. "Emma, take care of my dude!" I salute him and he salutes me back before walking back inside.

JAKE IS A GREAT DRIVER. He's cautious but not neurotic. No road rage. He leaves the appropriate three car lengths distance between us and the car in front of us. He asks me if I want to stop every time we see a rest area sign.

And he lets me be in charge of the playlist since he's driving. So far he hasn't complained when I want to listen to some songs three times in a row. And he seems to appreciate the diversity of my mix, with everything ranging from Stone Temple Pilots to TOAD to Backstreet Boys to Live (*Throwing Copper* of course) to Taylor Swift to Juvenile.

I've caught him singing along to several of the songs and each time I've felt the tiniest of flutters, especially on "Quit Playing Games with my Heart." Teenage me would've drawn his name in bubble letters inside a heart on my notebook. Adult me was temped to put the car in park, adjust his seat backwards, and climb onto his lap. A very large part of me hates we met filming this show together and not out somewhere—like the grocery store, or a restaurant, or ooh maybe a farmer's market? Or possibly even working out, because if we'd met each other working out I wouldn't feel so bad about wanting to work him *in*.

But I know we can't cross that line. We are colleagues. Nothing romantic about that.

"So have you been to San Luis Obispo before?" Jake rolls the windows up so we can talk. We've been blasting music with the windows down for the past hour and some change, barely saying a word to each other once we got out of L.A.

"I haven't. I haven't really been anywhere to be honest. Have you been?"

"Yeah, SLO is a beautiful place. Mountains and beach. Vineyards. Kind of a perfect place actually."

"Have you filmed there before? Is that how you know it?"

He's quiet for a moment like he's deciding how to answer me. "No. I went with a girl."

I am hit with a pang of jealousy and am immediately mad at myself about it. I have no claim over this man. No right to feel jealous. "Oooooh," is all I manage to say, drumming up enough internal strength to give him a little smirk like I'm intrigued. Intrigued and not at all envious.

He doesn't elaborate. "They have these amazing tri-tip steak sandwiches there at this place called Firestone Grill. We have to go there. And I had production book us at the Madonna Inn. I had to fight for it because it's more expensive and a little bit of a drive from both sets but it's too cool and fun to pass up. It's this old very ornate and funky hotel. I've never been to another place like it. The rooms are themed and borderline ridiculous, but in the best way. It's an...*experience*."

I feel the smile widen on my face. I'm genuinely excited. I've never traveled, never really gone anywhere beyond the casino, so this is uncharted territory for me. "I can't wait," I say honestly.

I've also never done a road trip with anyone. I didn't know

how fun they were. To ride for hours taking in the scenery and just talking and laughing with a friend. A really hot friend who I'm afraid I might be developing a raging crush on, but still—a friend.

"So what does your family think about all this? Do they realize you're about to be a star?" Jacob asks innocently, completely clueless about the emotional bomb he just detonated. My eyes instantly threaten to fill but I fight the tears back. I will not give them this. I won't give my family the kind of regard they never gave me.

I weigh how to handle his question, and then decide just to answer honestly and blow past it. I've been blowing past that part of my reality for years, so it should be second nature for me at this point.

"Okay, I'm going to answer you, but that is more of a loaded question than you realize, and the answer is equally loaded. I usually don't talk about it, but I'll tell you because we're going to know each other for a long time and it makes no sense to lie to you. But don't let it make you feel sad for me. I'm all good. So just promise me—no pity, no *poor Emma,* no sympathy. I'm a big girl and I made my peace with things a long time ago." I turn to face him. "Promise?"

He stares forward but looks completely stricken. "Promise," he says, his voice tight.

"I don't have a family." *There. I said it. That wasn't so hard. I can do this.*

"I lived in and out of foster care since I was eleven. My parents couldn't take care of me, or well...well, they didn't want to make the sacrifices to take care of me. They would've had to give up drugs to have the money to take care of a kid, and I guess I just didn't give them the same kind of high that drugs did."

I shrug like it's no big deal, but the tears are pooling and I already know I won't be able to keep them from falling. I don't ever talk about this. I know how to *exist* with these feelings stuffed way down deep inside, but not really how to talk about them openly.

I wipe my eyes and continue. "I never got adopted because I was older when I entered foster care and..." I turn to face him. "You know how everyone wants a puppy but no one really wants to bring home an older dog?" I pause but it's a rhetorical question. I don't expect him to answer. "Well, it's kind of like that with older children in the foster system. Sometimes people might *think* they want a teenager, but it turns out they usually don't. Old dogs come with a lot of baggage, and neglected teenagers do, too." I take a deep breath.

"Do you have any siblings?"

"No. I don't think my parents meant to have me. It was a mistake. And not one they made twice."

"Not a mistake, Emma. An accident maybe. But not a mistake."

I'm quiet for a moment, thinking about that. I'd always considered it a mistake, but maybe he's right. Just an accident. Those two things aren't the same.

"Do you have contact with them now?"

"No, they overdosed a couple of years after I went into foster care. The coroner said they'd gotten a bad batch, laced with fentanyl among other things." I shrug. "I don't fully know, I was young. I had to grow up way too fast, but I think I'm a better human for it now. But that's the reason it's hard for me to accept all these amazing things happening in my life. And why I'm so careful with my money. I've just never really had any type of security—financial or otherwise—except what I've been able to provide for myself, which hasn't been much—but it's been enough. And I've never had love that I could really feel secure in either. Every time I thought a family might love me enough to keep me... Anyways, this all just feels like so much more than I deserve. My life has never been one of *those* kinds of lives. And I didn't think it ever could be." I look at him, eyes and cheeks definitely mascara-stained, but not caring. "Until now," I say with a small smile.

He doesn't say a word. He doesn't even look at me. He blinks and...are those tears? Did I make him cry? He still doesn't speak, but he does reach over and take my hand in his and give it a strong squeeze. When the quiet continues to hang between us, I turn the music back up to fill the heavy silence and we still don't talk, until he takes an exit that I didn't know we were supposed to take.

"Wait why are we getting off here?" I ask, voice still a little shaky.

He just swallows and then pulls over at the first gas station we come to. He parks, gets out of his car, walks to my door and opens it. "Hop out." I look up at him quizzically, but do it anyways, only for him to wrap me in the biggest bear hug imaginable the second I climb out of the car. He doesn't even say anything. Just stands there holding me tightly, as if molding his body around mine can shield me from everything I just told him. It can't, of course, because those things are inside me and the only person who can shield me from them is *me*, but it still feels good.

He doesn't let go.

He's warm and though his body is hard because he's essentially just a giant slab of muscle, he feels like bubble wrap around me. Like I'm encased in protection. And like in his arms is my new favorite place. I've never been hugged quite like this and I'm not ready to let it end.

I'd read one time to never be the first one to break a hug. So I don't let go either.

I'm not sure how long we stand there, just hugging, tears silently streaming down my face. I use all of my resolve to not let the real sobs loose because I know he'd feel my body heave with them. I've never cried like that in front of someone and I'm not ready to start now. I strain to keep the ugly cry at bay but can't help but let some tears fall. There are years' worth of tears in me. Almost two decades worth, I'm sure. They're probably thrilled to have the chance to escape.

I barely shift in Jake's arms and he gives me one final squeeze before moving his lips to my ear. "You deserve every bit and so much more. Don't you dare sell yourself short just because no one ever told you what you're worth." Then he lets go of me and walks back to his side of the car, climbs in, and waits for me to do the same. I do, and we get right back on the road, like nothing happened. Like this man didn't just validate everything I've ever felt with merely one hug and two sentences.

"Bittersweet Symphony" by The Verve Pipe comes on next and I know it's my own playlist, but I swear it feels like someone is scoring my life in this moment. We ride and let it blare. I take in the landscape around us—the rolling hills, the open spaces— and know that "Wide Open Spaces" by The Dixie Chicks has to be our next song. And yes I know they're just "The Chicks" now, but it doesn't sound right when I just say *The Chicks*. I flip the visor down and assess the damage. Smeared mascara, of course. Dried tear marks. Swollen eyes. I lick my pointer finger and dab at my eyes, trying to lessen the damage. "I look like a hot mess."

"One of those words is true."

"I think we might disagree about which word that is." I laugh, thankful to him for lightening the mood a bit.

"Agree to disagree." He says it like it's not up for debate. And before I can say anything else, he asks, "So how do *you* feel about the show so far? Is filming what you expected?"

"Ummm no. Not even close." I glance over at him, but he's still looking at the road ahead. "It's...well, it's more fun than I expected for one thing. It's exciting and every day is like a giant adrenaline rush that I can't get enough of. But it's also way more technical than I realized. So much more goes into each scene than I ever would've thought. There are so many factors to consider when filming that had never even crossed my mind. Like with our steamy scenes, it still surprises me how orchestrated everything is. Filming is fun, but so *involved*."

Jake nods knowingly. "Yeah, I remember all that surprised me at first, too. Like I just expected to show up and say my lines and with my first real speaking role it was more like I had to wait hours while the lighting was perfected and the camera was placed before I ever got to be on set and say my handful of lines." He shakes his head. "So much work for about forty-five seconds of footage. It's crazy to me still."

"But also kind of fascinating," I offer. "Like sometimes I want to walk over to video village and watch the playback so I can see what it really looks like, but I don't want to overstep or infringe on Alex. But like on our love scenes, I'm dying to know if those parts look good. If they look *real*. You *know* how I feel about that stuff looking real."

"Emma, you can watch playback anytime you want. You are the star of this show. If you don't like the way something looks, you can ask to reshoot. Not even *ask*, you can *demand* it. This is your show. Don't be afraid to act like it. This show..." He shakes his head and steals a quick look at me, taking his eyes off the road for barely a breath. "You're not just along for the ride, Emma. You are the entire attraction."

Welp. It looks like Mandy's panty joke was spot on.

34

EMMA

The Madonna Inn is spectacular. It's gaudy and over the top and I absolutely love it.

Jacob is checking us in and I'm just taking in this spectacle of a place. I almost hate that we have to film while we're here, because I think I could spend weeks just exploring all the nooks of this place.

"Okay, so I had them book you the Madonna Suite because it's the most famous one. It looks beautiful and has one of their famous rock bathrooms, but if you don't like it, you can switch. Honestly they all look really awesome." Jake hands me my room cards.

"Rock bathrooms?"

"You'll see," he says with a huge grin.

"So wait, what room are *you* in?"

He raises his eyebrows twice like he's about to tell me the sexiest thing. "The Caveman Suite."

I bark out a laugh. "Planning to succumb to your baser instincts?"

"Maybe something like that," he says on a chuckle.

I wonder if he could be thinking about me, or if he even *would* think that way about me, but I push that thought away immediately. *No no no.* Can't go there. *Won't* go there.

"I'll show you mine if you show me yours," I blurt out. So apparently I *can* and *will* go there. He quirks one eyebrow at me and I feign offense. "I'm talking about our *rooms*. Get your mind out of the gutter."

THE MADONNA SUITE IS *SENSATIONAL*. It has pink walls, a pink ceiling, pink carpet with giant roses all over it, crystal chandeliers, gold throne chairs with pink rose upholstery, and various stone walls. I have never seen anything like it. I might want to stay here forever. I flop onto the king-sized bed and let out a dramatic *Ahhhh*.

"You like?" Jacob sinks down in one of the thrones. They're oversized chairs but he makes them look regular sized.

"I *love*."

"Told you this place was outrageous."

"Outrageously *awesome*. I feel like "Pink" by Aerosmith should start playing on a loop the second the door is opened."

"That'd definitely be fitting."

I lean up on my elbows to look at him as he studies the room, and—this man. *Whew* this man. His hair is a little extra disheveled from being windblown and the ends are curling up, inadvertently calling to my fingers. He's in a light grey t-shirt that shouldn't look that good on anyone, but it perfectly accentuates his big arms and his broad chest. He's completely unaware that I'm ogling him, so I let myself stare a little longer.

I haven't really let myself take him in like this, and now I know why. It's dangerous. A slippery slope I could easily fall down. Because in this moment...well in this moment in which I'm sliding too far down, all I want is to *climb him* back up.

But I don't *want* to want to climb him. That's highly inappropriate and I would never cross that line with a coworker. Especially when I have everything to lose. Like literally everything.

"Want to see mine?" Jacob asks innocently, completely oblivious to the fact that I'm internally drooling over him.

If my very unwelcome thoughts are any indication—yeah. Yeah I just might want to see his.

AFTER A BRIEF TOUR of a man cave on steroids that I needed to exit as quickly as possible in order to keep *my* baser needs at bay, we're sitting at the hotel bar and I'm starving. Maybe that's what's wrong with me. I'm just hungry and I can't think straight because of it. Low blood sugar can do weird things to the mind. And body too apparently.

It's so early that the early bird special doesn't even start for another ten minutes, but here we are, looking at the menu and debating if eating dinner this early is sad or brilliant.

"Sometimes it just makes sense," Jake says with confidence. "We have an early call time, we ate shitty snacks all day, we just need some real food and then to call it a night."

I nod my head in agreement, barely able to process his words as I silently admit to myself that he's right—white cheddar Cheetos and granola bars do not a meal make. Except maybe girl dinner.

"Do you want a drink?" He asks, flipping the menu to look over the cocktails.

"If I had a drink right now I think I'd pass out on the spot. I need *food*."

"Got it."

We finally order but keep adding things to our order while the bartender tries to maintain his patience.

"Is that all?" he asks on a mildly annoyed but somewhat amused chuckle. Well at least he has a sense of humor.

Jake and I look at each other and I answer. "Yeah, that oughtta do it."

We crush the food and talk like we're buddies. Which, I guess maybe we are at this point. We talk about favorite TV shows and food genres, the actors we think are underrated and the ones we think are overrated, our shared love/hate with working out, and he shares all his favorite restaurants, none of which have queso, forcing me to proclaim my disappointment several times.

"Okay I'll find the best queso in L.A. and then I'll take you there. How about that?"

"I accept."

I honestly think we'd be happy sitting here all night, but the bartender brings the check and it pulls me back into reality. The reality that we have a very early call time in the morning and I need to sleep. And the other absolutely enigmatic reality that I'm so comfortable around Jake that it actually makes me uncomfortable how comfortable I am.

Yes, I hear myself.

And yes, I'm annoyed with me, too.

35

JAKE

Once again, the studio offered to send a car for Emma and me, but I wanted to drive and she said she was happy to ride with me. I always prefer to drive when I have the chance, especially somewhere like out here where it's not congested.

It was early and we didn't talk much on the way to the vineyard, but it was a comfortable silence. Not the awkward kind where you don't know what to say. But the easy, effortless kind where you don't have to fill the space with small talk.

It was nice.

As if she could read my thoughts, Emma walks over as they set the next scene. "What are you thinking about all quiet over here by yourself?"

"Nothing really."

"*Something,*" she smarts.

"If you must know, I was thinking about how nice the ride with you was this morning." May as well just lay it all out there.

She flinches, and I can tell that's not what she was expecting me to say. "But…" she starts. "But we hardly spoke."

"I know." I shrug. "Still."

She squints at me for a long moment. "I can't decide if you're saying you like being around me or like when I'm not talking." Her lips tilt up the slightest bit. "Which is it?"

"Either? Both?" I'm a liar. I'm a liar and she knows it. Before I can say anything else, we're called to our spots.

I'M WAITING on Emma to come out of wardrobe so we can head back to the Madonna Inn, and I'm contemplating asking her if she'd be down for a detour. Our call time isn't as early tomorrow and I think we deserve a little fun. Plus, I know she'd love it.

I hear footsteps and turn to find Emma walking up. She couldn't be more casual, and she couldn't be more beautiful. Sneakers, yoga pants, t-shirt tied up in a little knot again so that the slightest hint of her stomach peeks out.

I officially have a crush. A raging, hormone-inducing, thought-consuming crush.

"Ready?"

"Ready Freddy," she says with a smile.

I don't even know what that means but because she said it, I somehow like it.

"So…" I stop and turn to fully face her. "How would you feel about a detour on the way back to the Inn? We can grab dinner there. I think you'll be a fan."

She shrugs happily. "Sure, let's do it."

"I think—and I don't want to overstate this—but *I think* you're about to love me."

"You say that as if I don't already," she says as she starts walking.

I feel that those words in the pit of my stomach. And I know she doesn't mean it like *that*, but it makes me imagine how it would feel if she did.

Verdict: it would feel fucking great.

"OKAY KEEP YOUR EYES CLOSED, we're almost there."

"Okay but I'm warning you that I'm starting to feel dizzy with my eyes closed. I don't have much food on my stomach and these roads aren't helping."

"Almost....almost..." I pull into the parking lot and wish I could act more chill, but I don't feel chill. I am too pumped about this. "Okay. Open them."

She does and blinks a few times as her eyes adjust. I can feel how annoyingly huge my smile must be and I don't even care.

"No way."

I nod. "Way."

"Pinch me." When I don't move she turns to face me. *"Pinch me."*

I do, gently, and she shakes her head, her smile threatening to overtake her entire face. She shoves at my shoulder. "You remembered. That night I told you how much I love them. You remembered."

"Of course I did."

She shakes her head in disbelief. "I can't believe you found this place."

I have to actively keep my chest from puffing out. "I know it."

"Welp, you were right," she says, reaching for her door handle.

"About what?"

"If I didn't love you before, I definitely do now," she says on a laugh.

We hop out of the car and walk toward a little shack barely off the road where a tilted neon sign is flashing *Mojito Hut.*

"I'M JUST SAYING...WHY *can't* we go every night?" Emma is loading up at the craft services tent and has no more room on her tray but I can tell she wants that muffin she is lingering in front of.

I pick it up for her and then grab another for me. "For starters, our livers probably need a mojito-less night and also— they're closed on Tuesdays."

"That's ludicrous that they are closed on Tuesdays. That's the worst night of the week for them to close."

"Why?" I genuinely don't know the answer.

"Um hello? Taco Tuesday. Tuesdays are for tacos. Their marketing person needs to step it up."

"I think their marketing 'person' is Armando and Elena... meaning they have no marketing person. It's a shack on the road. They're just doing their thing."

"And doing it well, I might add," she says wistfully. "Except for the queso thing."

The "queso thing" is the fact that they don't have queso dip, just queso fundido which, in Emma's words, is "not even close to the same thing." But the salsa is amazing and their chips are homemade and they have twelve mojito flavors, so she let it slide.

We've gone to the mojito bar the past six nights. Emma is, in a word, *obsessed*. She wasn't kidding when she said she loved mojitos. And to find a place that doesn't act put out when you order a "high maintenance" drink that requires muddled mint is making her dreams come true.

And since I found the place, I'd like to think that *I'm* the one who's making her dreams come true.

After three nights in a row, we were on a first name basis with the owners, Armando and Elena. They're a very cool couple who opened this hole in the wall place and I'm not sure they've ever had more than four people there at a time before this week.

On night five we took some of the cast and crew with us. Last night we took even more. Today Armando and Elena are probably thrilled to be closed and also probably need to restock... everything.

"Let's hang at the hotel bar tonight. We haven't done that yet and it looks pretty fun."

She exaggeratedly pouts but then nods in acquiescence. "What do you think the chances are that they have mojitos?"

36

JAKE

The fun thing about shooting on location somewhere is how close the cast and crew get. You're stuck with each other and not much else for the duration of filming in that location, and you find yourselves just hanging out in your off time because it's not like you can go home after work anyways. And we've needed daylight so we've been shooting during the days which means we've been going out every night after we wrap.

It started as just me and Emma, and then DJ, the wardrobe assistant, joined us, and then our second assistant director Jan and some of the set crew came, and now everyone from the director to the production assistants are hanging together. It doesn't happen like this on every set, but we have a solid team and they're genuinely fun to hang out with.

We've been alternating between the mojito bar and the hotel bar at the Madonna Inn. Emma is partial to the mojito bar, but the Inn is way bigger and can fit our group much better. Plus, it has an enormous food menu and can accommodate all the gluten free, keto, vegan requests much better than a place that serves exclusively tacos, burritos, and queso fundido.

Which is why I find myself at the Madonna Inn bar surrounded by the same people I just spent the entire day—and nearly every day for the past four weeks—with. We're a big group and everyone is chatting, so we're loud and probably obnoxious, but this hotel bar is raking it in from us so we've gotten no complaints. I've been talking with Tommy, our cinematographer, and not to say he's a downer, but he's kind of a downer. Not in a bad way, but because he really, really misses his wife and kids and he can't stop talking about them and it's making me sad.

But it's making the women around us have googley eyes because he's so lovesick for his family. Note to self: women like a man who wears his heart on his sleeve a la Travis Kelce.

I'm listening to the conversations around me and joining in here and there, but I'm never not tracking Emma. She's magnetic and even when I actively try not to look at her every second of the day, I fail.

The problem is, every guy in here feels the same way. Every guy except maybe Tommy.

The bartender we've grown to like, Trey, suddenly yells out across the bar, breaking into all conversations. "Hey any of you actors know how to play a bartender? Because I'm drowning back here." The bar just cheers him on. And then I see Emma slip through the crowd up to the bar. Leaning over the counter as far as she can, she beckons Trey over and says something to him that I can't make out. But I can very easily make out the way he acts like he can't hear her and pulls her head closer, so her mouth is right at his ear. I swear her lips might have just brushed against his ear.

I hate him.

Okay, maybe he really *couldn't* hear her. Benefit of the doubt. I try to shake it off but then I see him nodding with a huge smile and offering his hand, which she takes and then abruptly climbs over the bar. Yes, *over* the bar.

"Turns out I got myself a real bartender here, so the rest of you can stand down!" Trey announces to shouts of "Emma! Emma!" She's shaking her head at the onslaught of attention, but I can tell she's happy.

I watch as she gets to work, making drink concoctions I've never seen before and clearly comfortable in this element. She's laughing, playing around with everyone, and I want in. I want those laughs directed at *me*. I want her to lean over close to me when she can't hear *my* order. I want her to notice, well, *me*.

"Emma!" I yell it out, much louder than I'd intended to. She doesn't look my way. Doesn't even register me over the rising bar chatter. Screw it. I half-stand and yell it out even louder. "EMMA!" Her head whips around and she gives me that damn wink as she walks toward me. The same one that unnerved me the day we had that impromptu lunch at Stella's.

"What can I get you, good sir?"

You. Your body. Your attention. But I say, "Make me something. Anything. Please."

She taps her finger to her lips like she's thinking hard about it. She cocks a brow at me. "Spirit?"

"Gin." She shifts under my stare, and I can tell my eyes are too intense on her. So I blink.

"Stiff?"

God am I.

I have to close my eyes at that question. I make a so-so gesture with my hand.

"Got it." I can feel the moment she moves away and I dare to open my eyes back up. She's grabbing a couple things and when she can't reach one, Trey walks over and takes it down for her.

But not before ogling her entire backside, from top to bottom and back up.

Their hands brush when he gives her the bottle of purple liquid. I shift in my seat, suddenly wanting to switch places with Trey.

A few moments later, Emma delivers a beautiful cocktail in front of me. It's in a coupe glass, with a lemon twist and a muted lavender color. She leans in close and says, "It looks fancy but guys love it."

I take a sip and damn if I'm not *guys*. Because I do. I do love it. "Wow. That's really good. What is it?"

She makes a fist and pulls her arm down in victory, mouthing an exaggerated but silent "yessss" before answering me. "An Aviation. I knew you'd like it."

"How do you know how to do all this?"

She shrugs. "I used to bartend, remember?"

"Yeah but—"

She casually cuts me off. "There's a lot you don't know about me."

My blood heats and I can feel it in my veins. Maybe it's just the drink beelining into my bloodstream. "*Yet.*" I say it before I can stop myself. "There's a lot I don't know about you *yet*." I think I catch her eyes flare but then she looks to the side of me, where I can feel movement, but I don't take my eyes off her. "Where?" I don't even know why I ask, other than the fact that I have her attention and I'm not ready to let it go.

"A casino. I didn't love it, but the money was good and it was never boring."

"But you—"

I'm cut off again as she turns to hear who's calling her name. She turns back to me. "Gotta get back to it. That one's on me." She smiles at me for a split second before she's pulled away by another order.

"What's Emma's deal?"

I don't recognize the voice. I turn to my left to find a face I *do* recognize—slightly—sitting next to me. Tommy must've left. Poor guy.

This guy is one of the production assistants I'm pretty sure. I definitely have seen his face around set a lot but I haven't had much interaction with him yet.

He holds out a hand. "Ben. I'm a PA on the show."

"Yeah, that's what I was thinking." I shake his hand. "Jake. Nice to officially meet you Ben."

I take a sip of my drink and damn it really is good. *She's* good.

"So what's the deal with Emma?" He asks again.

"Oh, the bartender was swamped and she jumped in to help him. Turns out she used to bartend."

I look over at him and he nods before gesturing between me and Emma across the bar. "But you two aren't...right?"

"Aren't?"

"Together?"

This guy. This fucking guy. I clear my throat. "No." One word shouldn't sound so defensive, but I can tell it does the second it leaves my mouth.

"Okay. Just wanted to be sure. Thanks man."

I nod and take another sip.

Ben raises his hand up and calls out her name. It takes a couple of times but she comes over.

"Hey Ben, what can I get you?"

She knows his name.

She knows his name.

"Am I allowed to ask for your number?" He has a deep laugh and damn, he's charming as hell.

Emma playfully rolls her eyes. "We already talked about this, mister."

Already talked about what?

"I just meant if this is your new gig then technically..."

Technically what?

He shrugs but it's good-natured. Like they have an inside joke or something. "A guy's gotta try. Again." He's smiling and seems relaxed. "Can you do an old fashioned?"

She scoffs. "*Can I?*" She gives him a quick smile as she turns back to the towering wall of spirits.

I don't want to ask. I don't want to be that guy. But I really do want to ask. But I shouldn't. But I'm absolutely going to.

I angle towards Ben. "What was that about?"

He sighs as if in defeat. "Gotta shoot your shot, right?"

I'm pretty sure I know what he means and I'm a hundred percent sure I don't like it. I press him anyways. "What shot?"

"I asked Emma out a few weeks ago, not long after we first got here."

"And?"

"And she said no." We both go silent when she slides him his old fashioned before being summoned by Lin, one of the "hair wizards" as Emma calls them.

"Sorry man." *I'm not.*

"Me too. She's pretty awesome."

Tell me something I don't know. "Did she say why?"

"Yeah, she pulled the work card. Said she can't date someone she works with. That it would be unprofessional and it's all too new to her and it wouldn't be the right thing to do." He takes a sip of his drink. "And she thinks working on set together almost every day would make things complicated and awkward. I mean, I get it, but damn, you know?"

I nod and try to swallow around the enormous lump that just formed in my throat, wondering if this rule of hers is a Ben rule or a universal co-worker rule. The real question is—*is it also a Jake rule?*

And I can't help but feel hypocritical because I have the

same rule. No coworkers. It's easier that way. Cleaner. Nothing extra. But I'd break it for Emma in a second.

Because man do I want all the extra I can get of her. And forget clean. I want dirty. Rules schmules. Dating costars is back on.

Ben and I talk the rest of the night. Turns out he is super nice.

He's also pretty damn funny. I like him, and that makes me hate him.

Because he likes her.

And I don't want *her* to like *him*.

But sitting next to him most of the night makes me think that it'd be pretty hard not to like this guy.

Fuck Ben. But also, I'd hang with him again no questions asked.

But also, fuck Ben.

37

Jake: Have you ever dated a coworker?

Lilah: Yeah.

Jake: And?

Lilah: Never again.

Lilah: It got too messy.

Jake: Were you guys okay working together after?

Lilah: No. Still work together, still aren't okay.

Jake: Thx.

Lilah: Ummmm...

Lilah: That's it?

Jake: Yeah. That's what I needed to know.

Lilah: You want to date her?

Jake: I want to do more than date her.

Lilah: Ew, gross. I'm your sister. Don't tell me stuff like that.

Jake: I meant I don't want to JUST date her. I want more with her. Get your mind out of the gutter sis.

Lilah: Omg. You like like her.

Jake: Yeah

Lilah: Does she like you?

Jake: I don't know.

Lilah: Ooh, sounds like a no then.

Jake: Thanks for that.

Lilah: 🩶

Jake: Have you ever dated someone you worked with?

Gray: . . .

Gray: . . .

Jake: Great conversation, thanks bro.

Jake: Have you ever dated someone you worked with?

Timbo: Define "dated"

Jake: Nevermind.

38

EMMA

Just like there are far more worse things than groping your gorgeous costar all day, there are also much worse things than frolicking in a vineyard with said gorgeous costar. Sure, we're about to be ambushed by a couple of assassins in the next scene, but the lead up to the action has been nice.

And not just nice. It's been fun. Working on this show, working with Jake and this whole crew has been like a salve to my soul. A soul I didn't fully realize needed healing. It feels like I've finally found somewhere I belong. Somewhere I fit into comfortably. This entire process has made me fall in love with acting. And I'm self-aware enough to realize that Jake is the single largest part of that.

He makes me feel safe. He looks out for me. Guides me. He's the one to make sure we have a closed set for any scene that is remotely intimate. He's the one who asks me a million times if I'm comfortable before and after he touches me for those scenes.

The first one to yell for someone to grab my robe. The one who says "We're done" when he thinks we've shot enough takes. The one who whispers jokes in my ear to take the edge off when I start to tense up.

But he's also the one who makes me tense up in the first place. The one who makes my stomach dip a hundred times a day. And the one who makes me laugh just as many times. The one who makes me question if he really does want me or if he's just *that* good of an actor. The one who makes me wonder if that's how he really touches a woman or if he just knows what an audience wants to see.

Because while Jake makes it incredibly easy to round the bases with him on set, he also makes it incredibly difficult for me to *not* want him to hit first, second and third base *off* set, too.

And that, my friends, is a complication I didn't foresee.

After the whole fake kiss debacle, I was worried that filming romantic scenes would be difficult because it would be awkward and uncomfortable, and yeah, sometimes it can be. But mostly it's difficult because making out with Jake and declaring my love for him every day on set toys with my mind—and body—in ways I didn't anticipate.

Spoiler alert: I didn't expect to want him *for real*.

"Hey Emma, Alex wants you on your mark." The voice breaks through my thoughts and saves me from my imagination running wild. I follow Ben with a mild sense of relief. I'd been contemplating asking Jake if he feels these same things, too. If he has the same confusion as me about what's real and what's just the byproduct of filming a show like this together.

I take my mark and look around to take everything in. *Everyone* in. Tommy, the cinematographer, is speaking with Raphael, the lighting gaffer. Alex, our director and Willa, our first AD, are chatting animatedly at video village. Wardrobe is talking amongst themselves. Jake is looking over the sides for the next scene. And Ben is next to me listening to his earpiece. He nods and then puts his hand on my arm, as if to pause me from moving. "Makeup wants to touch you up real quick."

I nod and offer a gentle, "Thanks Ben."

"Not that you need it." He winks as our head makeup artist Janine takes over.

I can't help but let out a small laugh because Ben is handsome and sweet and harmless, and in another world where I didn't work with him, I'm sure I'd want to go out with him. But that other world would have to be a Jake-less world, because in a world where I didn't work with Ben or Jake, I'm going Jake every time.

When I lift my eyes back up I find Jake's own drilling into me with an intensity that makes my breath catch. His eyes shift to track Ben walking away before looking back down at the script in his hand.

I'm not sure what that was but it didn't feel like nothing.

39

EMMA

"Once again, let me just say you are a peak road tripper."

We're headed back to L.A. after six weeks in San Luis Obispo and I'm low-key bummed to be leaving. We were supposed to finish this weekend but we wrapped a couple days early. I was tempted to stay those couple extra days because I really did love being there. We had the best time filming and the best time just...living. The Madonna Inn and the Mojito Hut treated us right and I'll genuinely miss our nightly hangs. Filming at Hearst Castle made me feel like *actual* royalty, and running through vineyards made me feel as free as I've ever felt, even though none of it was real.

I pop a couple more white cheddar Cheetos in my mouth and say, "Turns out I love being a total passenger princess and I'm not even ashamed of it."

"You shouldn't be." Jacob doesn't miss a beat.

"I mean, I probably kind of should be if we're being honest.

I'm a capable, independent woman and yet I'm over here just snacking and picking songs while you're navigating what seems to be a fairly stressful freeway system."

"Well when you put it like that..." He chuckles and then elbows me across the center console. "Can I be a passenger *prince* for awhile?"

"Not a chance." I offer him some Cheetos as a peace offering and he takes them.

"Since we're going to get back a little late I thought I could just drop you by your place on the way in. And then if you're okay with it Timbo and I will bring your car to you tomorrow. That way you don't have to come out of your way with me and then drive back where we already passed."

Um no. That will not work.

"No, that's okay, I don't mind driving back with you and grabbing my car."

"But it's going to be late when we get there and it'll make you like an hour later getting home."

I think about how to remain casual but not give away the fact that my place is currently not *my* place. "I just... I just think I'd feel more comfortable to have my car with me. I know it sounds silly, but just in case anything happened and I needed it."

Jake nods. "No that's not silly, I get that. Okay, I'll take you to your car."

I silently let out the breath I'd been holding. Phew. I'll stay with Mandy again until my trailer is back on site. It strikes me that I should probably tell Mandy this so I grab my phone more as a courtesy check than anything else.

> Me: Hey, we're headed back. Just making sure it's still okay for me to stay until my trailer gets back. I can't wait to see you!

Mandy: Wait what?? I thought you were headed back on Sunday?

Mandy: My sis is in town crashing on the couch and she's not leaving until Sunday morning. I need a bigger place!

Me: Oh okay, no worries. I'll figure it out! No prob.

Mandy: But how will you figure it out? Where will you stay? Dammit I really do need a bigger place.

Me: No you don't. You never have more than one other person there. It's my bad, I should've checked with you when I found out we were finishing ahead of schedule. I got it, don't worry!

Mandy: Well now I have ALL the worry. How close are you?

Me: An hour or so. I got it :)

I DEFINITELY, definitely don't got it. Sal sleeps on the couch in his own apartment. He has a fold out couch and his roommate has the bedroom. So that's a no go.

I try to think of answers but the only answer I come up with is that I'm a short-sighted idiot.

Why did I sublet my apartment? Why did I think I was allowed to live in my trailer full time? Why did I not line things up better with Mandy?

Probably because I've been swooning over my costar and living in a dream world and forgot to come back to reality.

"You're quiet." Jake's voice cuts through my silence.

"Just thinking." It's the truth.

"About?"

"Okay, if I tell you something I need you to promise not to judge me. Like, I did something extremely dumb without fully thinking through the logistics and consequences and now I'm kind of stuck and it's all because of my own stupidity."

He's quiet.

"So I need you to promise no judgment. And also no trying to *fix* anything. Don't be a fixer, just be a listener. Promise?" I hold my pinky out to him.

He hooks his with mine.

I take a breath and sigh it out slowly. "Okay. So I sublet my place out to one of Mandy and Sal's coworkers at the restaurant."

He just nods. Listening.

Another big breath. "I knew I could get decent money for it and I had my trailer and it just seemed so silly to have two places. And you know I like that trailer. So I just moved into it and rented my place out. But I didn't realize they actually *moved* the trailers. And I know that's so dumb and saying it out loud makes me feel like an actual idiot, but I really didn't know. I just thought they stayed there and were ours the whole time we film. And then I was going to move back into my place when shooting wraps and I had to give up the trailer anyways."

I massage my temples. "I *thought* I was being smart because I wasn't wasting money and was able to save that rent but now I'm momentarily homeless for a couple days and I'm realizing that I will be off and on during filming whenever they need to move our trailers."

I chance a glance at him. He still doesn't say anything so I give him a conclusion. "And that, my friend, is what I was thinking about."

Now *he* lets out a deep breath.

"Okay, so, let me just make sure I understand. You rented your place out because you thought you didn't need it anymore, and you've been actually *living* in the trailer, but now you have no place to stay anytime the trailers are moved. Or serviced."

"In a nutshell."

"Emma! Why didn't you talk to me about this before? Why didn't you ask me about living in the trailers? I mean, I knew you spent the night there sometimes but I thought that was just when you had a really early call time or when we wrapped late at night. Wait—where did you stay when they were moving them to SLO?"

"Okay—first, why *would* I talk to you about this? It doesn't have anything to do with you. Second, I didn't ask because it seemed obvious. We spend so much time in the trailers that I was never going home anyways and it seemed redundant and wasteful to have two places. And third—Mandy's house."

Jake holds his hands up in surrender for a split second before putting them back on the wheel. "I'm sorry, I'm sorry. I didn't mean to put you on the defensive. I just...I'm just trying to help you figure this out. Okay so when is the sublet up?"

"Well it *sounds* like you're trying to fix it. And you pinkied." I shoot a glare at him. "I did a six month sublet so about three more months."

I see realization dawn on his face. "Oh. *This* is why you didn't want me to drop you at home tonight."

It's not a question but I answer anyway. "Yep."

"So are you going back to Mandy's for a couple days?"

"Well that was the plan, but we wrapped a few days early and her sister is staying on her couch right now."

"Okay. What about Sal?"

"Sal is basically crashing in his own apartment. His bed *is* the couch. And it's not even a true couch. It's a pseudo couch. And there's not another one for me."

"Emma—" He shakes his head. "You can't sleep on a couch."

"Of course I can. I love a good couch. But there's not an extra. Mandy and Sal are out this go round so I'm going to a hotel for a couple nights. I already got it figured out. And I'm pumped about it. Hotels are great. I love a hotel."

"Yeah, we just left a hotel after being in one for six weeks." He cuts his eyes over at me. "Which hotel?"

"Holiday Inn." *Thank gosh for ubiquitous hotel chains.*

"Which location?"

"The one near set." *Boom. Take that, detective.*

"Ahhh." He nods like that makes perfect sense. But then he raises a brow and I know I've messed up. "There isn't a Holiday Inn near set. You mean the Hampton Inn?"

"Yeah." I shake my head. "I always get those two mixed up." *Look at me honing my acting chops like I'm a professional.*

"Got it." Jake signals to get over so an overly aggressive car behind us can pass. "The thing is, there's no Hampton Inn near set either."

Dammit.

"Alright, fine, Jake. Geez, who made you the truth police? I don't know which one yet, but thankfully we have another hour in the car for me to figure it out."

"Stay at my place."

"What? No. No way. Maybe you don't know me as well as you think, but I have some pride and *I would never.* I'm not looking for a handout."

"Emma, I have three extra rooms. Timbo lives there. And I'm a great roommate."

"Jake, this isn't why I told you about this. That's such an imposition. It's actually easier for me to get a hotel for a few days."

"How so?" But he doesn't give me time to answer. "And in general I don't love the idea of you living in the set trailer."

"Why?"

"I don't think it's safe for you to be there alone every night."

"It's been several weeks and I'm safe so far."

"Several *weeks?* How did I not realize? It doesn't even have a real kitchen."

"I'm used to less."

"But it's not even a real home."

"It's more than I've ever had."

"More than your apartment?"

"Yeah, it's a thousand times nicer than my apartment."

I don't want to jump to conclusions, but I think I've just rendered him speechless. Because the silence is *silencing.*

"I still don't like it." He's quiet for a few beats more and then shakes his head. "Yeah, I don't. And I have plenty of space. Stay with me until your subletter leaves. We can even ride together when our call times are together, which they usually are. It makes a lot of sense actually."

I mean, he has a point. But still. I was looking forward to a break from him because I can only control myself for so long. Being in the same house with him has *disaster* written all over it.

"I don't think it's smart."

"I think it's smarter than subletting your only place to live and trying to live in a trailer that isn't designed for actual living."

I wince. "Ouch."

"Sorry, but true," he says on a shrug. "Listen, it'll be fun. Timbo is an absurdity. Highly entertaining. You'll love being around him. And I'm clearly amazing." He gives me his heart-throbbiest smile. "My beds are really comfortable, or so I'm told. Timbo cooks amazing dinners. And there's one more thing."

"What?"

"I have to warn you that we have *Is it Cake?* marathons."

"I don't know what that is but I'm intrigued."

"So you'll stay?"

"*Only* for the next few nights until our trailers get back, yes I'll stay." I squeeze his arm. "Thank you. Like really, really thank you."

"You'll stay longer than that. And you're welcome. Now stop second-guessing it and turn on some tunes."

40

JAKE

"I'm just saying, it was surprising," Timbo says, throwing the door open for me to walk through. My hands are full of Huang's Chinese takeout. He hasn't stopped talking about this since we left the gym and he's driving me insane.

"What was surprising?" Emma perks up from her spot on the couch. She's reading. I love having her here, even though she's so stubborn and promises she's leaving tomorrow when the trailers get back.

"This girl at the gym." Timbo grabs a bag from me and sets it on the counter before turning back to face me. "Are you worried she doesn't find you attractive anymore?"

"Um, no I *wasn't* worried about that." I set my bag down on the counter, too.

"Pfft. Impossible." Emma chimes in, walking into the kitchen. She takes a big inhale of the food and moans. "Mmmmm. That smells *so* good."

That tiny moan could undo me if I let it.

"What's impossible?" I ask.

"Huh?" she crinkles her nose in confusion.

"You said something was impossible." I *really* want her to finish that thought.

"Oh—that someone wouldn't find you attractive."

A few seconds of silence hang in the air, only to be broken by Timbo who throws his arm around her shoulders, shaking his head. "Emma, don't throw him a pity compliment. You're better than that."

She laughs. "I'm not. It's true! You know it. I know it. He knows it." She turns to face me square on.

I think my eyes must look like they're super glued open because I'm a little shocked she just blurted that out so casually. And in front of Timbo, no less. "So wait, wait wait wait. You think I'm attractive?"

"Of course."

"You've never told me you find me attractive."

She shrugs. "One," she holds up a finger. "That'd be like telling a turtle it's a turtle. I mean, *obviously* it's a turtle." She laughs at her own joke. "And two," she holds up a second finger. "It never came up." She shrugs and then cocks an eyebrow. "Do you find me attractive?"

I swallow slowly, probably too slowly, then say simply. "Yes."

Timbo, channeling Olaf, barks out: "You hesitated."

If a look could kill, the look I give Timbo should render him pulse-free. "I did not."

Emma moves closer to Timbo, crossing her arms and nodding. "Yeah, he's right. You totally hesitated."

"No I didn't. I was...thinking."

Emma cringes dramatically, like I'm making it worse with every word I say. "I mean, if you have to *think* about it that's not a good thing. See watch this." She turns to face Timbo. "Beau, do you find me attractive?"

Timbo instantly replies, with complete confidence. "Total smoke show."

She raises her eyebrows as if she'd just solved a case. "See?"

Timbo nods in agreement, like they're conducting a science experiment and they just proved their hypothesis correct.

You know what? I'm not sure I enjoy this living arrangement after all. It feels very *them against me* right about now.

Emma nudges Timbo. "By the way, thanks Beau. You're a smoke show, too."

She starts unpacking the takeout and then looks at me. "And you are too, Jake. Even if you don't reciprocate, I'm big enough to say the truth. I've got hot friends and I cannot lie."

"I do reciprocate!" My protest is a little too loud. "I just—"

She holds up a hand, stopping me. "Oh my gosh please don't make it worse." She laughs. "It's okay that I'm not your type but I don't need a detailed thesis on it." She laughs again, shaking her head. "I don't think you're my type either so no hard feelings." She holds her hands up in mock surrender.

Timbo pipes up, because of course he does. "Am I your type?"

"Not even close."

"That's fair." He shrugs and they both nod in agreement.

"What *is* your type?" I muster up the courage to ask. I try to sound casual, like I couldn't care less. But I'm pretty sure I come off as desperately invested.

"Not you guys." She holds up her fork, "Shall we?"

41

EMMA

The trailers have been back for a few weeks and I relish being back in my own space, but I'm also not too prideful to admit that staying with Jake and Beau was fun. They're shockingly easy to be around.

They both tried to convince me to stay, I refused, and the compromise is that I will on weekends sometimes or days off from shooting.

My apartment will be mine again in just a couple months, and I'm kind of enjoying the fact that I can float between a few places, Mandy's included. That's such a luxury to me. I've never had anything even close to that. Though I have to admit that the comfy bed at Jake's house definitely trumps the lumpy couch at Mandy's. She and Sal give me shit about "moving up in the world" but they not-so-secretly love it, especially when I invite them over to hang out at Jake's.

Shooting has been going great. It's one of those things that the more you do it, the easier it gets. I still have a raging case of imposter syndrome, but at least I can silence it most of the time now.

The intimate scenes have gotten easier, too. The lingering confusion I'm left with after filming scenes like that with Jake... not so much. The lines are super blurry, at least for me.

Hierarchy is a sexy show. I have no doubt that *watching* Daniel put his hands all over Annabelle will make the viewers swoon, if *feeling* him put his hands all over *me* is any indication. Because the response he elicits from my body is borderline unbearable. Even if he's playing a part, those rough and skilled hands still belong to *Jake*.

I push those thoughts from my mind approximately 20,000 times a day. I just can't go there. I know I can't.

It's not worth ruining this opportunity just because my costar is a walking god I'm dying to experience in every way possible.

It's not worth gambling with this show when it has all the makings of a hit series that could last for years, and maybe even set me up for life.

And it's not worth risking the inevitable rejection that comes down the line when the excitement fades.

A rejection I know well.

How many times have I gotten my hopes up that someone really wants me? That's not rhetorical. I can answer it.

Seven.

Yes, *seven*.

Seven homes I started to get comfortable in. Seven families who said they wanted me. Seven times I tried to make it work, tried to make them see that they should keep me past a couple months.

And how many times did they want me after the novelty wore off?

Zero. None. Nada. Nil.

I know how to expertly deal with both hope and rejection now: If you don't hope, you don't feel rejection.

Boom.

I've been living my life that way for years and I'm so much happier than when I used to get my hopes up. *Unaffected* even. I don't let people fully in, and then I don't have to let them out. Except Mandy and Sal, who relentlessly weaseled their way into my life. I love them and love having them in my life, but still—I *would* be okay if they left me behind.

See? Unaffected.

Same for Jake. Maybe not *physically* unaffected (not even close), but emotionally unaffected?

Yeah, probably not that either as it turns out. Which is precisely why I can't let myself go there.

I just can't get invested. Every time I've ever let myself get invested in someone, I've never seen even a tiny return.

42

Emma: Yes, I think I have a crush.

Emma: No, I'm not going to act on it.

Emma: Yes, sometimes I think he might have a crush, too.

Emma: No, he has not acted on it.

Emma: Yes, that makes me think he actually doesn't have a crush.

Emma: No, I'm not 13 but I know it sounds like I am. I don't have anyone else to talk to about this and I've got to let it out.

Mandy: Sounds like maybe you need to let it IN.

Emma: Not helping.

Sal: She's not wrong.

Emma: I can't go out with him anyways so I don't even know why I care.

Mandy: Ummm I think we need to go get a drink together.

Sal: Or maybe coffee because I feel like I'm going to need some energy to unpack all this.

Mandy: Ooooh let's do Espresso Martinis!

43

JAKE

I walk in my house, slam the door behind me and fall on the couch before letting out a dramatic groan.

Timbo is standing in the kitchen unwrapping little aluminum foil tents. He loves to cook veggies on the grill that way. "Okay. So you clearly had a rough day."

"Yes. Every day is a rough day right now."

"Care to elaborate?"

"I mean it's Emma. You know it's Emma."

"But what about Emma?"

"She's driving me insane."

"Good or bad insane?"

"Bad insane."

"Okay well that's good. That's progress, right? I mean, she *was* making you crazy because you wanted her. So if she's making you crazy because you don't want her that's a definite improvement, right? Well, except for the fact that you have to work with her almost every day, I guess." He shrugs.

"No dude, I still want her. I want her so badly it's *making* me insane. Every day is fucking torture. I'm with her all day, we eat our meals together, have our coffee together, run lines together. And then when we shoot I have to hold her hand, kiss her, put my hands all over her body, act like I'm fucking her. It's brutal."

I glance over at Timbo. He looks disgusted. *"What?"* I challenge.

"Oh, I don't know man..." he starts. "Fuck my life, I make millions for a job where I literally just play make believe, I travel all over the world, people swoon over me everywhere I go, I have a personal assistant to handle all my stupid shit, and my coworker is the hottest, coolest girl I've ever met. Every day I have to go to work and see her and they even make me kiss her and feel her up. And then to make it worse, they pay me a shit-load of money to do that."

He narrows his eyes at me.

"Anything else?" I ask sarcastically.

"Yeah. And I also have the best friend in history. He's an awesome wingman, a beast in the gym and is the reason I have the body girls drool over. He doesn't put up with my shit, doesn't hit on the girl I like even though I won't make a move on her, and he's a damn great cook who makes sure I eat well on long shoot days. My life blows."

He turns to leave. "The steaks are on the grill. They needed to come off forty-five seconds ago. Call me when you grow the fuck up and stop being such a whiny punk."

He walks out the door. I immediately pick up my phone and go to my favorites. I push his name.

"Yeah?" he answers. I can hear him on the phone *and* right outside the door.

"Alright alright, I'm done being such a whiny punk."

He walks right back in the door, shaking his head. "About damn time, dude."

I get up and clap him on the back. "Okay, I hear you. Thanks for the reality check. I *am* being a punk. I know I am. It's not like me." I punch his arm. "But you're right, I'm being ridiculous. My life is amazing. *Beyond* amazing." I sigh. "I'm just sore because I can't have the girl I want. She doesn't date coworkers."

He nods. "Might I remind you that you literally had that same rule after Claudia. So she's not off base." He lifts his brows for emphasis. "And might I also remind you that you miss all the shots you don't take, man. Either get over it or do something about it. Take your pick. But you can't complain *and* do nothing. That's not allowed."

He shoves the tongs in my hand. "And go get the steaks. Because of your bullshit we're eating them well done tonight."

44

Jake: Got a minute?

Emma: Like 90 of them.

Jake: Lines?

Emma: Sure!

Jake: Are you in your trailer?

Emma: Where else? ;)

45

EMMA

I'm putting in my earrings when there's a knock at my trailer.

"Come in!" I shout, knowing it's Jacob. He walks in and freezes.

"*Wow*. Wow, you look *unbelievable*," he blurts out, and I wonder if he meant to say it aloud.

"Thank you." I feel a little uncomfortable, though I know I shouldn't. Maybe even a little guilty but I know I shouldn't feel that either. That wouldn't be fair to me. We've worked together for months now and we've flirted a little, yeah, but Jake has never asked me out. Never even alluded to asking me out. Hell he could barely say he found me attractive. He's had every chance in the world and hasn't taken it. Someone else did, though. They took a chance and I'm taking one, too.

"I thought we could run through tomorrow's lines together." He closes the door behind him.

We do this all the time. We run our lines. Give each other

feedback on inflection and facial expressions. Laugh when a line is too cheesy and make a joint executive decision that no human would ever say that and thus we must change the line immediately. It's fun. It's helpful. And it makes me so much more confident. Sure we have table reads, but being surrounded by the writers is just not the same as walking through things just the two of us.

We sit on either end of the couch and start the scene. It's a more dramatic one and seeing how Jake is playing it helps shape my approach. He's really talented. I can't help but think about the fact that although this show is shaping up to be really great, I do think it's probably beneath him. He could be doing so much more.

We finish the scene and I lean back on the couch, stretching. "Okay, pretty sure we nailed it. We got it. Good?"

He smiles. "Yeah, good."

We fist bump. "Alright so what are you up to the rest of the night?" I start to stand and he pulls me back down.

"Wait. I thought we'd run through the next one, too."

Is it my imagination or does he look mildly panicked? I look at him like he's crazy. "Ummm, the extremely sexy one?"

"Yeah." And is it my imagination again or does he now look overly nonchalant? Like *too* nonchalant.

I tilt my head, honestly thinking about it, weighing the need —or lack of—for rehearsing the next scene. "I mean...do we need to? I feel good about it. I think we're kind of natural at those things together at this point. We've shot so many scenes like that and they don't unnerve me like they did in the beginning. I think we could shoot them in our sleep. It's the more dramatic stuff like the scene we just did that throws me off a little bit." I stand up to grab my shoes and sit back on the couch, putting them on. "I honestly haven't thought too much about the next one. Should I?"

"Yeah, I mean, probably? *I* think so. It's the *finale* for our first season. Kind of a big deal. I think it'd be helpful to feel it out together. Kind of like we did for the very first scene we ever shot."

I shoot him a knowing look. "Practicing *that* went a little awry. And we both know it."

Silence.

I think back to how kind and patient, and even gentle he'd been when I was nervous and wanted to practice. And not just a scene, but a straight up *kiss* for that scene.

Ugh. I break the silence. "Okay you're right. It can only help us. Let's do it."

He breathes what sounds like a sigh of relief. "Thanks Em."

No one has ever called me that. *I love it.*

I roll my shoulders a few times and chuckle. "I've just got to get in that zone. I wasn't prepared for this."

"What can I do to help?"

"Oh, I don't know." I shrug. "Look sexy and say something dirty to me. Or grab me by the waist hard. And kind of dig your fingers in. Or tell me I'm beautiful. Actually scratch that. I know what would do it. Do the dishes. Ooh! And take out the trash." I chuckle. "Any or all of the above."

He pushes himself off the couch, walks to the sink and then checks the drying rack. The dishes are dry so he puts them away. Then he begins washing the two cups in the sink—lids, straws and all. He casually puts the pieces on the drying rack like he's not fulfilling every girl's fantasy right now. Then he walks to the trash can and opens it to take the bag out. *But* I just took the trash out this morning so it is essentially empty. Yet he still grabs the nearly empty bag, holds it in the air and says simply, "It's symbolic. And I'll take it with me when I leave," before dropping it beside the front door.

I feel...god, I don't know what I feel. But I definitely feel *something*, and I feel it both high in my body and *low* in my body. Flutters, I think. Flutters in my chest and flutters below my navel.

Jake walks toward me and grabs my hips, pulling me super close.

Oh.

He puts his lips less than an inch from my ear and whispers, "Emma, you're beautiful and I'm dying to do things to you that I can't say out loud for fear that you'll never speak to me again."

My stomach clenches, among other things. *What. Just. Happened.*

He understood the assignment. Even though the assignment was a joke.

Wasn't it?

I push him back, laughing nervously. "Ummm okay Jake. *Damn.* You didn't have to sell it so well." I give him a playful push. "Overachiever."

I step back a couple steps for some much-needed distance and breathe out in a way that makes me sound a little breathless *and I hate it.*

I clear my throat and then slow clap. "Bravo. You're a pro. Well done. You're hired."

46

JAKE

I wasn't selling anything. And I wasn't kidding. She gave me permission to say and do those things, and even though I know *she* was kidding, that didn't mean *I* was. I took the opening. Even if it was a fake one. When it comes to Emma, I'm going to take what I can get. Starting now.

Because Timbo is right. I can't keep complaining about something without doing anything about it.

And it felt good to be that close to her. Without all the cameras panning our every move. Or surrounded by even a limited crew.

"Well if you're *that* far past it, why are you here?"

Emma's voice cuts through my thoughts. *What?* What's she talking about?

"Your line, mister."

Oh shit. Yes. We're supposed to be doing the scene.

She starts again. "Well if you're that far past it, why are you here?"

"You."

"Me, what?"

I step toward her. "I'm here for you. Well actually I'm here... *because* of you."

"Well what'd *I* do?" Emma asks incredulously. She's gotten really good. She makes it so easy to get lost in a scene with her.

I step even closer. Crowding her.

"It's not what you did or didn't do, it's what I *want* to do."

She holds my glare. Swallows. Audibly.

Was that Emma swallowing slowly like that? Like she can't breathe with me that close? Or was it Annabelle? She's so in character I can't freaking tell. And it's frustrating that I can't tell where Emma ends and Annabelle begins right now. Maddening even.

"Can we?" I break character and gesture toward her body. "Is it okay if I...?"

"Yeah, sure. We can keep going. I think we're build—"

I step forward again and press my body right up to hers. With Timbo's words flooding my ears, I take the shot and push a little closer.

She lets out the slightest gasp. It's nearly imperceptible. But I caught it. "Oh. Oh so you're going...oh so you mean like *really* do this scene." She's talking more to herself than to me.

"Yes," I manage to get out.

She pauses and I can feel her thinking. Weighing things.

Then she puts her hand on my chest, looks down and lingers there while she skims the sides in her other hand.

She looks back up. "So show me what you want to do." I know that was Annabelle's line but Emma said it like it was hers.

Fuck it.

I'm going to. I'm going to show her. Not Daniel. *Me*. Daniel's not showing her shit. *I'm* going to show her.

You miss all the shots you don't take. I can't unhear those words.

I kiss her. My lips connect with hers and I feel like I might explode on the spot. The script calls for it so I'm not completely out of line. Technically I'm well *inside* the lines, but it doesn't feel like I will be able to stay there, because my mind is reeling with possibilities and my body is thrumming with want. *How far will she let us go under the guise of rehearsing? How much will she let us "practice?"*

I think about pulling back just to see if she'll lean back in. But what if she actually *doesn't* want me and this *is* just acting for her? I don't want to risk that truth. At least if we keep going we can play it off as getting lost in a scene.

I slide my tongue into her mouth, toeing the line but not crossing it. I know she likes to "real" kiss. None of that fake no-tongue nonsense. She thinks it looks too pretend for two people who are supposed to be ravenous with each other. I tease her tongue with mine. Testing. Waiting.

She doesn't kiss me back.

Instead, she pulls back.

No.

No.

I don't move. I don't even breathe. I'm suspended in time, my lips achingly close to hers, but not touching.

She lifts her eyes to mine. And stares. It feels like a thousand words pass between us, though neither of us utters a word.

But I realize we must have arrived at the same conclusion, because as suddenly as she pulled back a moment ago, now she quickly closes that fraction of distance between us as she presses her lips back to mine.

I honestly think I might happy cry.

But I don't have the chance to, because now *she's* the one setting the pace. A pace I'm scrambling to keep up with. She's kissing me wildly, almost greedily, like she needs me to breathe.

I love it. Her hands are combing over me. *Everywhere*. It's furiously messy and hungry, with an urgency so palpable I could slice through it. She's right there with me and I'm internally dying over the fact that I'm actually, *finally* making out with my dream girl.

I think.

I feel myself losing control. I've kept that control tethered so tightly for months now and I don't think I can hold it a second longer.

She moans ever so softly and *nope*. The tether is broken. My restraint has left the building.

I walk her back until she's pinned against the kitchen island and then nudge her legs apart with my knee, settling myself between them. We kiss for several long moments. It's perfect. It's exactly what I need and not even close to what I need at the same time. I'm insatiable. I need *more*. Of this. Of *her*. I lift her onto the counter and the little red floral sundress she's wearing rides up several inches. This *body*. This *girl*. I grip her thighs and am immediately overwhelmed with how fucking good it feels to have permission to finally touch her like this. The groan that escapes me sounds unrecognizable. Almost feral. Nothing like myself.

I feel like a teenager who is going to blow before anything even happens.

I squeeze my eyes shut in an attempt to abate the nearly consuming pleasure that just washed over me. Pleasure just from touching her. *Barely* touching her.

Emma wraps her legs around my waist and cinches them in so it propels me forward. I wasn't expecting it, and I topple forward on top of her, smushing her back onto the counter. She laughs. A nervous, adorable laugh.

I don't.

Instead, I drop down to my knees.

She's not laughing anymore. She's dead silent. And dead still.

This is where the scene ends. We've taken immense creative liberties in the past few minutes. Yes, Daniel and Annabelle *do* make out in this scene. Yes, it *is* one of the sexiest scenes of this entire season. No, he *doesn't* put her on a kitchen counter. And no, she *doesn't* wrap her beautiful legs around his waist. But he *does* walk her backwards into a wall. And she *does* say, "On your knees." In the scene, he kneels down and it fades to black.

I dropped to my knees too soon. I should've waited on her line. But my body is moving faster than my mind can keep up with.

We *should* be done. But I'm pretty positive we're just getting started.

I look up at Emma and hold her stare, our eyes locked together in what feels like an iron clad understanding of what just happened and what *could* happen. My eyes are boring into hers. Beseeching. Asking what to do. Maybe, in my dream scenario, even asking for permission. But more probably giving her the chance to come to her senses and kick my ass to the ground.

But she doesn't move. Doesn't speak. Doesn't even blink. And then, in what has to be the greatest moment of my thirty-two years on this earth, she responds to my unspoken question with an unspoken, yet very clear, answer.

She nods.

It feels like the wind just got sucker-punched out of me, in the best way imaginable. I can barely breathe.

"On your knees." Her voice is a gentle command.

I curse myself for hesitating even a fraction of a second, but I have to be sure. We've been rehearsing, and that *is* the line, and I just...I have to be sure. I care about her too much to not check. I will hate myself for eternity if this backfires, but I have to check. *I have to.* "Emma, I need to know what you want. I need you to say it."

"I want you where you are." She leans back onto her forearms and lets her legs fall open even more. *An invitation.* "I want you on your knees, Jake."

I squeeze my eyes shut and moan. My blood is on fire and I'm pretty sure every last drop of it just rushed to my dick with those seven words. Seven words that I take as the green light they are, as I lower my head in between her thighs and breathe in all of her.

In the span of the past several moments—mere *minutes*—I have confirmed what I long suspected: Emma Watts is my favorite flavor, my favorite scent, and my new favorite place to be is between her legs.

I brush my lips over her, at once loving and hating the thin fabric of her panties that's keeping me from her skin. Bright coral little cotton panties that I've dreamed of seeing. Sporty and girly and soft. I stay on top of them and pepper her with kisses all over, feeling her body soften more with each one, any lingering tension fleeing her body. I lick her straight through the fabric and then trace kisses back along the same path. And though I know that shadow of dampness is partly from the trail I just licked, I know it's also from *her.* I nip at her clit, and *oh.* She clearly loves that. Now I have a new thing to add to my favorites —her soft, throaty moan is my new favorite sound. I could listen to it on repeat for the rest of my existence.

And I'd bet my life that I know what my new favorite *feeling* will be. Unmistakably, *her.* Wrapped around *me.*

"Jake." She squirms under my mouth. "I—I need more."

I keep my face planted between her thighs and take the deepest inhale I can manage. "I know you do. And I'll give it to you." I lick another trail up one side, then the other, before dropping my head against her. "But I'm living out a dream right now and I don't ever want to wake up. And Emma, you *undo* me, so I have to pace myself."

I want to devour her. Consume her. *Claim* her. But I also want to take my time with her and make this one perfect moment stretch for a million more. Just as I tuck my fingers into the waistband of her panties to peel them down, there is a knock at the door.

My heart hits the floor.

Are you fucking kidding me? I'm going to kill that person. And the descendants of whoever invented knocking. And doors.

I freeze, not moving up or down. She scoots down toward me and I don't want to mistake it for her demanding more when she might just be trying to get down and answer the door, but damn if that doesn't feel like *exactly* what she's doing.

She doesn't get up. Did she hear the door? Is she just ignoring it?

Another few knocks.

"Oh my gosh!" She jerks up abruptly, eyes panicked. "Oh my gosh. Oh my gosh. Shit. *SHIT!*"

She jumps up, knocking me off balance in the process. She turns back to face me, still wide-eyed. "Jake, I—Oh. Oh wow. This is...um..." She doesn't finish that thought. Instead she brushes her dress down and clears her throat. "The door is for me. I...I need a minute. Oh my gosh, I need *a lot* of minutes." She laughs a laugh that is borderline hysterical and paces around in front of me. "Where did the time go? Can you stall?" She stops pacing and walks right up to me. "Let me see you."

She tries to pat down my hair and then straightens my shirt. She tugs at the bottom of it to pull it straight and then she sees it. The huge bulge in my jeans. Don't get me wrong—I know she already felt it through my pants. But seeing her *see* what she does to me? It's about to unravel me.

And clearly it unravels her a little too, because she doesn't look away for several long seconds.

"Emma." She's still holding the hem of my shirt, one hand now twisting into it.

She drops her hands and shakes her head, wordlessly asking me to *not go there*.

I respect it. I won't push her right now.

"You want me to stall? For what?" I ask, following her like a puppy as she walks toward the bathroom.

"Yes, *please*. Could you?"

Well, I mean, technically I guess I can. "Okay. What am I stalling for?"

She's quiet a few beats too long and I'm instantly uneasy.

"Well, this may be the weirdest timing of my life."

"Emma, what am I stalling for?"

"My...date." She nods to herself in the mirror as she touches up her makeup. "And I know this would look weird to anyone who isn't us. Or isn't in the business at least."

"Meaning?" It comes out more as a grumble than a word.

She sets her lip liner down. Of course I know what lip liner is, I have a mom and a sister. And I've been with a lot of women. Give me a little credit.

"*Meaning* that if he weren't familiar with stuff like this, he probably wouldn't understand that it's no big deal and we were just rehearsing a scene."

"Oh is *that* all it was?" There's a slight edge in my voice. It was either an edge in my voice or a crack in my voice and I went with the edge because I don't want her to know I am on the verge of crying.

Me. A grown man. Crying because the girl he wants is about to go on a date and clearly doesn't want him back.

"Emma." It's a protest, the way I say her name.

She shakes her head—again—and levels me with a look like only she can.

"Well it's not like any scene *I've* ever done before," I mumble.

"Of course it's not, and that's part of what is going to make our show such a hit. We just got caught up in it. How could we not? It's a great script. And a great scene. And you're a great actor." She says it so dismissively that I'm wondering if I imagined the near combustion of a few minutes ago.

Another, louder, knock at the door.

I nod slowly. Exaggeratedly. Sarcastically. "Caught up?" I say it as more of a statement than a question.

She nods. "Yeah, it's bound to happen sometimes with what we do."

"Emma."

"Yeah?" Her tone is casual.

"I bit your clit, Emma. And you asked for *more*."

She sucks in a breath and squeezes her eyes shut. I can tell she's replaying it. And I can tell by the way she clenches her legs together ever so slightly that she *loved* it.

"Would you let me do that on camera?" I know I'm pushing her. But she's acting way too coy and too casual for what just happened. Too *unphased*.

And I don't like it.

"Yeah, I would." There's hesitation in her voice she can't quite mask. "I would," she repeats. *Bullshit*. It sounds to me like she's trying to convince herself. And then she adds, softly, "I would, because it's *you,* and I trust you, Jake." She holds my gaze a few beats before adding, "And I mean, the script called for it..."

"The script called for *fade to black*, Emma."

"...and we've filmed a bunch of scenes like that together before."

Not like *that*. Never like that. She knows it and I know it. That went way beyond anything we've ever filmed together and anything we ever *would* film together since *Hierarchy* is not a "*Skin*emax" series. But if she doesn't want to admit that then *fine*.

I'm standing in the bathroom doorway and she looks at my reflection in the mirror, pleading with her eyes. "Jake. Jake, please."

I sigh and adjust myself as best I can but these aren't magic pants and they definitely aren't winning any awards for trying to conceal the raging hard on I'm sporting. I try to wrangle my emotions in but there are a lot of conflicting ones so it's easier said than done. I walk to her door and swing it open.

To find a face I know all too well staring right back at me.

Dammit.

And he has flowers.

Damn it all to hell.

So it really is a date? A freaking date? With *him*?

"Hey man, I'm here for Emma."

He smiles good-naturedly.

I don't.

"Yeah, she'll be right out. We were running lines. Sorry we ran over." *I'm not.*

"No problem." He shrugs casually. "I know how it goes."

I just nod.

"How's the show going?"

So I guess we're doing small talk. "Good. Haven't seen you lately..." I shake my head and decide I'm just going to say what's on my mind. "What happened to not dating people she works with?"

My tone is accusatory and I don't even mean for it to be. I feel like I'm floating a few feet above, watching myself handle this situation utterly terribly.

"Yeah," he laughs again. "Well, she really meant it, huh?"

"So then what's this?" I snap out.

He shrugs. "I quit."

He *what?*

He quit? I knew I hadn't seen him lately but I was low-key thankful he hadn't been around so I didn't ask any questions. I just thought he was working less or something. "You *quit?* Why?"

"I mean, I couldn't get her out of my head, you know?"

I do know.

He continues, "Got to shoot your shot with someone like her. I've already found another PA position on a film a couple of soundstages over so it's all good."

This son of a bitch. This amazingly *brilliant* son of a bitch. He quit so he could ask her out? That's such a baller move. It makes me like him even more, which makes me dislike him even more.

If *I* didn't want her, he's exactly the kind of guy I would want *for* her.

Emma's voice breaks through my spiral.

"Hey Ben! Sorry I'm a little bit late. We got totally caught up rehearsing!"

"*Wow.* You look...gorgeous. *Wow.*" He looks elated. *Of course he does. She's perfect.* "Shall we?" He reaches out his hand.

It's all I can do not to slap it back down.

Screw him for getting to be so free with his emotions with her. For getting to say whatever he's thinking.

"Yeah but um..." She nods toward the flowers in his hand. "Should we put those in water? They're beautiful."

"Oh, yes." He holds them out to her. "I forgot all about them when you walked in."

Okay, Cassanova. Calm the fuck down.

In the span of five minutes I watch her thank him, grab a vase, and make small talk as she quickly arranges the flowers. Here she is chatting away with ease, and here I am absolutely battling to take each breath. I don't take my eyes off of her once but she doesn't even look at me until she says goodbye and walks out.

Leaving *me* in *her* doorway.

Like a rejected buffoon.

I'm just standing there, in *her* trailer, staring after her. Literally just watching her walk away. With another guy. Like a lovesick...what's more pathetic than a buffoon?

Whatever it is, I'm that.

47

JAKE

I slam the door so hard the entire doorframe rattles precariously.

"Woah. What's got your panties in a wad?" Timbo calls out from the den.

"*Who.*" I correct him.

He shifts on the couch to face me. "Let me guess." He pretends to be thinking hard. "Emma?"

"Among others." I slam my hand down on the counter in frustration.

"Dude, calm down. Who's *others?*"

"Fucking Ben."

"Okay obviously I don't know who *Fucking Ben* is."

"Ben that production assistant who is extremely jacked and liked Emma so much he actually quit his job on the show so he could ask her out."

"Oh, because of the whole not dating people she works with thing?"

"Yeah so he literally *quit*."

"Damn that's good. He's *good*."

"I know. And now she's going to fall in love with him and they'll get married because clearly he's a great guy and I'll never have a chance with her. And it's on me. I blew it. I was too slow to act and now I missed out."

"I mean, I don't want to say *I told you so*, but—actually I kind of do want to say it. I warned you man."

I groan and fall back on the couch next to him. "Why didn't *I* quit to be with her? Why didn't *I* think of that?"

Timbo looks at me like I'm an idiot. "Dude, it's *your* show. You can't quit. You're literally starring in it and running it. That's stupidity talking."

"But I can't compete with something like that. Like in a show or movie, or *shit*, even worse—in a romance book—the guy who quits his job to be with the girl is going to win every time."

"Honestly you're right. That's so good you should write it into the show somehow."

"You know you're zero help, right?"

"I mean if you had listened to me..."

"I did listen to you!" I jump up in exasperation. "I did! *Today*. I made a move and she was right there with me."

"Wait, what? You made a move today and *then* she went on a date?"

"Yes." I hang my head in frustration.

"I mean, what move? Because it sounds like it didn't work."

"You can be such a jackass."

"No, I'm really asking. Because if you made a move today and then she went out with another guy...I'm just saying I don't know about your move man."

"I kissed her. And she kissed me back." I close my eyes remembering how it felt. "We made out, and...I kind of went down on her, and it was incredible. And then he knocked at the door to pick her up and it was just...it was over."

Now Timbo is standing up, shaking his head like he doesn't understand. "Woah woah woah. What do you mean you *kind of* went down on her? You either did or you didn't. Kind of going down on someone isn't a thing."

"I'm not going to kiss and tell man. That would be disrespectful to her."

"Well you'd better tell because if"—he frames his next words in air quotes—"*kind of going down on her* was your move then yeah of course it didn't work you idiot."

"No, you don't get it. You *won't* get it. We were rehearsing a scene. A hot one. And it...turned real."

"Was going down on her part of the scene?"

"Yeah."

"Like was it written in the show that you go down on her?"

"Yes."

He looks at me with an unmistakable look of pity. "Is it possible *she* was just rehearsing?" He cringes at the question hanging between us.

"No." I shake my head. "No. *No.* It was hot. And she let me *actually* kiss her." I glance at him. "*Everywhere.*"

Timbo's eyebrows shoot up. "Everywhere?"

"Everywhere."

"She let you actually kiss her pussy?"

"Yes. I mean, it was through her underwear, but...yeah."

"Okay that's not exactly the same thing, but we'll roll with it. And that happens in the script?"

"I mean it *alludes* to it. Geez, why do you keep fixating on that?"

"Two reasons. One—I've got to freaking watch this show when it comes out. And two—it's kind of an important distinction to make. If all of it was written in the scene you were rehearsing together, then how do you know it was real?"

"You had to be there."

"I mean, I wish I had been. Emma's smoking."

"Shut up." I sit back down. "Yeah, she is. And now she's out with Ben, who seems really nice and he's handsome and he drinks bourbon and he brought flowers and he quit his job so he could ask her out. He quit for the fucking *chance* to ask her out. I mean, hell. *I* want to date him after all that."

"Me too."

"Did I mention you're zero help?"

48

EMMA

"I'm just saying, it's impressive." Mandy takes a sip of her espresso martini.

I nod, taking a sip of my Moscow Mule. I'm not an espresso martini girl, and this place does not have mojito vibes. "Agreed."

"A guy who quit his job so he could ask you out? He's not messing around." Sal is already on his second espresso martini, but he's at least twice the size of Mandy and me so it basically counts as his first.

"Yeah, it was a bold move. And admittedly really hot." And flattering as hell. A guy who wants to ask you out so badly that he quits his job so he can? *Whew.*

"*But...?*" Mandy raises a brow.

"Why is there a *but?*"

"Because there's a certain *other* great man in the picture who takes up a lot of your headspace. And I'm not talking about myself." Sal winks at me.

"Guys, listen. Yes, Jacob is a great guy. And yes I might be somewhat obsessed with him. But you guys already know the deal." I hold up a finger. "We work together." I hold up another finger. "And we will continue to work together for hopefully years to come." I add a third finger. "And not to mention, he's never made a *real* move on me anyways. I think he feels as confused about not crossing the lines as I do."

"Except the move he made on you a few days ago." Mandy always plays the devil's advocate. I love it about her. *Usually*. Just not tonight.

"That wasn't a real move."

"Yeah, because I make out with my friends and push them onto countertops and kiss them over their panties all the time." Sal rolls his eyes.

"Hey! *I'm* your friend. How come I don't get that kind of treatment?" Mandy asks, feigning offense.

"Ohmygosh." *Why did I tell them about that?* "I already told you that it was part of the scene. It was in the script. It wasn't real." I don't dare admit that it *was* real. That we crossed the line from playing a part to playing with each other. That the script didn't call for his head between my thighs. And it sure as hell didn't call for him kissing and licking me while I leaned back and spread my legs wider for him, asking for more. Nope, definitely not going to mention all the artistic freedom we took with that scene.

"The lady doth protest too much, methinks."

I glare at Sal. "Shut up, Shakespeare."

My phone chirps. Speak of the devil. The devastatingly gorgeous, devastatingly confusing devil.

Jake: Want to meet Timbo and me for dinner?

Me: I'm out with Mandy and Sal.

Jake: Good. Bring them.

Me: Let me check with them. I'll let you know in a few.

Jake: We can go get queso.

Me: I'm making an executive decision. We're in.

"Do you two get turned on when you're shooting sexy scenes together?"

Mandy is three margaritas in, not to mention the martini from earlier, and it *shows*.

I side-eye her and straight up lie. "No."

"Yes."

I whip my head toward Jake so fast I might have residual whiplash tomorrow.

So I guess we're just saying whatever is on our minds tonight.

I shake my head. "Nuh uh. I've never noticed." *Except when we were rehearsing in my trailer.*

"I'm an actor. I'm good at acting like I don't."

"But I never...*feel* you."

"That's because I—"

Mandy cuts him off. "Do you do the tuck?"

Jake's mouth drops open for a millisecond. "How do you know about the tuck?"

"Of course girls know about the tuck." I roll my eyes. "But you can usually still feel it...*tucked*."

Mandy and Sal's heads are on a swivel watching this interaction.

Timbo laughs. "Oh, well it might be because Jake isn't big enough to—"

Jake bites out, "You don't feel it because I try to be a gentleman and conceal it from you so I don't make you uncomfortable."

Mandy sighs. "Awww." Okay so Mandy might be further past tipsy than I realized. If she thinks a man tucking his cock into his waistband so I won't feel it is swoon-worthy then Mandy needs some water *stat*.

My brows furrow. "That's your whip."

"It's both. I tuck the handle of my whip into my waistband, too, so you don't feel...*me*."

Timbo starts to speak again and Jake side eyes him so hard he shuts his mouth and takes a sip of his drink instead.

But Sal does no such thing. "So you really get hard during your scenes with Emma?"

Wow. Just wow. Group dinners are off the table after tonight. Terrible vibes. Zero stars. Would not recommend.

Jake, more brazen than I've ever seen him before, gestures toward me. "Have you *seen* Emma?"

So everyone really is just saying whatever tf they want tonight, huh?

"Awww." And just like that, Mandy is fired from being my best friend.

Sal mimics a mic drop before turning to me and saying, "*There's* your move."

He's fired, too.

Jake looks quizzically between us. "Move?"

But Timbo clears his throat, and I'm saved from having to acknowledge Sal's statement and Jake's question. I'm so grateful for Timbo's impeccable timing—that is, until he speaks. "By the way, I was kidding about Jake's dick not being big enough to notice. He's got a big hog. Just putting that out there." He claps Jake on the back. "I got your back, bro."

Timbo nods. Mandy awwws. Sal shakes his head. Jake face palms. And I raise my hand.

"Check please."

49

JAKE

I t's been two weeks since the "trailer incident" that plays on a loop in my mind all day, every day. Emma and I haven't talked about it since she claimed that we just got a little "caught up" rehearsing in the moments after Ben knocked at the door for their date.

We pretend like it never happened. Actually, *she* pretends like it never happened, and I let her.

She's still seeing him. I've seen his car at her trailer several times. It makes me both mad and sad. It's my own doing. I could've told her how I felt, I could've gone for it like ole Benny Ben did. But I was trying to do the right thing. I knew she didn't want to date someone she even *casually* worked with, so how could she ever justify dating me when everything hinges on the two of us intimately working together for a long time to come? And I know she might be right. It probably wouldn't be smart. So I tried to do right by her, but somehow it feels really, really wrong.

Today is our last day shooting season one. We shot most of the season finale a couple weeks ago and we've been shooting daily since, wrapping things up. I'm mostly used to it now after years in this business, but sometimes it still throws me to shoot things so out of order. Post-production work is its own kind of magic, though, so I no longer worry about how it will all come together. It just does.

It's always bittersweet to close a season, but it's been such a great shoot that nearly the whole team is coming back for season two. And the network wants to push the seasons out closer together while the *Hierarchy* book hype is so strong, so we are only breaking for a couple months before starting season two. The script is already done, casting is working on the new characters, and since we've been greenlit for three seasons, we'll already be shooting season two when season one premieres. I've never been on a series that moved this fast, but I'm glad we're not letting things stall out in between seasons. Or even episodes. We're releasing season one in two phases—six episodes at once with a mid-season break followed by six more episodes. It's a newer approach and I think viewers will like it. I hate when a show you love makes you wait an eternity for a new season. And people almost expect to be able to binge watch a show now, so this model ticks all those boxes.

"LET'S REVERSE THAT."

Willa is in video village just off set but her voice carries throughout the room. She leans into Alex and listens, nodding, then walks over to Emma and me. "Alex wants to reverse that. Emma, *you* shove Jake into the wall instead. This is Annabelle's moment. She feels powerful, *she* is going to take control."

I think back through the books. It's hard to remember where

each one ends and the next begins, but I'm pretty sure Annabelle doesn't shove Daniel. That's hot and I feel like I would've remembered it. "Do we need Lisa to sign off on that change?"

Alex's voice comes through on Willa's walkie talkie. "Jake, it's not reading right with you doing the shove. Try it reversed and see what you think. And Emma, put your hand on his whip like you're going to disarm him."

I nod and look to Emma. She smirks and says, "Sounds great to me. I, for one, am a big fan of the change."

"Yeah I bet you are."

"Alright, roll it back to the top." Willa walks back over to take her place at video village.

We begin the scene and I grab Emma's wrists like the take we just shot, but this time she breaks away and shoves *me* into the wall before sidling right up to me, mere centimeters from my face. And *oh fuck*. I am instantly turned on.

She reaches down and grabs me. My dick. *She grabs my dick.* I'm immensely thankful for the many layers we're wearing and hope all the loose fabric hanging off her is concealing the fact that her hand is wrapped around my cock.

"Cut! That was perfect."

I don't have a free hand to make any adjustments so I slump against the wall as much as I can with Emma still pinning me, trying to make my body as concave as possible and my dick disappear in the process. She doesn't release me.

"Emma."

"Yeah?"

I swallow and she watches my Adam's apple bob.

"That's um...that's my dick." It's barely a whisper, lest anyone hear me.

Her hand jerks back like I spontaneously caught on fire and she doesn't want to get burned. "Oh my god!" It's the loudest whisper ever. Then much quieter, "Oh my god, Jake. I'm sorry. I thought—"

"Let's do this in a minute when we don't have an entire crew surrounding us." I nod reassuringly to her, then lift my head and shout loud enough for Alex and Willa to hear me. "Good call, Alex. I like it better."

He holds his hand up signaling me to wait silently as they watch the playback. Emma takes this as her cue to continue the conversation. This time, she leans up to my ear and whispers directly into it so no one else can hear.

"I thought that was the handle of your whip and your dick was *behind* that."

She takes a deep breath and continues. "I mean, I *have* thought about how you said you get hard and hide it with your whip a lot since the other night, because that would mean you've successfully hidden that from me for several months. But I thought..."

She's completely spiraling. "Are you *sure* that was your penis?"

"Quite."

"But..." She squints at me. "But, it was really...solid. Like a hard handle you can hold onto."

That's what you do to me, I want to say. But instead I can only manage a nod.

Her eyes go wide as saucers. "*Oh*. Timbo was right."

Now my dick isn't the only thing inflated. My ego is right up there with it. I will myself to think of the least sexy thing I can.

For inexplicable reasons, my mind goes straight to rabbits. Cute. Fluffy. And they like to—

Nope.

Snails.

Perfect. Snails aren't sexy. They're slow and well, their eyes are actually kind of cute, but they're so slick and—*oh for fuck's sake.*

Alex's voice breaks through my unsuccessful redirect. "We got it." He stands and holds his arms out wide. "And *that*, ladies and gentlemen, is a wrap!"

The entire room breaks into immediate mayhem. There's applause. There are hoots and yells. High fives and hugs are flowing. I glance at Emma who looks somewhat shell-shocked. "That's a wrap, baby!" I shake her shoulders. "That's a wrap! We did it! *You* did it!"

She shakes her head as if to shake off her daze. A huge smile breaks loose and suddenly she's in my arms.

And I'm futilely calculating what I can possibly do to keep her in them forever.

50

EMMA

"When do you leave for the down under?" Willa takes a giant bite of her truffle mac and cheese.

"In two days." Jake is polishing off his plate which mere minutes ago was piled sky high from the buffet.

We're at the wrap party and I know this is only my second one ever, but man do I love a wrap party. Everyone is happy and relaxed and that *we made it* energy is electric. From here, it's out of our hands. Post-production takes over and Jake swears we've got an incredible team in place for it.

"Oh man, no down time, huh?"

He laughs. "No rest for the weary, I guess. But it'll be good. I haven't seen my costars since I came back to the States. And we worked together for years so I'm looking forward to catching up with them, especially Alissa."

Jake is headed to Australia to shoot a special episode arc on *Sunset Cove*. He said he'd sworn that he would never go back, but it's his former costar Alissa's last season and she begged him to come back so the show could right the wrong of ruining their relationship on the show. He gave them three episodes.

Not going to lie, I binged the entire *Sunset Cove* series over the past few months and I admit that I am *invested*. I'm as hungry for a Sean/Sam reunion as the rest of the world. So much so that I encouraged him to go back and shoot the episodes. We need *closure* on that love triangle.

And as much as I'm going to miss him while he's gone, I think it will be good for us to have some distance. Necessary, even. Every day I'm with him I like him a little bit more, so I'm hoping every day I'm *not* with him I'll like him a little bit less. I've got roughly sixty days to shake it off and *unlike* him so we can start season two without me harboring a completely inappropriate crush on him.

I speak up, "I personally am relieved we get to finally see Sean and Sam be together." Relieved and not at all jealous that he'll be shooting sexy scenes with someone else.

Jake nods. "Me too." *Nope, not jealous at all.*

"What's the time difference?" Willa asks.

"Seventeen hours."

"Ouch."

"Yeah, ouch," I chime in. "So I guess we'll talk in two months." I chuckle half-heartedly. "I'll miss you." I blurt it out without thinking.

His gaze lands on me. It's soft but piercing. "I'll miss you, too."

"And I'll miss you both," Willa throws in, putting a much-needed damper on the moment.

"IF YOU NEED me I'm just a short fifteen hours away." Jake's hands are on my shoulders.

I laugh. "Noted."

"And if you need *me*, I'm just a short fifteen minutes away," Beau adds.

"Also noted." I turn to face him. "I can't believe you aren't going with him. It feels weird for you two to be apart."

"That it does. But I've taken on some big name clients and I can't leave for two months. My sun doesn't rise and fall on this jackass like it used to." He nods his head toward Jake.

"Dude, go get in the car. I'll be there in a minute." Beau takes the hint and walks out. They stopped by to see me on their way to the airport. I'm packing up my trailer in preparation to move back into my apartment.

"I wish I could stay and help you."

"I'm good. Does it look like I have a lot of baggage?" I think about that question. "Actually, don't answer that."

"Come here." Jake holds out his arms for a hug.

I walk straight into him, wrapping my arms fully around him. We haven't hugged like this since that day he pulled off the interstate on the way to San Luis Obispo. It feels...right.

It also feels...well *damn*. I put my hand between us and *yep*.

"Jake?"

"Hmm?"

"You're...hard."

"I am."

"And big."

"I am."

My hand is cupping him. I let go and take a few steps back, putting much-needed distance between us.

I stare at him. He stares right back at me, a hint of challenge in his eyes. I try to think of if I've ever seen that look in his eyes before. I don't think I have. This is a different Jake.

"Why?"

"You."

"Me?"

"Yes."

I shake my head, not accepting this revelation. "Because you hugged me?"

"No."

He takes a step toward me and I take another step back.

"Because you came within a hundred feet of me." Another step forward. "Because I'm so into you I can hardly function." He steps forward. "Because you're you." Another step. "Because you *exist*."

My stomach somersaults before bottoming out. Did someone just suck all of the oxygen out of the room? Because I suddenly cannot breathe.

"I—I don't understand." I take yet another step back.

"This is my default when I'm near you."

"Where—where is this coming from?"

"It's been there, Emma. I just haven't had the balls to do anything about it."

"So you spend months with me almost every day and then wait until you leave the country to drop a bomb like this?" My voice rises with each word, frustration and confusion taking hold of me.

He takes another step toward me. "Don't! Don't take another step." My eyes are starting to prickle. "I—I can't handle this right now. I can't handle *you* right now."

His mouth tilts up. "Am *I* allowed to handle *you*?"

He has never been this bold with me. I'm completely taken aback. I walk in a circle. Am I about to spiral? A thousand percent yes. "What is happening right now?" Then I answer my own question before he can. "No. *No no no.* This is too much. I—I can't process this in real time." I feel the tears start to pool in my eyes. Nope. Not happening. Head tilted back so the tears don't fall, I ask "Since when?"

"Always?"

I feel like the Grinch. Like my heart just grew three sizes and my body cannot accommodate it if it gets any bigger.

"You *like* me?"

"That's an intense understatement."

"Jake." I look at him and I know he can read the panic etched all over my face. "Jake, we can't. It could mess everything up. We work together. And we will for a long time, I hope. And now we aren't going to see each other for two months and the next time we see each other we will be right back to shooting together again. This...this just can't...*We*..." I trail off before gathering my thoughts. "Can we go back? Can we still be friends? Like we have been?"

"Can we be more? Because that's what I want."

"No! We can't! You *know* we can't." A few beats pass. "Not now anyways. Not while we're on the show together. It's just risking way too much. It could ruin everything."

"Well, good thing I'm an executive producer then. I think maybe I'll let our writers go and hire the writers of the last episode of *Lost* or *Seinfeld* instead for next season. Let them botch it so this thing can crash and burn to the ground. And then I can walk out of the fire with you."

Oh my god. Can you come from words alone? Is that a thing?

"You don't mean that."

"Look at me and tell me I don't."

I can't seem to do that. "You said the script for next season was already finished and that it was great," I retort.

"Yeah but now I'm thinking it needs a rewrite. For selfish purposes."

This man. "This isn't smart."

"Actually, I'd argue that sitting on the sidelines for almost a year was the dumbest thing I've ever done."

My stomach clenches and my heart flips. I shield my eyes.

"Don't look me in the eye right now. That's an order. Shut your eyes. I have to shield myself. I'm...confused." I peek through my hands. "You're making me think about things I can't have."

"But you can."

"Jake you know we can't! Even if we want to, we can't!" I'm all but yelling.

"Do *you* want to?"

I think about it for a moment. Part of me wants to scream *YES of course I want to!* I've wanted him more each day for months on end. But the other part of me can't dare risking it. Not the show. But *him*. "It's not worth the risk to me."

"You care that much about the show?"

"I care that much about *you*."

He holds up his hands as if to say *then why can't we?*

The tears are falling now and I can't seem to stop them. I wipe my eyes.

"Jake, don't do this. Let's go back. Like it has been. I need you in my life."

"Emma, that's exactly what I'm telling you. I want to be in it. *Need* to be in it, I think."

"No, I don't mean like that. I mean like you have been. Like my best friend."

"You won't take the risk to have me?"

I shake my head. "I won't take the risk to *lose* you."

"But you *won't*. I'm right here. I'm staying right here." He breathes out a little laugh. "I mean, yeah, I'm leaving for a couple months, but I'll be back." He tilts his head. "And you could come with me, you know."

I drop my head back. "What are you doing to me right now?"

"Emma, I—"

"Don't." I hold my hand up to stop him. "Just, don't. Please. Jake, you're...important to me."

"What every guy wants to hear."

"No, let me finish." I wipe my eyes again, though it seems pointless because they immediately well up again. "Everything that has ever seemed too good to be true in my life has been. Until this. All of this. The show. Friends. And most of all, *you*." I take a breath and keep going. "I have dealt with a lot of loss. A lot of disappointment. A lot of losing something right when I thought it was finally mine. And I think—I think I'm stronger for all of that. But, I can't stomach the thought of all this goodness I finally have in my life ending. And it all starts with *you*. You're the root that everything branches from. If we give in and things go south, where would that leave us?" I shake my head. "I learned a long time ago that if you don't let it start you don't have to see it end."

His eyes are glassy when he asks, "What makes you so sure it would end?"

"It always has." I shrug. "But I mean, I'm not. I'm not sure. I can't be. Maybe it would, maybe it wouldn't. We can't know. But I'm not sure I want to find out. Because if things go the wrong way...I don't think I could take one more thing like that. Especially if it would mean losing you."

"So you'd rather not try? You'd rather not give it a chance?"

"Yes."

"You want to keep being how we have been? Friends and nothing more?"

"Yes."

"Like this never happened? Like that day right here—" He glances over at the kitchen countertop—"never happened?"

"Yes."

"Like I haven't wanted you with every fiber of my being for the past year?"

That one is harder to answer. The lump in my throat is impossible to swallow around so I just nod.

His shoulders slump in defeat, and he nods, too. "Okay then."

He turns to leave, and as he walks down the stairs to my trailer I hear Beau yell through the car window. "You told her?" He sounds excited.

"Yep." *Jake.*

"And?"

"Nope."

51

EMMA

Two months later

My life has become unrecognizable.

It's a life I never could've imagined in my wildest dreams. It's at once amazing and completely overwhelming. I'm on billboards. I'm on commercial previews for *Hierarchy*. I'm plastered to the sides of buses. I'm in the tabloids. I'm *everywhere*.

For a girl who is trying to not have feelings for her costar, seeing larger than life images of us being romantic everywhere isn't exactly helping.

I've started to notice photographers trailing me sometimes and that is something you never get used to. And everything the press picks up is so sensationalized. A shot of Ben and I out at dinner and *Emma's Boy Toy* is the next day's headline. A photo of Mandy and me hugging outside an Aerie store is printed alongside *Friend consoles Emma after big break up.* A picture of Sal and me grabbing coffee is run with an *Emma's new boyfriend?* headline. It's so ridiculous you almost can't help but laugh. *Almost.*

And Jake's getting the same treatment. Headlines claiming he and his *Sunset Cove* costar Alissa are dating are relentless. Pictures of him out with the model Daphne Jones are everywhere. But I have to admit that even *I* am wondering how true the news with Daphne is. I mean, pictures *do* lie as evidenced by all the headlines about me, but also, there sure are a lot of pictures of them together. And the internet tells me she lives here in L.A. So if she's with him in Australia...

I should be glad. He's seeing someone. That's good. I want that for him. He gave me the chance to have him and I rebuked him. He *should* be dating someone. And I can't be jealous. Hell, I'm still dating Ben. We're not at all serious, so I don't feel too guilty about harboring confusing feelings for Jake. Because they're feelings I would never act on. Feelings I *can't* act on. And I really do like Ben. He's a great guy and all the publicity absurdity doesn't bother him. He's actually awesome. So awesome that sometimes I wonder if I should fully cut him loose since I'm not hook, line and sinker for him.

Then again, I've never been hook, line and sinker for anyone. I don't really know how to be all in with someone. I've always got one foot out the door. I think that's part of what growing up with no one stable in my life did to me. Yep, that really screwed me up. Thanks mom and dad.

Ben and I are essentially glorified friends with benefits. He knows I don't want to be exclusive or in a relationship and he's fine with just the occasional dinner and movie dates—and frequent bed dates. It works for us and I appreciate the lack of expectations.

Jake and I have texted sporadically since he left. But *casually.*

The question game. Lots of *How's it going?* small talk type texts. Nothing deep or too real.

I think we're good. I think he gets it. I think we're past it.

52

JAKE

I got back last night and only have a few days to adjust to the insane jet lag that comes with a seventeen hour time difference and a fifteen hour flight. I literally traveled for a full twenty-four hours. I'm strung out as hell.

But I'm also ready.

We start pre-production on season two in a matter of days. The script is excellent. The OG team is in place. And season one premieres next month.

I think the distance from Emma was vital for me. I handled nearly a year of being obsessed with her and not acting on it until the very last fucking minute, and after two months away I feel like I can do it all over again. I'm prepared to see her. I'm all good.

At Timbo's urging, I finally went out with someone and getting laid definitely helped take the edge off. I hadn't slept with anyone since I'd met Emma. I just hadn't *wanted* anyone else. And not that that's really changed, but a man can only go so long. So when Daphne Jones, a model Timbo has been training and who is objectively stunning, asked him for my number since she was coming to Melbourne to shoot a commercial, I told him to give it to her. She texted and asked if I could show her a good time while she was there, and I obliged.

Did I think about Emma while I was inside of her? Every time.

Does that make me a bad person? Probably.

Am I going to see Daphne now that we're both back in Los Angeles? That depends.

If Emma is still seeing Ben, and it seems like she *is* if the tabloids are to be believed, then yeah I'll see Daphne. She's a great girl.

But if she's not still seeing him? Then fuck no I won't see Daphne. Or anyone else. I'll figure out how to pull a Ben and shoot my shot without scaring her off. I mean, I can't quit the show or anything, and I have to be careful not to freak her out, but I'll be on standby for when she finally realizes I'm worth taking a chance on.

"Dude, get your lazy ass up." Timbo throws on the lights and jerks my blackout shades up.

"I know you did not just bust in here when it took me almost five hours to fall asleep last night. My sleep schedule is way out of wack."

"I did and I'd do it again. Sleeping all day won't get you back on schedule. You've got to power through the day so you can go to sleep tonight. You know this." He puts a mug of coffee on my nightstand. He really is a great friend. I hate him in this exact moment, but man do I love him.

I groan. "Alright alright, I see your point." I sit up and rub my eyes. "Jesus I'm beat."

"And I'm about to beat you up even more. We're going to the gym. You look weaker than you did a couple months ago. Gotta get you back in heartthrob form."

"I look weak because I'm exhausted. And I worked out while I was there. Followed your regimen to a freaking tee, so if I look weak that's on you."

"Touché."

I take a sip of my coffee. Damn that tastes good. "So catch me up." It was impossible to keep up with him in real time with nearly a full day's time difference between us.

"I'm good man. My client list is growing. I'm getting some big marquee names. I got laid a lot."

"What's new?"

"I've just been keeping busy man. I saw Emma a few times."

I perk up. "You didn't tell me that."

"It didn't seem important."

"You saw the girl who dominated my every thought for almost a year and it didn't seem important to mention that to me?"

"Well when you put it like that..."

"How is she? I barely talked to her either."

"She's good. I hung out with her and Sal and Mandy some. Two bad things, though, and one good."

I feel worry creep in. "Start with the bad."

"She's as gorgeous as ever. And she's still seeing Ben."

Yep. Stings a bit. "What's the good?"

"She knows you're dating Daphne. You're welcome."

"Am I?" I set my coffee down so I don't spill it in anger. And by spill it I mean throw it at him. "Why would I be thankful for that?"

"I was thinking it might make her jealous."

"And did it?"

"Well, she *is* still seeing him so...I don't know man. It seemed like a good idea at the time."

"What exactly did you say to her?"

"Just that you were dating a client of mine so not to worry about what happened before you left."

"Dammit Timbo."

"What?"

"And I'm *not* even really dating Daphne."

"Well *dating* sounded a lot better than saying you were *fucking* her."

"Get out."

He walks to my door. "Glad to see you, too, man."

Emma: Hey. Welcome back!

Me: Hey yourself

Emma: Are you a zombie right about now?

Me: 100% yes

Emma: . . .

Emma: . . .

Emma: Are we good?

Me: Yeah. Why?

Emma: Well, I haven't seen you since you left for the airport and we barely talked while you were gone. I just want to make sure you and I are okay.

Me: Never better. Promise. All good.

Emma: 😄 Can't wait to see you in a couple days.

Me: Me too.

I WALK into the table read and my eyes are scanning every inch of the room. For her. I had wanted to see her before this but there just hasn't been a chance. She's not here yet and I feel relieved and disappointed at the same time.

I greet everyone who is already there and make small talk. I'm fully aware that I'm not really absorbing any of the conversations I'm participating in, because I'm much too distracted thinking about seeing Emma for the first time in two entire months.

I give myself a rousing internal pep talk. *I'm good. We're good. Everything is good.* If I say it enough maybe I'll believe it. I'm prepared to see her. I've *got* this.

Midway through a conversation with Tommy, our cinematographer, I know she's gotten there. I swear I can *feel* her before I even hear her voice.

And I'm right. I turn to see her setting her things on the table.

I'm *so* not prepared.

And I most definitely do not *got* this.

She's...exuberant. She's perfect. She's everything.

Sixty days of trying to wash and fuck away my feelings for her is out the window in a single heartbeat.

Well, shit.

I'm absolutely, categorically, unmistakably still in love with my costar.

53

EMMA

"I need a favor," Jake says, angling his body toward me. We're sitting on the stairs to my trailer eating lunch and running lines just like we did so often last season. We've been filming for almost three weeks and it's like we never stopped.

"Shoot," I reply, taking a giant bite of my chicken salad sandwich. It's gorgeous outside and the sun is hitting the perfect spot on my steps.

"So my family is coming to town this week so they can celebrate the show with me—my parents *and* my brother *and* my sister."

"Oh how awesome is that?" I know it's been a while since he's seen his family. He's gone back to Florida a few times for holidays—he and Timbo even invited me to come along a couple times, but for someone who doesn't like to feel like an imposition that was way too much for me. But I know his family hasn't been out to visit him in Los Angeles since we started shooting *Hierarchy*.

He nods. "Yeah, it'll be great."

"And also a bit nerve-wracking because there are going to be some *scenes* in that first episode." I eye him knowingly.

"Yeah, no. They're not staying to watch the premiere with me. Had to eighty-six that idea. I don't want to watch it with them. But I absolutely want to celebrate it with them."

I nod. "How long do they get to stay?"

"Just four nights. But yeah, I'm pumped."

I wait for him to continue. He doesn't, but I can sense there is more as the silence hangs between us. "*And?*" I elbow him.

"And they want to meet my people here. My friends. My *squad* if you will." He shakes his head before explaining. "My mom is really into T-Swift circa *1989* era right now and she can't stop talking about squads. And, well, for me that's pretty much you and Timbo."

I put my hand over my heart. "I'm honored to make squad status. So what are we going to do? Dinner?"

"Yeah, they all want to go out to dinner together. I got a big table at El Fuego on Thursday."

I waggle my eyebrows. "Where there's queso, there's me. I'm in." I take another bite. "Is Timbo coming?"

"Yeah of course. And he's bringing that girl he met at the gym last week."

"Doesn't he meet a girl at the gym every week?" I raise a brow.

"You're not wrong."

He takes a bite and before *I* can bite—my tongue, that is—I blurt out, "Is Daphne coming?" Silence. Might as well just break that ice.

"No."

"Aren't you two dating?"

He doesn't answer. Instead he flips the question on me. "Are you and Ben?"

I think about how to answer that. *"Ish."* Yeah, that feels right.

"Ish?"

"Yeah, *ish*." I shrug. "I have a hard time letting people in."

"I've noticed."

Welp. I've got to steer this conversation back on track. "I just thought that if Timbo was bringing someone and you are bringing someone...I just don't want to be a fifth wheel. Or more like...an eleventh wheel?"

"You'll be the eighth wheel. Perfectly balanced." He nods at me with the softest smile. "Timbo's date will be the ninth. And Daphne is meeting them the night before."

So she *is* meeting the family. My heart drops. But I'm not allowed to feel disappointed. It could've been me meeting the family. But I'm the one who shot him down. And yet—it hits me that I *am* still meeting the family. Huh. *Take that Daphne.*

"It's Thursday night at 7:00. Does that work for you? We wrap early that day."

"Yeah. I'll be there. You know I can't say no to queso. Or margaritas. Or you."

His jaw clenches but he keeps his voice light. "Actually, you've proven that you definitely *can* say no to me."

Damn. I think I need some aloe for that burn.

54

JAKE

I wasn't lying about Daphne. I *am* introducing her to my family. Tonight. More out of obligation than really wanting to. I mean, she's nice. And really beautiful. But she's just not...Well, she's not Emma. In general I think she's a total catch, but we've hung out for a few months at this point and I don't feel a spark with her.

Still, I can't seem to cut her loose quite yet. The sex is good and she's a beautiful, sweet woman. And since Emma is still dating Ben, it makes no sense to break things off with Daphne. So, I'm taking her to meet the fam. And even though he's the one who encouraged me to go out with her in the first place, Timbo thinks it's a terrible idea since I don't even want to be with her. I think he's right (per usual but I'd never tell him that), but I mentioned that my family was coming to town and she asked if she was going to meet them...and here we are.

We don't have firm plans for tonight and I knew I wanted to save El Fuego for Emma, because queso is her love language.

That's much more of an Emma thing and it would be sacrilegious for me to not take her. And I really do want my family to meet her. She's a big part of my life, even if it's not in the way I want her to be. A bigger part of my life than Daphne by a landslide.

I made reservations for tomorrow but didn't for tonight. I was about to just make it easy and have everyone over to my place and order pizza since I'd totally dropped the ball, but then I decided the hole in the wall pizza joint Emma and I love would be right up my brother Gray's alley.

"Benny's is an interesting choice, huh?" Daphne says on the way there. "I mean, definitely fun for a group though." She looks over at me and squeezes my hand. "I can't wait to meet your family."

"Yeah, me too." I answer. "They're good people."

I don't know why I feel so out of sorts. I feel like I'm cheating on Emma. Which is total bullshit. We're not together. She doesn't see me that way. And I can eat at Benny's without her if I want. I'm not doing anything wrong. She literally doesn't even care. I go out with Daphne. I stay in with Daphne. Emma does the same with Ben. So I don't know why tonight feels different. But it just doesn't feel right to me. The only thing I can figure is because introducing her to my family maybe is a "big step" that I don't want to really take. And yet here I am, stepping away.

I'm an idiot.

"You are quiet tonight."

"Yeah sorry, I think I'm just tired."

"Well get your energy up because I think you'll need it later." She looks over at me and winks. I laugh, a kind of forced laugh, and wonder what the hell is wrong with me that I laugh a forced laugh when a beautiful girl tells me I'm going to get laid later.

I'm in love with someone who's not her, that's what's wrong with me.

We pull up and park and as we get out of the car I see my entire family waiting out front. Eager much? I chuckle. I put a hand on Daphne's back as we walk up to meet them. Mom and Dad are overcome with emotion the second they spot me. Lilah's with her husband Aaron and my brother Gray is flying solo per usual. He would never bring a girl on a plane unless it was serious, which it never has been for him. And he likes it that way. As we say our hellos, Gray comes in for a rare bro hug. He's not an overly affectionate human being. Never has been. And since he's my big brother, any show of love from him feels like winning the lottery. That pseudo-hug just made my whole damn night.

Dinner is smooth, Daphne is gracious and polite. The conversation is easy and everyone is just happy to have time together. It's not awkward and I really do enjoy it. It honestly just feels good to see my people. It's been too long.

My parents, Lilah, and Aaron are staying at one of the hotels under the umbrella of Lilah's company, and Gray is staying with me. We say our goodbyes and Gray comes with Daphne and me.

As we hop in the car, I wonder if I'm dropping Daphne at her house or bringing her home to mine. Honestly, I do need to get laid tonight to take the edge off, but I am full and not really feeling it. Not really feeling *her*. Still, I know I should offer to bring her home with me.

"I can't wait to see Timbo's ridiculous ass tomorrow. It's been a minute." Gray is in the back, windows rolled down and enjoying the cool night air. You don't get nights like this in Florida. "And looking forward to meeting Emma, too."

"Yeah, it'll be a good time," I agree with him.

Daphne cuts in. "You're taking Emma tomorrow night to dinner with your family?" She has a very slight edge to her voice, borderline imperceptible, but it's there.

Well, I guess that might answer the question of where she's

staying tonight. "Yeah, my family wanted to meet my friends here and they've never met her before."

"Who else is going?"

"Timbo."

"And Emma." She says it slowly. Too slowly.

"Yeah, and Emma." The silence is so thick it's suffocating. I don't really know what to say, so I don't say anything. Instead, I turn up the music to fill the silence. I glance at Gray in the rearview mirror and he gives me a *Did I just mess up?* look.

Daphne remains quiet the rest of the ride but as we pull onto her street Gray says, "Daphne, it was great to meet you. I'm sure we'll see you again while we're here."

I'm pretty sure he won't. But he doesn't know that, and neither does she. I've just decided it.

As I walk her to her door she asks, "Why didn't you invite me to come tomorrow night?"

How do I even answer this? "Well, I brought you tonight. Tomorrow night is more of a friend thing."

I'm definitely not going to mention that Timbo is bringing a date.

Things have never felt awkward with Daphne before, but then again I've never brought her into any parts of my life before. She's just not really part of my equation. Not even a factor in it. We've been casual, just sharing each other's beds. And now I'm kicking myself for not listening to Timbo about tonight. "Thank you for coming tonight," I say somewhat robotically. She doesn't respond, and not knowing what else to say and because I am apparently a complete amateur, I follow up with, "Do you *want* to come tomorrow night?"

"Do *you* want me to come tomorrow night?" She throws the ball right back at me.

And I royally fumble it. Because I don't answer immediately.

Daphne nods. "That's all I need to know." She unlocks her door and shuts it without another word.

And all I feel is...*relief*.

I get back in my car only to find Gray still sitting in the back seat. "Dude, why are you still back there? This feels like I'm your Uber driver. Get in the front."

I hear his seatbelt unbuckle. "I didn't want to make any sudden movements to spook her more than I already did." He climbs out of the car and drops into the front seat. As I shift into gear he turns to face me. "So is she or isn't she your girlfriend?"

"No, she's not my girlfriend. We are just sleeping together."

"Then why the hell would you bring her to meet us?"

I sigh. "Because I'm an idiot."

I see him nod in agreement in my peripheral vision. "Well, yeah, but that's old news." He turns the music down—typical Gray acting like an old grump who can't hear over the music. "Where does Emma fit in all this? Because she seemed like a touchy subject with Daphne."

I shrug. "Nowhere. Everywhere."

"Don't speak in riddles."

"Emma wants nothing to do with me in that way and I want everything to do with her."

"Ouch."

"Exactly."

"Have you tried?"

"Yes." I groan in frustration. "It's complicated." I turn the music back up and Gray, ever the astute observer he is, gets the hint and doesn't say another word the rest of the ride home.

THE NEXT MORNING I wake up to a faint buzz.

It took me forever to go to sleep last night because my mind was racing. What do you call it when something consumes your mind to the point that it drives you crazy? Obsessive? Am I actually obsessed with Emma to the point that it is taking over my life?

I think I might be.

I reach and grab my phone to check the time, only to find seven new texts.

> Timbo: What time tonight? Who all is going again? And where? I know, I know. You already told me. But tell me again.

> Lilah: It was nice meeting Daphne last night. Is she coming tonight? I know Beau and Emma are, and he's bringing someone, right? Do we need to add another seat on the rez for Daphne?

> Emma: How did last night go? Did she get the parental check of approval? Or more importantly, the Lilah check of approval? Bc I know you always say she's the one who has the most to say about your life choices :P

> Daphne: Hi, good morning. I think we should talk?

> Mom: I'm so happy to have some time with you, Jake. We miss you. And I'm so happy to see you happy...

> Mom: Are you happy?

> Gray: Dude wtf. Get up. I'm on my second cup of coffee down here.

UGGGGH. I roll onto my back and stretch. It's barely after eight. Why is everyone so freaking energetic this morning?

Me: 7:00, El Fuego. My parents, sister, brother, me, you, your date, and Emma.

Timbo: Is Lilah bringing A-A-ron?

Me: Of course she's bringing her husband dumbass.

Timbo: Still not a fan.

Me: He's harmless. Maybe not who I would've picked for her, but at least he's not a bad guy.

Timbo: He's a douche and you know it. We never liked him in high school.

Me: Maybe we were jealous. He was captain of everything and girls loved him.

Timbo: Might I remind you that neither of us has ever struggled in the girl department.

Me: Speak for yourself man. I'm struggling like hell right now.

Timbo: Roger that.

Me: Thanks sis. No, she's not coming tonight. I'm bringing Emma so you can all meet her. I'll call you soon.

Lilah: 😊

Me: It was good. Pumped for tonight? I looked and you can get a triple dipper with just two quesos and salsa if you want. They let you sub the guac.

Emma: Oh I'm planning on it. Unless they have that good kind and then I want that, too. I'll let you pilot the guac.

Me: …

Me: …

I LITERALLY CANNOT THINK of what to say to Daphne. So I just leave it. And I don't really care. What kind of jackass does that make me? A lovesick one I guess.

Me: I am happy, Mom. And I'm mainly happy to have time with you and Dad. And Gray. And Lilah. I've missed you, too.

Me: Don't drink all my coffee, jackass.

SUFFICE IT TO SAY MOM, Dad, Lilah and Aaron are probably getting better treatment at their swanky hotel than Gray is at my place.

55

JAKE

I pull up to El Fuego and man is it packed. I knew I should've Ubered. Parking is going to be impossible to find.

> Me: I'm in the parking lot but no parking. Where are you?

>> Emma: Should've Ubered. They have killer margaritas. Ask me how I know.

A beat passes and I'm waiting on a follow up text that doesn't come.

Instead she emphasizes (!!) her own text to elicit a response. Got to love her.

> Me: "How do you know?"

I think I see a couple walking out to their car, so I slowly hover behind them like a creeper.

Ding. A picture comes through. It's Emma with a giant margarita. Next to...Lilah...with a giant margarita.

> Me: Wtf? How did you two know who the other was?

>> Emma: We recognized each other you dingus. She recognized me from the show and I recognized her from the pics around your house.

Dammit. That couple walked across the street to an ice cream shop. I'm weirdly nervous. My people in there mixing without me. It makes me feel uneasy. I wanted to introduce them.

I see a family walk out. Bingo. I idle and just kind of lurk until I see what direction they're going. An old boxy Dodge truck is going to snag it. He's closer. Dang. But I'm not even really mad about it because his truck is badass and he deserves that spot. Way cooler than my Audi hatchback. I've always wanted an old Bronco and I've just decided I'm going to trade my Audi in for a Bronco next week. Decision made.

Ding. Another picture comes through. This time it's my Mom flanked by Lilah and Emma, all three of them hiding the bottom halves of their faces behind giant margarita glasses with just their eyes showing.

My heart lurches in my chest. God. Is this what it could be like? To have a girl who fits in with your family like this? Who you also love? Who is the hottest thing you've ever seen?

> Me: I'm literally in the parking lot. This is not fair.
> Also, you three are adorable.

>> Emma: Should've Ubered bro.

I spot someone coming out of El Fuego and this time I'm not

taking any chances. I roll down my window, tell them I've been trying to find a spot for fifteen minutes, that my whole family is inside waiting on me, and beg them for their spot. I sound desperate enough that they promise to not turn on their car until I am behind their spot so no one else sees their lights go on and scoops it.

Five minutes later I finally walk into El Fuego and my people —*all* my people—are saddled up to the bar laughing and chatting animatedly. My frustration instantly fades to happiness. The realization that this is how it *should* be overtakes me and just like my decision to trade my Audi for an old Bronco, I promise myself that I will make this happen and show Emma that she wants this, too—that she wants *me*, too. I'm not waiting around another year or two for her to figure out what I've already figured out. I won't be aggressive about it because I know I have to tread lightly so I don't scare her, but I'm in it for the long game.

"WHAT THE HELL IS GOING ON HERE?" I yell out to the entire bar. Emma, Lilah and my mom swivel on their bar stools and Gray and my dad turn around. Emma playfully rolls her eyes. "About time!"

The Patrons at El Fuego don't know what hit them tonight. When I walked in I noticed all the people trying to be stealthy with their phones snapping pictures of Emma at the bar. Probably asking themselves, "Is that the girl from that new show?" that they've seen plastered on advertisements all over the place. And now those same phones are turned—not stealthily at all— on me. I don't even care. It kind of makes me want to walk over and plant a kiss on Emma right now just to start an absolute riot but she would kill me. The tabloids are already going to have a field day with this. *Hierarchy costars out to dinner together* blah blah blah. Who freaking cares? Well, Emma might. Because she doesn't want people to get the wrong idea. And because I think she is still pseudo-seeing Ben. But *I* don't care. I'm tired of caring about that stuff.

I walk over and dish out hugs like I didn't just see everyone last night. Emma passes me a Michelada and I want to hug her for knowing me so well. The hostess comes over to ask if we're ready to be seated but Lilah pipes up. "We're waiting on two more. Can we have ten more minutes and then if they're not here we'll go ahead and sit down?" The hostess nods kindly.

Hell I hadn't even realized Timbo wasn't here yet. I was so caught up in the parking fiasco and then the falling in love with seeing all my family together with Emma that it didn't hit me. I pull my phone out of my pocket and give him a call.

He answers immediately. "Hey man, we're in the parking lot but parking is a nightmare."

I laugh, "Dude same thing happened with me. We should've Ubered."

"Hindsight. Is everyone there?"

"Yeah we're at the bar. We'll sit down when you get in here."

A few minutes later Timbo comes walking through the door with an absolute bombshell I've never seen before. He introduces us to Alma and I elbow him and ask through closed teeth, "Dude who the hell is this?" It's not the girl from the gym he had told me about it, I know that much.

"Man, don't even…" he starts, shaking his head. "But she's sweet."

"Among other things," I say under my breath, nodding approvingly.

We pile in around a giant half-moon booth with a dark green bench seat curving around it and chairs on the straight side. After we're all seated the hostess asks if we'd like her to take away the extra chair or if we'll be needing it. Emma quickly but very casually says, "We don't need it, thanks!" and shoots a soft smile to Lilah, who gives her a subtle nod. It's borderline awkward because I want to ask where Aaron is. It's also awkward because I somehow didn't even realize he was missing until right this second. Not winning any brother *or* brother-in-law awards over here. I glance around the table and when I land on Timbo two seats down from me, he is shooting absolute daggers in my direction. I shrug at him as if to ask *What?*

There's a heavy silence at the table for just a second before my mom starts telling everyone how happy she is we all made time to come together tonight.

With everyone immersed in my mom's convo, I lean into Emma and quietly ask, "Wait, where's Aaron? And how did you know we didn't need that chair?"

"He's not coming and I'll tell you later," she says through a plastered on smile.

Suddenly Timbo stands and holds his hand out to Alma to follow him. "Be right back," he says and they walk toward the bar. Timbo comes back about five minutes later with the hostess who takes away the chair next to *him*—the one Alma had been sitting in—and clears the silverware in front of it. He doesn't say a word, just smiles and joins back in the conversation like he didn't just ditch his date.

Wtf.

Lilah speaks up first. "Wait, where did Alma go?"

Timbo shrugs casually. "She had something come up. Where's Aaron?" he counters.

She stares at him, unblinking. "Same."

Okayyy.

My mom pipes in, "Is she okay? Will we see her again?"

"I'm not sure," answers Timbo as he grabs a chip and scoops an obnoxiously large amount of salsa on it.

"Yes you are." Lilah shakes her head in annoyance. "And no we won't see her again, Mom."

"And how do you know that, *Delilah*?" Timbo asks defiantly.

"Because you're kind of a slut when it comes to women, *Beau*."

"Damn, tell me what you really think." He puts his hand over his chest like she wounded him.

"Just did."

"Hey hey hey," I interject, coming to my longtime best friend's defense. "That's not true. Well it *is* true, but I did find out that Timbo's been in love before."

You could hear a pin drop.

"What?" Lilah asks incredulously.

"Yeah, *what?*" Timbo echoes her, glaring at me.

"I'm just saying, you're not a total caveman. You've been in love."

"Oh my god, who?" Lilah can't let it go.

The daggers still shooting from Timbo's eyes in my direction are terrifying. I think he might actually kill me.

But then he does something far, far worse.

"Yeah," Timbo starts. "It's true. I have been in love. It's the reason I could recognize what Jake's going through."

And now every head at the table whips toward *me*.

That motherfucker.

"Oh honey, *who?*" My mom puts a hand on her cheek, like she's *shook*. "Who is she? Daphne?"

I'm going to destroy Timbo.

I don't want to say it's Daphne, because it's obviously not and I don't want to give Emma the wrong idea. But how can I deny that it's Daphne without seeming like an unfaithful jerk? I'm stuck, and I have no idea how to answer.

The silence at our table hangs heavy in the air. A table that had been so boisterously loud just moments ago.

"Could you idiots grow up?" Gray cuts in, absolutely commanding the table because he's a man of very sparse words.

"Your teenage boy drama doesn't have a place at this table so cut the shit." He shakes his head like he's fed up with us.

We're all wedged into this giant booth and I can feel Emma start shaking beside me. I steal a glance at her and her head's down and her shoulders are moving up and down. Suddenly she can't hold it in anymore and she starts clapping for Gray, which in turn relaxes everyone else and the next thing I know the entire table is laughing. I look over at Timbo and I can tell he's about to give in, too.

I tip my drink toward Gray and mouth, "Thank you." He just nods back. Not sure I've ever loved him more.

The rest of the dinner is a blast. We've ordered five (yes, *five*) quesos so far because Emma has consumed two of them herself. Our server asks if we want to add any guacamole to go with the chips and salsa (and queso) and I look at Emma who raises an eyebrow at me. I speak up and ask the server, "Can you tell us more about the guacamole?" They must not make it at the table because we haven't seen that happen at any table since we've been seated. I continue, "Like is it chunky or creamy or..."

"Dude, why are you being weird about the guac?" Gray asks pointedly.

Emma pipes up. "He knows I love guacamole if it's the chunky fresh kind but if it's the blobby kind it's a hard pass for me."

"Hear hear!" My dad says raising his glass.

The server laughs and says, "It's chunky, fresh, not at all blobby, and completely delicious."

"Four orders of guac then please," I say.

"And another peach margarita please," Emma requests.

"Ooh me too!" chimes in Lilah.

"Me three!" says my Mom.

"To hell with it. Me four," adds my Dad.

Timbo raises his hand and hangs his head in mock embarrassment. "Make it five."

I amend our order."Okay, Sarah is it? Let's have four guacs and peach margaritas for everyone at this entire table."

Gray speaks up, "Not everyone," he says tipping his Dos Equis toward her.

"Okay, Sarah, peach margaritas for everyone *except* him," I say, tilting my head in Gray's direction.

Emma was spot on with her ordering because the peach margaritas *are* delicious. The girls are all a little tipsy and I think my dad would be wasted if he wasn't such a big dude because he has been downing them like there's no tomorrow.

"Emma, great call on these margaritas," he praises her. "And for clarifying about the guacamole."

"Yeah, ain't nobody likes blobby guac." Lilah bursts out laughing, followed by the entire table.

So Lilah is *more* than a little tipsy.

Emma adds, "The only better kind of guac is when they make it in front of you at the table. I love when they do that."

"We will follow you to any Mexican restaurant you go to," says my dad, with his hand over his chest like he's making a pledge. Christ. I think he's in love with her.

"Amen to that!" says my mom, holding up her nearly empty glass in Emma's direction. God I think she's in love with her, too.

Well that makes three of us.

We talk and laugh and eat and drink and just generally have the best time. It's like I never want the night to end. It's a far cry from our pizza dinner last night, which was nice, yeah, but just so much more...subdued? Tonight has been so relaxed but also hilarious and fun, and I chalk most of that up to Emma's presence. She's just magnetic.

Sarah comes back to the table to clear some of the dishes (ahem, margarita glasses), and I try to slip her my card for the bill. Emma suddenly snaps to attention and gently puts her hand on my arm. "Wait."

Just as I think she's going to lean in and say she'll pay for her own or something ridiculous like that, she moves her hand from my arm to Sarah's—halting her—and then brings her lips to my ear.

"We *have* to get churros," she whispers into my ear like she's telling me something genuinely important.

I chuckle. "Of course we do." I look to Sarah and hand her my card while adding, "But may we have some churros for the table also please?"

Emma clarifies, "Jake, you have to be more specific. Like four orders, two with dulce de leche and two with chocolate *puhleaseeeeee and thank you.*"

"You heard the girl," I nod to Sarah.

You heard my girl, I wanted to say.

She just doesn't know it yet.

But she will.

I HUG my parents goodbye as their Uber pulls up, and Lilah comes over to me before she hops in with them to head back to the hotel. Timbo left a few minutes ago, Gray is waiting on me, and Emma already grabbed her own Uber.

I face her. "Why didn't Aaron come tonight?"

She flinches but recovers in less than a second. "He had to handle some work stuff."

"You've always been a terrible liar."

"I'm too pure of heart."

"That's not even close to true."

She elbows me and we're quiet for a few beats. "Things are a bit rocky there."

I put an arm around her and squeeze her in. "I had no idea. I'm sorry sis. Want to talk about it?"

"One day. But not today." She hugs me and turns to her ride, but then turns back to me. "I can see why you said the whole world's going to fall in love with her."

"Yeah," I say, nodding.

"Does she know *you* are?"

My head snaps to her so fast I think I pull something. "What? I'm—I'm not." I say it like it's a completely absurd notion. Then more softly, "She doesn't feel the same."

"I'm not so sure about that, little bro."

56

EMMA

"By the way, your family is amazing."

We're walking back to our trailers after a long day of shooting. I've been wanting to tell him how much I loved meeting his family all day but we haven't really had even a moment alone.

"Thank you. I definitely hit the family jackpot." He looks over at me. "It was a lot of fun. I'm so glad you came."

We reach my steps. It's our natural rhythm—we walk to our trailers together, Jake drops me at mine and then goes to his. But today I feel like I have more to say, and I don't really know why. I feel introspective and like I want to talk at the same time. I open my door and gesture for him to come in. He walks right in and goes to my fridge to grab a sparkling water for each of us. So comfortable, so *easy*.

"They thought you were amazing, too." He sits on my couch and hands me a water. "Couldn't stop talking about you."

"They were so nice to me. Like such a warm family." I think

for a moment, trying to put into words what I'm feeling. "You're just so...insulated. In the best way."

He quirks a brow. "Insulated?"

"Yeah, insulated. Like you're surrounded by love. By security. If you screw up, they'll still love you. God forbid you lose someone, there will still be people left to love you." I feel my eyes start to prickle and curse them for always giving me away.

Jake senses my turn of emotions and puts a hand on my knee. "Hey," he says gently, trying to get me to look at him.

"It's just crazy to witness in person because I've never really seen a family like yours before. I have no insulation. Like not even a knock off brand North Face that kind of works but not really. I just...when you don't have that kind of thing, it's shocking to see how much others have sometimes."

"Feels unfair?"

"Am I a bad person if I admit that it does?"

"No."

A tear slides down my face and he wipes it away with his thumb.

"I know it's not what you're talking about, and I can't give you that. I know I can't fill that past void of family that you never got to experience. But, *I'm* here and if you'll let me, I'd love to insulate the hell out of you. With all of me—my body, my heart, my mind, and with every good thing and good person in my life. And I think, if you'd let yourself have everything I want to give, you won't...there wouldn't be such a void in the future, Emma."

"Jake." I stand up. "I'm not—I wasn't asking you to fix it, Jake. I was just..." I drop my head back. "I don't know what I was doing. I guess just saying how I felt. I know you can't fix it or change that. I'm not asking you to."

"Good. Because I'm not sure I'd want to change anything about your life because it made you who you are, and I fucking love who you are."

Why do I feel so frustrated by everything he says when he is quite literally saying the sweetest things imaginable? What is wrong with me?

A *lot*, I think.

When I don't say anything, Jake keeps going. "And I don't just love *who* you are, Emma. I love *you*."

I love him, too. Even *I* can admit that. He's my best friend. But I've only ever said *I love you* to my parents when I was a little girl, and they always responded with *You too* but never the word *love*. They never said it and I always suspected that meant they didn't.

His eye contact is unwavering. When I still don't say anything, he repeats himself but changes the emphasis. "I *love* you."

"You don't love me. Not like that."

He closes his eyes in frustration. "Take it how you want, Emma. I'm not going to argue with you about how I do or don't feel." He shakes his head, exasperated. "Besides, saying I love you is just that—it's simple and true and doesn't need to be more than it is. I love Timbo, too, okay? So you don't have to get defensive. It's okay that someone loves you."

Ugh. I want to tell him to get out right now and also to never leave.

"Jake, why are you making it about this? About you and me? It's not about us. It's just about life and how it can be sometimes."

"I'm just saying that it doesn't *have* to be, Emma. *You* keep yourself closed off. Life doesn't have to be you against the world. Maybe it has been in the past, but that doesn't mean it has to stay that way. You're *keeping* it that way. Maybe out of self-protection, I'm not sure. But I am sure that you could have a lot more than you allow yourself to."

Okay now he's starting to piss me off. Making it out like *I'm* the problem. Realistically, yeah, I probably am.

"Jake, I'm not the problem." *Lies.*

"I absolutely didn't say that."

"But I do have two problems and I can admit them. I don't know how to *be* loved because I never have been. And I don't know how to *believe* I'm loved. They sound like the same thing, but I don't think they are. And I don't know how to do either of those things. And when you say all of this kind of stuff, it messes with me. It might not seem like a big deal to you because you grew up with all this love and so throwing the word around like it's candy is no big deal to you, but to me it's huge and I just don't—I don't really know what to do with it. It's hard for me to know what to say or do and you keep saying things that I don't know how to process." I finally take a breath. "And then you act like I'm the problem for not seeing all this stuff. And you're probably right. I'm broken. I know I am. But I don't know how to fix it and also—I don't want you to fix it either."

I sigh and fall onto the couch. "I don't know what I want. And I don't know how we got to this conversation when I just wanted to tell you that I thought your family was really incredible."

He's quiet for several long beats. "Okay."

"Okay?"

He nods. "Okay." He's quiet for a few more moments before asking, "Emma, can you trust me for a minute? Can you just let me see something?"

How do I answer that when I have no idea what he's asking of me? "I mean, I do trust you already, Jake."

"Good. So you trust me, but you're just not sure if you can *believe* me when I say things about how I care about you?"

Well that makes it sound like I'm completely nonsensical,

which I guess I am, because he just hit the nail on the head. I nod.

"Okay." He nods, too, and then scoots a little closer. "Well can you believe *this?*" He brings my knuckles to his lips and presses a gentle kiss.

It's as if a swarm of butterflies has just commandeered my stomach. I stare back at him.

"And this?" He drops my hand and runs his hand through my hair before cupping both sides of my face and bringing his forehead to rest against mine, noses touching. He's waiting for my response. I nod. And then he moves just a whisper back and forth, effectively giving me an eskimo kiss.

It's so tender that I think I might melt right then. Or explode. I'm not sure which.

Just when I think he is going to kiss me, *just when I'm dying for him to kiss me*, he instead scoots closer and wraps his long legs around me and cinches me in toward him, cocooning himself around me entirely.

I know what he's doing. He's seeing how close I will let him. What level of intimacy is too much for me.

But it feels good to have him around me like this. I feel safe. He holds me for a few beats in total silence before whispering, "What about this, Emma? Do you believe this?"

I am still for a moment, and then nod, tears falling with that dip of my head.

"Good." Jake gives me a tight squeeze and then scoots back, placing both hands on my shoulders as if to steady me and make me look at him.

"I *do* love you, Emma." My eyes widen in what I'm sure looks like fear, and this time, *he* nods, knowingly. "Is that too much for you to believe right now?"

Tears are streaming down my face and I don't even care. Looking at this man, listening to what he's saying...it should be so easy to believe him. But when you've never had someone tell you they love you, when you're not sure anyone has ever *actually* loved you...the idea that someone might is inconceivable. I finally speak. "Yes."

"Okay. I see that." He gives me the tiniest reassuring smile. "What about the fact that I *want* you? Can you believe that?"

I choke out a laugh and he echoes that laugh.

"Well?" He asks, drawing out the word dramatically.

He is perfect. I think this man might actually be perfect.

"That I think I *can* believe," I say on a teary chuckle.

"And how about this—I don't just *want* you, Emma, I want to *be* with you."

His gaze is so intense, so direct, that I squirm just a bit under his unwavering attention. But he doesn't flinch. I think about his question. I *do* believe him, at least I think I do. But I also think he might just *think* he wants to be with me, and then when he has me he'll change his mind. I know my hesitation stems from all the times I thought a family wanted me to be theirs only to not move forward with adoption when the time came. And I realize this is some deep-rooted trauma that I probably need loads of therapy for...but I mean, I deserve *some* credit for at least having that sense of self-awareness, right?

My quiet speaks for itself and Jake looks at me with a mix of emotions behind his eyes that I can't quite decipher.

"Okay." He says it with the softest tone. "Okay. So physical closeness is maybe a little easier for you than emotional closeness? Easier than hearing the words?"

"Maybe?" I shrug slightly. "I'm not really sure, but I think maybe?" I hold his gaze. "It does feel easier for me to be close to you physically than it does for me to"—I gesture between us—"pretend like this is real."

"Not *pretend*, Emma. *Accept*. The word you're looking for is *accept*." His eyes sear into me. "There is no pretending between us, except when we're on set in a make believe world. And even then, much of what I do and say is an extension of what I feel."

I nod, knowing deep down that he's right.

"So I'm not going to scare you away with words. I'm not going to push my feelings on you. I'm not going to pressure you. Okay? I successfully kept from doing that all last year, until I just couldn't take it anymore..." He trails off with a laugh before continuing. "...and decided I was going to go for it. And you told me you wanted to stay like things were and I respected it. I've respected it until right this second. And I can see that you still want things to stay like they have been so I will respect that as long as it takes."

My head bobs. I could win an award for my nodding skills at this point.

"But I want to be clear about something." His stare is lethal. "I *do* love you. I *do* want you. I *do* want to be with you. I'll be here when you're ready, if you ever get there. I'll wait until you *believe* me. Until you feel the same about me or until you know for sure that you don't."

He takes a deep breath and blows it out so slowly that I drop his gaze, not being able to sit still under the magnitude of it all. "Look at me," he commands me gently. I do. "You *will* love and be loved, whether it's with me or someone else. That will happen for you in this life. I want you to know that. *Need* you to know that, I think." He cups my face again, like he did earlier, and lowers his head so we're eye level. "Selfishly, I hope it's with me. I want to be the one to love you, the one to show you that love isn't conditional, the one *you* love back. But, it might not be me and I know that. And that's okay. Your life will be full of love either way, of all different kinds. You'll be loved, and you'll love back."

I launch myself into his arms, wrapping my arms so tightly around his neck that I know there's no way he has a clear airway for breathing. I don't have words to say back to him. There are no words that would even do justice to what he just did for me. He gave me permission.

Permission to believe. Permission to trust. Permission to not rush it.

Permission to experiment with something I've never had, never known or understood.

Permission to open myself up to something I've spent years working to close myself off from.

Permission to maybe, one day, love.

57

Jake: Tonight's the night

Emma: Don't remind me.

Jake: Nervous?

Emma: Of course I'm nervous. I'm shaking in my fluffy slippers.

Jake: What time are you coming over? Bring Mandy and Sal, too.

Emma: Umm, I'm not and no.

Jake: What? We're not going to watch it together?

Emma: Hard no.

Jake: Really? I just assumed we would.

Emma: Really. Let's go out tomorrow night to celebrate it. Mandy and Sal will want to talk it out. Tell Timbo to come, too.

Jake: You're joking. You're really going to watch it alone tonight? With no emotional support person?

Emma: 100% yes. I need to watch it alone so I can crawl in a hole and hide forever if I'm not good.

Jake: They're going to love you.

Emma: How do you know?

Jake: It's impossible not to.

Emma: You're extremely biased.

Jake: You know I have evidence.

Emma: What evidence?

Jake: Me.

58

JAKE

Timbo walks in with his arms full of groceries.

"Woah. That's a lot of stuff my man."

"Yeah I picked up some things for tonight. Figured we'd all need some sustenance for all the stress-eating while we watch."

Timbo is a great dude. He's massively underrated. The rest of the world doesn't know how kind and thoughtful he is, but I do.

"It's just you and me, man."

"What? I figured Emma and her friends were coming to watch it together."

"I kind of figured that, too. But she wants to watch it alone because she's so nervous."

"That's ridiculous. It would take the edge off to be around people."

"I mean, her being around never takes the edge off *me*, but I hear you."

Timbo starts to set things out on the counter. Barbecue

chips, Fritos, french onion dip, a fruit platter, fruit dip, Oreos, and what looks to be four different flavors of sparkling water. When he notices me staring at the variety of snacks, he holds his hands up. "What? I didn't know what everyone would like. And I was going to throw some wings on the grill, too."

I shrug. "Didn't say anything. I'm down."

He clears his throat. "Speaking of not saying anything...and maybe of being down, too...where are you at on the Emma circuit these days?"

"Circuit?"

"Yeah, circuit." Then he mocks me. "I love her, I'm over her, we can't date because we work together, we're just friends, I love her, I'm over her, we can't date because—"

I stand up and cut him off. "Okay, okay. Enough." I shoot him a pointed look daring him to do that again.

"Just wondering what version of you I'm getting tonight, that's all man."

"An immaculately controlled yet hopeful version."

Timbo plops down on the couch and I sit back down. "You know, I was thinking about something."

"Oh no."

"No, hear me out. Have you ever been in love before? I mean, I know you and Cecilia were together for a long time, and then Sara and you seemed really great. But I guess we never talked about if you were in love with them?"

"I mean, I thought I had been for sure. A few times even. Definitely with both of them and also Erica, I think. But based on how I feel now...I don't think I've ever *actually* been in love before."

"Okay so hear me out and don't get mad at me for asking this."

"Can you not?"

It's as if I didn't speak. Timbo completely ignores me,

pressing on with this train of thought that he is forcing me to board. "Do you think there's a chance that you are just *infatuated* with her because you can't have her? And that is making you feel like your feelings are more intense than they are? Like maybe you aren't in love with her, maybe you're just obsessed with her because she's taboo and that just makes you want her more?" He nods, like he's just cracked the case. "I've felt like that before."

"When have you ever wanted someone you couldn't have?"

"Plenty of times." He stands up and walks into the kitchen before amending his answer. "Once." He starts pulling out bowls and platters for the snacks. I want to remind him it's just the two of us and we can just eat out of the bags, but I want him to tell me who he couldn't have more, so I keep our conversation on track.

"Name her."

When he doesn't, I raise my eyebrows as if to say *exactly*. "And by the way, this is kind of weird to say, but I hope you're wearing condoms. No one needs a bunch of little Timbos bouncing around out there."

"Dude, I always suit up. You better watch your own self. Now that your new show is about to blow up, everyone will be wanting a slice. Not just of you but of your bank account, too."

"Please. And I'm always safe, too."

"I bet you wouldn't want to be with Emma."

"Dude, stop putting those images in my head."

"Pretty sure they're already there."

"Of course they are. They live rent free in my head."

Timbo lets out a long whistle. "You're so whipped. You're whipped and you haven't even had her. God knows what you'll be like once you get her."

I lean back against the couch and sigh. "Happy."

59

Jake: Verdict?

Emma: If I wasn't on the show I'd STILL want to watch it!

Jake: So you're happy?

Emma: YES! I loved it. I mean I know we already screened the episode with Willa and Alex, but it felt different watching it on a network like that. It just felt so real.

Jake: It IS real.

Emma: I'm going straight into episode two. I might binge it all night. The world is my oyster. Or actually I might stop here and space it out. What about you? What'd you think?

Jake: Thought we crushed it.

Emma: Reviews are already all over the internet. I can't believe it. I've gotten like 40,000 new followers on Instagram and it just ended a half hour ago. I'm shook.

Jake: This is just the beginning, Emma.

> Emma: Are you reading what everyone is saying? I tried not to but I can't look away.

Jake: Yeah. I'm letting myself read it all tonight. So far it seems really positive.

> Emma: Very. And the world already wants us to be together in real life, which is a great sign! I always feel like that when two characters are really good together.

Jake: Oh I've been meaning to tell you.

> Emma: What?

Jake: It's me. I'm the world.

> Emma: Jake.

Jake: Yeah?

> Emma: You're doing that thing again.

Jake: What thing?

> Emma: Confusing me.

Jake: Really? I feel like I'm being incredibly clear.

> Emma: Jake.

Jake: Emma.

Jake: Sorry. I'm working on it.

60

JAKE

"For someone whose new show just went insanely viral last night, you're sure in a bad mood." Lilah is on the line, and she's not wrong.

"I'm just having a bad day." *Because I had the worst night of my life* I don't add.

"How could you have a bad day when the project you've been working on for well over a year is a success? Not even a success—it's a smash hit and it literally *just* got released! You two are all over the place. And by the way, I still deeply regret that you were cast in this role because I swooned for Daniel Teller when I read the series and now I can't thanks to you, but I've got to say—you and Emma are perfect together."

"Ughhh." I throw my head back and let out a frustrated groan. Kill me now.

"So I take it things aren't great there?"

"Not especially." I take a sip of my coffee. It's cold now but I don't even want to get up to heat it up. "I mean, she probably thinks things are fine."

"And you don't."

"I don't know, Lilah. Stop peppering me with questions. Timbo has already been trying to help me, and I just can't—"

"Beau? *Beau* has been giving you advice?"

"Yeah, of course."

"Timbo the Himbo? You're taking relationship advice from a guy with a name like that? No wonder everything is screwed up."

"Why are you always so down on Timbo? He's actually been giving me great advice. I'm the one screwing things up and he's the one trying to help me make it right. He's actually very thoughtful and practical."

"Maybe you should just date *him*."

"What are you? Five? I'm hanging up."

"I GIVE it five stars and if you had released all the episodes at once I would've binged it all night. When the sixth episode ended, I was all..." Sal stands up at the table and slow claps for all of us to see.

I don't even know why I came tonight. It's honestly the last place I want to be. I want to break the table. I want to yell. I want to punch something. I want to punch *someone*. And more than anything else, I think I want to cry.

"Agreed. I was freaking out. And I mean I don't want to make it weird and say this, but I am totally going to make it weird and say this." Mandy gestures between Emma and me. "You two were scorching together. Like I just...I mean it was almost hard to watch it was so good, you know?"

I chance a glance at Emma, and she looks the tiniest bit uncomfortable.

Good. She should be.

Emma looks over at me. "Jake, what did Timbo think?"

Timbo bailed on tonight. I assume it's because he's hooking up, but I gave him a pass because he celebrated with me last night. And then talked me off a cliff for hours. He deserves a night off from my drama if I'm being honest. "He loved it. Said he'd watch it even if I wasn't in it, which is high marks coming from him because the guy basically only watches shows about drugs. *The Wire, Narcos, Breaking Bad*. Well, except *Is it Cake?* Never something like this though. I don't think he watched a single episode of *Sunset Cove* in four years."

Emma nods in approval. "Wow. Okay, I'll take it then." She's smiling and it's such a genuinely beautiful smile that it hurts to look directly at her. I want to hate her. I probably *should* hate her. I definitely shouldn't love her.

Sal claps his hands together. "So all around, a huge success, right? This is *it*. The moment every actor dreams of."

Mandy turns to Emma and shakes her shoulders in excitement. "You made it! You really did it!"

Emma laughs. "Okay calm down with that." She shakes her head but can't erase the perma-smile etched on her face.

"And you got the flowers to prove it." Sal sounds like a proud brother. "The biggest bouquet she's ever seen in real life." Emma has the tiniest blush. She hardly ever blushes.

"Oh my gosh, what? Why didn't you tell me?" Mandy is basically bubbling over with the announcement. "Who were they from? Ah, this is such a real life movie moment!"

"It's not a big deal." She tries to kill the conversation.

But Mandy isn't having it. "I want the details right this second."

"Okay, *okay*. I was on the phone with Sal when I opened my door to leave and they were sitting on the floor right in front of me. That's the only reason he knows." Emma shrugs. "I honestly don't know. There was no card or anything. Not even a flower shop for me to trace them back to." She smiles, "But wow are they beautiful."

Sal claps his hands together. "I told her I think it's Ben. Sounds like something he would do."

Mandy jumps in, "Ooooh, or could it be that guy from the other night?

I immediately perk up. "What guy from the other night?"

Emma rolls her eyes at Mandy. "No! I didn't give him my name much less my number or address, you ridiculous woman. Good lord."

Mandy nods. "Oh, true." She laughs. "I just got carried away. What about the hottie from the gym? He's asked you about the show before so maybe it was him."

Emma shakes her head. "I was actually thinking it could be Marci. That would make sense because she'd want to congratulate her client for great viewer numbers." She takes a sip of her drink. "Or maybe Dante and Peter. They've been so supportive."

Sal pipes up, "Let's say it's not Marci or Dante and Peter because that's not as fun. What about that guy at the exhibit last week? Didn't he know your director? So maybe he could've found—"

I suddenly blurt out, "Geez, how many guys are there?"

I didn't mean to sound so accusatory. I really didn't. But man do I feel it.

Emma bristles and Mandy answers defensively, "That's kind of a dick question, Jake."

"I haven't been with any of them, if that's what you're implying." Emma's glare is boring into my soul.

"Well, except Ben," Sal says under his breath.

"You're a grown woman and you can do what you want. Who cares if you *have* been?" Mandy asks defiantly.

Me. I care.

"You were last night." *Oh shit.* I cannot believe I just said that out loud. I am hit with instant regret and yet there's nothing I can do, because the words have already left my mouth.

"What? What do you mean?" Emma turns in her chair to face me head on, confusion all over her face.

I clear my throat, but don't meet her eyes. "I was just saying, you were with someone last night."

"What? How would you know?"

"Because I heard you." *May day, May day. Abort mission. Stop. Do not pass Go, do not collect $200.*

"What? How?" She shakes her head in disbelief. *"What?"*

"I could hear you from outside your door." It's like I'm in a self-imposed grave-digging contest to see how deep of a hole I can dig for myself. With every word I say it gets worse and worse. And yet I persist.

"Why would you listen if you heard—"

I cut her off. "Why would you be so loud?" *There it is.* Rock. Bottom.

"Maybe that's how good it felt!" She all but yells back at me.

"Well, I'd love to know who makes you feel *that* good. Actually, the better question is who you actually *let* make you feel that good."

Looks like I'm just burning the whole place down with me. And throwing a little gasoline on top for good measure.

"Oh, make it stop." *Mandy.*

"I can't not watch." *Sal.*

"You don't know that's what I was doing." There is a mix of anger and hurt in her voice, and I know I'm the one who put it there. I *wanted* to put it there. I have lost control and can't stop. I think I've reached my breaking point. Like I think I might honestly be having a break down in this very moment. I need Timbo to reel me back in, to talk me down, to not allow this bullshit I'm spewing, but he's not here and I'm apparently just going to spew away.

"All I know is for someone who says she has a hard time letting people *in*, it sure didn't sound like it."

Emma's face is stricken. That one got her. If my goal was to make her hurt like I am, I think I just succeeded.

"Dude, no. That's too far." Sal stands up and puts his arm out in my direction like he's stopping me from ever going near Emma again. "I like you, but don't ever talk to her like that again. That was over the line."

I look around the table and am met with four eyes staring back at me in disgust and two staring back at me in pain.

"You're right. I *am* over the line." I turn to face Emma. "It's pretty difficult to toe the line when the line you draw in the sand keeps moving. Or do you just have different lines for different people?"

She levels me with a look that I feel in my marrow and asks, voice quiet yet steady, "Why were you at my apartment last night, Jake?"

"To bring you flowers, Emma."

61

EMMA

Well, it turns out I wasn't totally off base about who could've sent the flowers. I'm staring at two bouquets—the giant one Jake brought over two nights ago and one Marci sent this morning—and even though size doesn't matter, if it did...well let's just say if Marci is proud of me then Jake is over the freaking moon for me.

That in no way excuses his behavior last night. Last night he was a version of himself I've never seen, and a version I definitely don't like. He was hurtful and purposely so. But I am trying to see things from his perspective, and I know it would've hurt—*badly*—to bring flowers over to surprise your friend-slash-girl-you-claim-to-love only to hear her fooling around with someone else.

I knew it was wrong. I had every alarm going off in my head when I texted Ben and I ignored them all. Was I self-sabotaging because I'm damaged beyond repair? Probably. Is that an excuse? Maybe? I guess at some point I have to take accountability instead of just blaming my emotional damage on my upbringing.

But still, I haven't misled Jacob. I've been honest the entire time. He knows I'm scared. And that I don't want to mix things up with our work and each other. He respected it for a long time and only recently has started to be more bold about the fact that he *does* want to mix things up. He'd be happy throwing it all together and blending it until it is so intertwined you can't tell one particle from the next.

And that sounds scary as hell to me.

My phone rings and it startles me. We're moving locations so we have several days off from shooting, and honestly the timing couldn't be better. Time is probably the only thing that will help the inevitable tension with Jake dissipate before we resume filming. I mean, we basically had the most vulnerable conversation I've ever had in my life and ended with him saying he'd wait until I was ready. And then I decided I was ready to be with someone else but still not him.

Yeah, we're going to need a lot of time to make things okay. At this point, I honestly don't even know why he likes me at all. Like not even as a human.

I answer the phone and Marci's on the other line. "Emma? Did you get my flowers? I have news."

"I did and they're beautiful, thank you, Marci. I was actually just looking at them." I find it funny she asks if I got her flowers considering I texted her a thank you for them just a few hours ago when they were delivered.

"Ready for some news?"

"Always."

"Do you want to go to New York? Because New York wants you!"

That is very mysterious but also exciting. "Um, yes please but also, tell me more."

"*Good Morning America and* Fallon both want you on! You and Jake. Next week. What do you think? We're going to run with it and make it an east coast press junket. Do a *Hierarchy* blitz!"

How is this my life right now? "Okay first—I mean, *wow*. I just never imagined all this. *Good Morning America*? Wow. And okay, second—Fallon? I'm not exactly sure what that means. All I can think of is Jimmy Fallon. And third—who's *we*? Who wants to make it a press junket? Fourth—what is a press junket?"

"That's a lot of questions when I expected blind joy, Emma."

I can't help but laugh. "Sorry. Just trying to get all the details and make sure I understand everything. I've never done a press blitz and—so wait, does production know? Like if it's next week..." I'm thinking out loud, total stream-of-consciousness style. "We're supposed to start back shooting next week."

"Oh my innocent, clueless star. Let's see—yes, Fallon is Jimmy Fallon—as in *The Tonight Show with Jimmy Fallon*. And *we* is Jake's agent and me along with the network. A press junket is when we slam your schedules with every press opportunity possible to drum up major excitement and exposure for the show. It's busy and crazy and effective. And yes production knows. The network is in favor and production will be pushed back a few days further to accommodate the junket."

Man am I glad to be surrounded by people who know what they're doing. "Does Jake know?"

"Of course. He's part of the production team."

I can't help but think about how desperately we need as much time as possible away from each other to let things cool off and now we won't have it. "Is he okay with it?"

"I haven't talked to him personally, Emma, but I'm sure that yes Jacob Morrow is thrilled that a show he is starring in and producing is blowing up right now."

Point taken.

"So when do we leave?"

"Three days. I'll send you the flight info. You two are booked together and we've also booked you at Essex House. A lot of the interviews will take place at the hotel and they're very accommodating."

"So you mean...you mean all this stuff has already happened and is already done? Like planned and booked and everything is set up...just like that?" I snap my fingers for effect even though I know she can't hear it.

"Yep. That's how it works. You just have to show up and dazzle them. Hour after hour, day after day. And then you'll be done and on your way back before you know it. Oh, and if you'd like a stylist they've already approved it. Might not be a bad idea considering this is your first real public appearance, and there will be a lot of them. We need you in different looks for each one. You can handle it yourself, but the network might ask to approve your selections."

I've said it before and I'll say it again. This whole world is just *wild*. Like who lives like this?

I guess I do now.

Me: Jake, can we talk?

Jake: What's up?

Me: Did you hear about the press junket? In NYC?

Jake: Of course.

Me: Sounds like a lot. But also important.

Jake: Yeah, it's both.

Jake: Are you good with it all?

Me: With that stuff? Yeah. Just have to figure out what to wear, pack, do and say. No big.

Me: With us? No.

Jake: We're fine.

Me: . . .

Me: Jake, I think we need to talk before we do all this stuff together. In person. Not over text.

Jake: I can come by later today.

Me: That would be great.

I'M PACING around my tiny apartment. I'm practicing what I want to say in my head. I'm on the verge of sweating. I'm both furious and incredibly remorseful. I want to scream at him and also have him hold me while I cry.

In short, I'm a disaster.

This is exactly why I never wanted to cross any lines with Jacob. Things are too intertwined with him and I knew it would be messy. And now it's somehow still messy and we didn't even cross those lines.

I wish I had a fancy apartment building with a doorman who would call up to me when someone came to see me. Or a buzzer. A buzzer would be *great*. They'd have to call up to me to buzz them in and I could've avoided the entire flower-delivery-slash-hearing-me-with-Ben fiasco.

And it would've given me a little preparation now—just about sixty seconds—but still. I could use every second I can get. Instead, I am jolted by the knock on the door and there is a part of me that wants to avoid any further tension so badly that I consider acting like I'm not home. But the tension is already too thick to ignore so that would be pointless. I open the door. He has a package in his hands but he doesn't hold it out to me. He doesn't even come in.

"Hey."

"Hey."

We stand there in an awkward silence for a few heavy seconds. I break first.

"Dammit Jake. This is what I wanted to avoid. How can we possibly go do a bunch of interviews together and film together and be normal together when things are like this?"

I hold my hands up in question, hoping he has an answer. When he doesn't, I launch back in. "See? *This*. This is exactly why I never wanted to cross any lines with you! Now it's complicated."

He finally takes the two steps required to be fully inside my apartment and closes the door before setting the package on the kitchen counter and turning back to face me. "It was always complicated. I've felt things for you since day one and I couldn't act on them. *Didn't* act on them."

"Until now. And now it's messed everything up."

"I haven't acted on anything. Not really. I've told you how I feel, yeah, but if I had really acted, you'd know it."

"Semantics."

"Maybe. And yeah, I think I probably have handled things pretty poorly. Especially the other night. And I really am sorry about that, Emma. What I said wasn't okay."

"I *know* it wasn't okay." I crinkle my face. "I don't like that side of you."

"And I don't like the side of you that is okay with sleeping with someone else the day after we had a talk like the one we had."

He's right. That was terrible of me. Unforgivable even.

"Jake, I'm pretty damaged. I know it about myself. Sometimes I don't even know why you like me as a human being, much less why you would want to be with me."

"So what if you're a little damaged? We all are. That's a byproduct of life. And you're not allowed to use that as an excuse for the other night." I can literally feel the exasperation emanating off of him. He sighs. "It's like when you're a kid and you find the most amazing toy you've ever seen but it has a little dent in it, do you still want it? *Of course* you do. Because it's the most special, rare, most perfect thing you've ever seen."

I have to squeeze my thighs together lest my traitorous body betray me and fling them wide open at that analogy.

"Listen, I hate that I said those things to you. I'm sorry. I left my house the other night with the intention of coming over here to tell you how amazing you were in the show while respecting your very strict boundaries, and when I heard you...and him— and I don't even know who *him* was—but the fact that you were with someone else after just watching our show on such an important night for us *and* after everything we'd said the day before...I guess it just broke me. And clearly broken me is not a good me."

"I was...I was confused. The show confused me. Our conversation confused me. Your text confused me. The show also turned me on, which is totally great for the show, but wasn't great for me in that moment because then I couldn't stop thinking about you and *what ifs* and if you were right that we could try and I just...I guess I just kind of broke down, too."

"Broke down and called someone else?"

I nod.

"God Emma, so you instigated it? Do you realize how screwed up that is? How much that hurts?"

"I—I needed...I was trying to get you out of my system!"

"And did you?"

I'm silent.

"So *I* get you riled up and someone else gets the benefits? Is that it? That's how this works? You film with me all day and spend your nights with someone else? You watch us be together on the show and get so turned on that you call someone else to take the edge off instead of calling the one who put the edge there in the first place? You let me pour my heart out to you and tell you I'll wait until you're ready and then decide you're ready for someone else?"

How can I answer these questions when I have no answer? I mean, I guess I technically *do* have an answer but saying *why yes I do work out my sexual and emotional frustration with Ben every time I want you and I've been doing that for months and it's kind of worked for me so I thought I would keep doing it* just feels tactless.

"Choosing me is so out of your realm of possibilities that you call someone else to take your mind off of me?"

I guess I am playing the quiet game. And winning, by the way.

Jake throws his hands up in complete exasperation. "You know, you're spending all your energy trying to get me out of your system when what you really should be doing is trying to get me *in* your system."

"Ahhhh!" Welp, there it is. An actual scream. I've just lost the quiet game I was playing with myself. My extended silence culminated in a ridiculous, frustrated scream.

Jake's eyes widen. I shocked him I think.

"Okay come on then! Let's try it. Do it."

His face is etched with confusion. "Do what?"

Now I throw *my* hands in the air. "Me! Get in my system! Maybe you're right. Maybe that *is* what I need."

He squeezes his eyes shut for the briefest of seconds. "Oh I have no question that's what you need. But I'm not going to have angry sex with you, Emma."

I throw my head back. "Ugh, why do you insist on making it so hard?"

"You think *I'm* making it hard?" He walks towards me. Crowds me.

"Yes!"

"Okay first of all *you're* the one making it hard." He grabs my hand and puts it on his cock through his pants. He holds it there against him and continues, "Because you're a brilliant gorgeous woman who I'm obsessed with and you're a really great human, too—the past few days aside, obviously, because at this exact moment you're acting completely insane."

I jerk my hand back off of him and glare.

"And no matter how mad you're making me right now—which by the way is really freaking mad—I'm not going to hate fuck you just to get in you, Emma. That's not what I want. Not even close. If anything, I want to love fuck you. I want to take you until you have no voice left and then I want to roll you over and hold you while you fall asleep. I want to listen to your breaths and try to make mine in rhythm with yours. And then in the middle of the night when I wake up hard from being next to your body, I want to dive right back in you and do it all over again. On repeat. Forever. So *no*, I don't want to have angry sex with you. I want to make love to you. But make no mistake that just because I want to make love doesn't mean I won't fuck you absolutely senseless in the process."

He turns to leave and looks back at me. "I can *lovingly* do that, just so you know."

He walks out the door and closes it behind him without another word.

I'm too shell shocked to move for what feels like several

minutes. Maybe even an hour. That is, until my eye lands on the package he'd set down on the counter when he first walked in.

I finally move and walk over to it, weighing it back and forth between my hands. It's puffy, with rounded edges and wrapped in kraft paper with packaging tape roughly holding it together. It looks like a man wrapped it. It looks like *he* wrapped it.

I love it.

I tear it open and can't subdue the sob that escapes me.

It's a North Face jacket. With a note taped to the tag.

Thought you could use this. Heard it's the next best thing to body temperature for insulating. If you ever get ready for an upgrade, I know just the thing.

62

EMMA

I walk into Daps to meet Mandy and am instantly suspicious when I find her at a table with Sal and Beau, of all people.

"What is this?" I ask as I get to the table. I don't sit down and I'm not going to until they answer.

Mandy clears her throat. "We just wanted to—"

I cut her off. "Oh my gosh, are you kidding me right now? Is this an intervention? Are you guys trying to stage an intervention?"

Mandy answers first. "We're calling it more of a group think." She nods with a smile, like she just nailed it.

Then Sal speaks up. "A group think with a side of a search and rescue."

I sit down. Slowly. Hesitantly. "What?"

"Well, clearly you've lost your mind and we're here to help you find it," Sal says seriously. He's not laughing. Not even smirking. And he always laughs at his own jokes.

I look to Beau. "And you?"

"I'm here because they had thoughts, I had thoughts, we all had thoughts, and it turns out they're the exact same thoughts."

"Which are?" I know how annoyed I must *look* if how annoyed I *feel* is any indication.

"We'll get to that." Okay so it seems like Mandy might've been the instigator here.

I roll my eyes. "Where's Jake?"

"He's on his way to New York."

I look at Beau like he's crazy. "What? No our flight isn't until Tuesday."

"He left a couple hours ago, he's taking a red eye."

I'm surprised. Bothered. Pissed. I don't even know why I'm feeling all those things. Jake doesn't have to tell me everything. But, I guess I'm mad that Beau knows this stuff and I don't.

Mandy claps her hands together and gives me a look of pity.

I said it once and I'll say it again. Group dinners with this crew are the worst.

She presses on. "Emma, we say this with nothing but love for you." She gestures to Sal and Beau and they both nod. "You've got to get over yourself. We know you've had a tough life, but you're going to sabotage the rest of it and any happiness you feel if you don't let yourself ever feel it. And you're never going to really live your life because you're so scared of losing everything you get attached to. What kind of life would that be?"

I can tell it's supposed to be a rhetorical question. I don't answer. And it's as if she passes an imaginary baton to Sal, signaling that it's his turn.

"She's right," he says with genuine concern. "For someone who says you don't want to let your past define you, you sure are letting it. For the love of god you need to get out of your own way because this is hard to watch."

Ouch.

I look to Beau knowing it must be his turn. But when he doesn't immediately say anything I wonder if he's just there because they asked him to come. I mean, he really doesn't know me, doesn't know about my life. Of course he doesn't have anything else to add.

But then he does. "I'm Team Jacob. Clearly."

"Me too." Sal and Mandy agree in unison.

"Are you kidding me? You guys are all Team Jacob? What happened to being on my side? What happened to being on *my* team?"

Sal shrugs like he feels sorry for me. "I mean, if I'm being honest, your team is definitely the losing team."

"Just gotta say, I'm having a little *Twilight* déjà vu right about now. Tempted to switch to Team Edward just to keep things interesting, but I'll stick with Jacob." Beau chuckles and honestly that was funny and it makes me almost want to laugh along with him. *Almost.*

"You didn't tell us the whole story or we would've been Team Jacob way sooner," Mandy says.

"What whole story?" I ask, genuinely wanting to know.

"You never told us Jake poured his heart out to you. Begged you for a chance last year. And *again* this year."

Sal chimes in. "And that he said he'd wait for you and then brought you flowers and you were with Ben."

Oof. That's embarrassing to hear if I'm being honest. How do they know all this?

"And you said he's always the first one to make sure you have a robe on any intimate scene. The second you stop filming." Mandy's voice sounds a little shaky.

"Before you ever arrived on set, he had them take his bigger trailer and your smaller trailer away and bring two equally-sized trailers." Beau throws out an absolute doozy.

"What?" I'm wondering if he's right and Jake really did do that.

"Yeah. He didn't want you to know. I probably shouldn't tell you but water under the bridge at this point."

I put my head in my hands. "Oh my god what are you guys doing to me?"

"Literally nothing except pointing out all the things you keep ignoring," Mandy states like it's obvious.

Sal piles on, "And what about the mojito bar he found for you?"

Beau nods and adds, "And we can never go to our favorite Mexican restaurants anymore because now he says the main parameter is that they have to have queso. None of our old favorites had it."

Mandy sighs, "And he really is so hot. Just so unbelievably hot."

"And he has a great family he's really close with. Including me. He gave me a home and a brother when I needed both. And he was so patient and had to stand by and watch while you were with another guy for months while he wanted to be that guy. And he never made you choose. And he did everything he could to not put pressure on you and respect that you didn't want to date someone you worked with. And he asked craft services to make sure they always had the cinnamon crumble muffins you love."

I am floored. My stomach feels like a pit. I think I might be sick. "Beau, how...how do you even know all that?"

He shrugs. "I know everything. Jake talks about you every minute of every freaking day. I could write a book about you just from listening to him opine about you for well over a year now."

He takes a sip of his beer and continues. "I know about your family. I know how you grew up. I know about the foster homes and never being in one school long enough to make friends, I know about the casino, I know about how you love to drink mojitos but you don't love to make them and you don't like to ask people to make them. I now know that queso fundido doesn't count as queso. I know that you don't like to let people in because then you don't have to deal with them going out of your life. I know he had his pick of some really cream of the crop actresses, but he wouldn't commit to any of them and then the second he read with you he wouldn't take no for an answer. I know he tried to respect what you wanted when he heard you wouldn't date Ben because you worked together. I saw his despair after he found out Ben quit so he could ask you out. I saw him beat himself up for not thinking to do that and I tried to reassure him that it's easy for a production assistant to quit and that Ben is not the pinnacle of greatness for that. I mean, you really don't have much to lose if you quit a PA job. Obviously Jake couldn't quit, it's *his* show. And I have seen him turn down woman after woman after woman. He gets hit on everywhere we go, all the time. I mean it's great for me because that means I get his overflow. But I also know that he did not go out or sleep with anyone from the day he met you until he had been in Australia for a few weeks. A *year*, Emma—that was a freaking year. And I'm the one who encouraged him to go out with Daphne because I couldn't watch my best friend flail any longer."

Mandy has tears running down her face. "I am so Team Jacob. Like the Team Jacobest Team Jacob there ever was."

Sal's brows are deeply furrowed and I think for the first time in his entire life he has no words.

I look around the table at each of them. "I think..." I swallow the huge lump that has formed in my throat. "I think I just became the *captain* of Team Jacob." I blink and tears stream down. I look to them with eyes that can't hide the suddenly overwhelming desperation I feel. "What do I do? I've been such an idiot. I was just so scared. I blew it. I don't even deserve him."

"You do." Sal says it without a shadow of a doubt.

"You definitely do." Mandy puts her hand on mine and squeezes.

Beau smiles and puts his hand on top of Mandy's on top of mine. "You do, but even if you didn't, I'm pretty sure he would move mountains to be with you. And not even regular-sized mountains. Like the tallest mountain. He would move Everest to be with you."

The tears are morphing into pseudo sobs. It can't be a pretty sight.

"Actually, did you know that Everest is not the tallest peak? I mean it is in terms of elevation above sea level but there are actually a few other—"

"Sal, we love the random knowledge you're dropping but—and I cannot overstate this—we absolutely do not give a shit about it in this moment." Mandy gives him a fake saccharin sweet smile followed by a very genuine look of frustration.

A ghost of a laugh breaks through my sobs. "So now what?"

Sal sits up straighter. "You go get him, Captain."

"But he's on his way to New York and my flight isn't for a couple days."

Mandy rolls her eyes. "Emma, there's this thing called money. And you can book a flight with it. And spoiler alert: you have it now."

63

EMMA

I hardly slept. Actually, maybe I didn't sleep at all. Maybe I just laid there all night in a state of partial consciousness. I don't even know. I booked the first flight of the day and am waiting to take off. I have no wardrobe for anything because I was supposed to meet with the stylist today. I look like death warmed over, but only slightly warmed over. More like lukewarm death which is just a terrible look all around and is unfortunate since I'd love to show up and see Jake and declare my love for him while looking like a million bucks. I'd say I'm looking like about five bucks, best case scenario. I'm wearing a big panama hat to hopefully hide behind and I'm hoping no one on this early flight recognizes me because this is not a moment I want immortalized on camera.

I've written and rewritten and deleted and edited and tweaked a text to Jake that is saved in the notes app on my phone. My plan is to send it and then put my phone on airplane mode so I don't have to process his response but can at least give him the heads up that I'm coming.

As the safety demonstration comes to an end I copy and paste the note into our text thread.

> Jake, you were right. I am the one who has made this hard. I'm on a flight to New York right now. I know you're already there. I'm coming to you. Believe me when I say I'm sorry, I feel the same, and I want to be with you, too. I know I've made our story hard. But what if up until now it has just been the prologue, and our real story starts now?

I wait until I'm sure it has sent and then I put my phone on airplane mode. Maybe I can get some sleep. I don't know how I possibly could when my mind is this restless but I might as well try.

"Oh my gosh, are you Emma Watts?"

Why? Why today? Why now? *Just why*?

I want to groan. I want to deny that I'm her, just in this one particular moment in time. I know what I *want* to do and I know what I *should* do.

I turn to face the voice. She's a beautiful girl sitting with two other girls in the row across from me. They all look giddy. My heart stutters to life for a moment. How could I be upset about this? I smile and nod, thankful for the distraction and bit of levity they're giving me.

The girl in the aisle seat shrieks and the girl in the center says "Can we get a picture with you?"

Oy. That is the one thing I don't want to do.

"If I wear sunglasses for it will you judge me?"

They all shake their heads.

"Okay then let's do it." I smile. She passes her phone to the girl by the window who holds it up for a selfie. I lean in towards them with hat and sunglasses securely in place. I probably look like I think I'm a diva, but I can't care. What I am is a mess and I don't feel like advertising that to the world right now. They check the photo and when they all do quiet little screams I know they must approve. They thank me profusely and I thank them right back. Then I slip in my ear plugs and lay back.

I'M AWAKENED by extreme turbulence and my stomach threatening to come out of my throat when our plane takes a steep dive. There are screams and I notice the fasten seatbelt sign is illuminated. The pilot comes over the intercom. His voice is calm and reassuring but what he says next is anything but. "This is your pilot, we have lost an engine and will need to make an emergency landing. We'll experience some strong turbulence as we decrease our altitude quickly but rest assured we are okay. Philadelphia is preparing for our arrival." Wait *what?*

The atmosphere in the plane devolves into an emotional frenzy. You can hear the panic in the air. There are screams. Sobs. Phone calls being made. Voicemails being left. Prayers being said. People all around me are taking action while I sit in my seat paralyzed by panic.

A flight attendant comes over the speaker next. "We ask that you remain seated, do not unfasten your belts, we will have a very bumpy descent and don't want anyone to get hurt. Upon landing we will evacuate the plane via the slides. Leave your belongings. Do not try to open the overhead bins. We need everyone to cooperate to get you off the plane safely."

The emotional mayhem on the plane doesn't lessen, but at least everyone does stay seated. I hear murmurings of an engine being on fire and that being the reason for the slide evacuation. The flight attendants are all seated and buckled so there's no one to fact check that with. It could be speculation from other passengers or it could've come from the top and trickled back to us. I have no idea.

I squeeze my hands into fists and steel myself to take breaths. For a moment, all I can think is *typical*. This is typical for my life. That whole *when something feels too good to be true it usually is* thing I've experienced every step of my life? Yep, this tracks. Because just when I'd accepted that maybe my life really *could* be this great, here it goes being jerked away. *Oh you were starting to like that life of yours? Well guess what? Too bad.*

And before I can even begin to process that, my mind pivots and lands on one thing and one thing only: Jake. And it stays on him the rest of the insanely terrifying flight. My mind is on autopilot, coasting through memory upon memory with Jake, unlike our plane which the pilots are piloting the hell out of as it pulses roughly through the sky. I replay every interaction I've ever had with Jake. I see his smiles, his laughs, his million different expressions. I can even hear his voice. I torture myself and let myself deep dive into what it would be like to really be with him.

As we near the ground and the haze and smell of smoke that has made its way into the cabin becomes unbearably strong, I tell myself that if we make it off this plane and I get a second chance, I won't waste it. I will spend it—*all of it*—on him.

64

JAKE

I've been waiting here for hours, since the news broke about the flight and I found out it was indeed the one she was on. I know she's okay. Her phone kept going straight to voicemail but the news reports said there were no injuries and that the passengers boarded a different flight in Philly.

I can't track her flight because I don't know her new flight number, but every time the doors to baggage claim open I look for her. I've lost track of how many people I've watched come through, and I'm not the only one. There are countless people around me who are anxiously awaiting the same plane's arrival.

And then, she's there.

She walks into the baggage claim area. She stops. The world around her stops. Everything stops. Everyone stops. Except me.

I don't stop.

I go running.

I shout her name and run up to her as fast as I can get there. I probably shouldn't have yelled her name, because now everyone is turning to see and there is no doubt they recognize us. Bystanders start going wild, hopeful they're witnessing the real life love affair they've been willing to happen since we released the previews for *Hierarchy*.

If I'm being honest, I'm hopeful for that, too.

Emma doesn't move, she doesn't even flinch among the craziness. Instead she just drops her crossbody bag to the floor and looks up at me with tears in her eyes threatening to spill out. I wrap myself around her and feel her entire body begin to shake in my arms. Shake with the sobs she'd been holding in, I'm sure. I reach one hand up and gently take the panama hat she's wearing off her head and shield her face with it from the many, many people around us snapping pics and videoing our extremely emotional greeting.

She lifts her arms beneath mine enough to wrap them around my waist. And then she just cries. The kind of cry that makes your whole body heave.

And we stay like that. People are shouting our names, asking us questions, paparazzi have entered the chat and are circling us. And still we just...stay.

I feel her barely shift in my arms and I hold her a little tighter.

"Am I too late?" Her voice is a whisper.

"For what?" I whisper back in her ear.

She tilts her head up. "For you?"

I don't know how to answer that because I feel like my ears are playing tricks on me, making up their own words. Making me hear what I want to hear.

She gives a quick but tight squeeze around my midsection, prompting me to look at her.

"Jake, am I too late? Did I miss my chance with you?"

My eyes are threatening to overflow and I know if I blink they will, but I can't help it. She's blurry to me and I have to see her clearly. I need to see her to know if this is real. I blink, and they fall. I don't even wipe them away, keeping one arm around her and the other still shielding her face with her hat.

I finally find my voice. "With me? *You really want me?*"

"Yes. I want all of you. Every bit. Now." She shrugs. "And forever, I'm pretty sure." She squeezes me again, tears falling down her beautiful, tear-blotched face. "Am I too late?"

My stomach drops to my feet and my heart threatens to jump out of my chest. I wonder if it's possible that I might literally float away as the heaviness I've felt for so long instantly lifts.

"No, I think you might be right on time." I take a deep breath and smile down at her. "I just got there a little early is all."

And then, she presses her lips up to mine. I'm so shocked that my arm briefly drops the hat I've been holding up to shield her and the growing crowd of people around us goes into hysterics. Daniel and Annabelle kissing, right in front of them. The cheers and screams are deafening. I quickly jerk the hat back in place and hold it a little higher this time so it obscures most of my face along with hers.

Thank god panama hats have such big freaking brims.

My mind is reeling. My heart is soaring. And sinking. And soaring again, then sinking again, all in the span of milliseconds.

Does she mean this? Does she really want me? To be with me? Or is this some type of impulsive emotional response to a traumatizing event?

No way am I going to break this kiss with this girl that I've wanted so badly for so long...but I'm not going to deepen it either. I don't know where she's really at, and I don't want to take advantage of her vulnerability in this moment.

Well I *want* to—god I want to—but I know I shouldn't.

Before I can overthink things any further, Emma brushes her tongue against mine. I feel her go up on her tip toes. She presses her body even closer into mine.

Oh.

Oh *shit.*

So she's really going all in. Does she realize all these people are staring at us? Does she hear the screams of *I knew it! I knew it!* Should I be protecting her from this? From...herself? Her clearly fragile emotions? What if she regrets this as soon as her emotional fog dissipates? What if she's upset I let it happen?

It takes all my willpower, but I pull back just enough to breathe her name out. "Emma."

She doesn't answer and immediately closes the tiny fragment of space I put between our lips.

I try one more time, pulling back just a hair. "Emma, people are everywhere, watching and taking pictures of us."

"Let them." Then she crushes her lips into mine and there is nothing soft about it. This kiss is urgent, needy. It's fucking delicious. I tighten my arm around her waist and cinch her into me. I want to let go of the hat so I can hold her face but I don't want to drop that shield just yet. This is *our* moment, well as much as it can be in the center of a packed airport baggage claim at one of the busiest airports in the country.

I lift her up against my body with the arm I have around her waist and let her feet just dangle, making a mental note to thank Timbo for the new upper body workout he's been killing me with. She wraps her legs around my torso and when I tell you I'm surprised all the glass in the airport didn't shatter in that moment because of the sheer pitch of the screaming, I mean it.

I don't know how many seconds pass, but when she finally pulls back from the kiss, she puts her head on my shoulder and just hugs me, suspended on my body like that. I finally drop the hat and hug her back with both hands. I feel her body shaking and know she's crying again.

With relief, I hope. If it's regret, I might never recover.

"What does your bag look like?" I ask her.

"I don't think our bags are here. They told us not to take anything so we left everything on the plane." I pick up her purse and carry her out to the car and once again silently thank Timbo for making me a strong fucker.

At least on the outside.

On the inside? On the inside I'm mush. I'm so damn weak for this girl. If she asked me to lie down I swear I think I'd roll over just for good measure.

65

EMMA

Jacob carries me out to his waiting car. I don't even care that he looks like he's saving me and I look like a damsel in distress.

I *am* in distress. I thought I was about to die and what flashed before my eyes when that realization hit?

Well, not *what*, but *who*.

Jacob Morrow.

So yeah, I am in distress. Distress about ignoring what I now see is the love of my life for well over a year. Distress about thinking I was going to die without being able to tell him. Distress about the fact that I thought I was never going to be able to kiss those lips again, to feel him against me, to have him inside me.

You want to talk about distressing? That's distressing as hell.

He opens the door to the blacked out SUV waiting by the curb and gingerly places me inside, standing to block me from all the cameras that have followed us while he shuts the door. Then he turns to face the muffled shouts of "Jake! Jake! Can we get a comment? Are you and Emma together? Have you been this whole—"

I hear his voice, loud enough to silence most everyone. "Thank you all for the concern, that was a super scary moment for a bit there and I know many of you went through that scare, too. I'm just thankful Emma is safe. Thank you for caring."

And then the car door opens on the driver's side back seat and Jake slides in beside me. "Go," he tells his driver.

He reaches over and puts his hand on my knee and then turns it over and wiggles his fingers signaling me to put my hand in his. So I do. I intertwine our fingers. It feels so good to hold his hand. We've never done that, except when we're on set.

I scoot closer and rest my head on his shoulder. We don't say a word. I must drift off, but I wake, suddenly very aware of an incessant buzzing. Sporadic but constant buzzes. Has his phone been blowing up like this the whole time? Is it my phone? Where *is* my phone? Was I just oblivious to this buzzing because I was so overwhelmed with all my emotions? Or did the screaming crowd just mask it?

I shift and he must realize I'm awake now, because he says quietly, "Your phone must still be off, because everyone you've ever met who has my number is freaking out to see if you're okay. The plane malfunction is all over the news and all the headlines mentioned that you were on it."

I take the breath I didn't realize I'd been holding.

"How would news outlets know I was on it?"

"You were tagged in some photos and I guess those same accounts posted about the emergency landing and people just pieced it together."

I nod.

"And..." He doesn't continue.

"And what?" I ask quietly.

"And..." He swallows, and I can feel his hesitation. "There are already photos and videos of us circulating." He shifts in his seat. "From the airport I mean."

I nod again. I mean, I knew that was coming. And as private as I've always kept things, it doesn't bother me. I've been denying Jake and my feelings for him for too long. Honestly, I'm ready to shout it from the highest rooftops. Like skyscraper rooftops. With a megaphone.

I'm not going to hide any of it. Not anymore.

I scoot away from him a couple inches so I can look at him. "I need to call Mandy."

"She knows you're okay, but I'm sure she'd love to hear your voice." Of course he updated her. Probably Sal, too.

I pull out my phone and turn off airplane mode. It's crazy to me that I never pulled it out during all that to send goodbye messages or something, but it seemed like a terrible idea to call Jake or Mandy or Sal just to say *hey I might be about to die but I want you to know I love you*. Actually, that probably would have been the right thing to do now that I think about it.

My phone regains signal and goes absolutely nuts. I have upwards of thirty text messages and eight voicemails. For a girl with only a couple of real friends, that's a *lot*.

I push "Mandy" in my favorites and she picks up immediately, sounding like the kind of stuffy that comes with crying. "You're really okay?" she asks through stifled sobs.

"Yes, I'm okay."

The sobs coming through the line make me sob all over again. Neither of us can speak. We just cry together. I feel Jake squeeze my hand but he doesn't say anything. He just lets me cry with my friend. And I hear Sal in the background chanting, "Thank gosh, thank gosh she's okay."

If I wasn't emotionally drained before, I am now.

I'd thought I was going to die.

The release that comes with the relief that I'm not is over-whelming. It's a delayed relief. Like I'm just now able to believe that I really am okay.

When I hang up I just lay my head on Jake's shoulder. My phone buzzes constantly but I just don't have it in me to talk right now. The people I care most about know I'm okay. And if Jake's right and footage is already circulating of us in the airport, the more distant people who care about me will know I'm at least safe and alive. And that's enough for me right now.

I must drift back off again because the next thing I know Jake is unbuckling me. I open my eyes. "We're here." His voice is so gentle. Almost timid even.

"Where?"

He chuckles softly, "At the hotel. We're at the back entrance so no one will see you."

God, this man. Always looking out for me. Protecting me. Don't think I didn't notice how he religiously held my hat in place to shield me from the hundreds of eyes on us in baggage claim.

I climb out behind him and feel like I'm in a trance, just going through the motions but not really registering anything. He has my hand in his and I hear him talking to someone about me having no bags and needing necessities brought up and I just...follow him. He takes me through a back hall, up a small flight of stairs, and to a private elevator. We don't say a word. He steps off the elevator and pulls me with him. Then he holds a card to the lock and opens the hotel door, gesturing for me to go in.

It's absolutely gorgeous.

"This is your room," he says. "They're bringing up some things for you until we can get your bags and whatever else you need and then everyone is under strict instructions to leave you alone so you can rest."

"But not you, right?"

He smiles. "I'm here. Right next door. I'm in the next room because we thought it would be convenient since we'll be doing all this press stuff together." He turns off the overhead bright lights so just the soft light from the lamps remains. "But that was before this obviously. We'll push back all the interviews we can. You don't have to worry about anything else right now."

He walks closer to me, but he's a little hesitant.

I look at him, a bit puzzled. "What?" I ask, tilting my head.

"Emma." He shakes his head and when he moves his eyes back to mine they're pooling. "I'm just so glad you're okay."

I nod.

"I really thought I'd lost—"

"Me too."

His eyes are so glassy I can barely make out his piercing brown irises from his pupils. "And I—"

I cut him off, taking a step closer. "I thought I lost you before I even got the chance to have you," I whisper through fractured breaths.

He barks out a shaky laugh. "You've had me since the day we met."

"No, I haven't. Maybe I could've, I definitely *should've*..." I trail off. "I love you, Jake."

"I love you, too."

I step even closer. "No, I *love* love you." I wrap my arms around him. "Not a friend love, though I do love you as a friend, too. But...a real love. I'm sorry I didn't realize before. I do love you. I believe I am in love with you and have been for...a while. Maybe even always." I draw in a huge breath and let it go slowly. "I'm sorry it took me so long to realize it."

He's quiet.

"Say something," I look up at him.

He barely shakes his head. "I...I can't." His voice cracks with emotion.

"Do you still want me?"

He nods.

"To be with me I mean. Want. To. Be. With. Me." I clarify, punctuating every word so he knows exactly what I'm asking him.

He nods.

"But you're not acting like it."

He is silent for a moment but then speaks, slowly, like he's measuring his words. "I'm worried you don't really feel like this about me. I'm worried you *think* you do because you had a very near death experience and you're reeling from that. I'm worried that in a few days or a few weeks you will be back to where you were and just chalk this—chalk *me*—up as a..." I can tell he's thinking of the right words. "A heightened response to a trau-matic experience."

"You're wrong." I shake my head.

"I want to be." He lifts the corner of his mouth hopefully. "But you don't know that, and neither do I. People react all kinds of ways after a terrifying experience like what you just went through. I just..." He shifts on his feet a few times. "I didn't need a near death experience to show me that I loved you, you know? And I'm not discounting that you really might have feelings for me, but you had no problem letting me walk away. Twice. So I can't get my hopes up too much because if you end up not *love* loving me...I don't think I could make it through that rejection, especially after thinking I get to finally have you." He hangs his head.

Oh.

Oh.

What have I done to this man? Why did I have to break him out of my own stubbornness? My very much displaced denial?

"Jake. You're right." I nod in agreement and put my hand on his arm. "You didn't need a near death experience to make you realize you love me." Now *my* voice cracks. "But here's the thing. Thinking I was about to die didn't make me realize I love you. I had already realized that on my own. But it did make me realize I'd *loved* you all along. And I was just too stubborn and too protective to see it, much less admit it."

I blink the swelling tears from my eyes and then continue. "But your life *does* flash before your eyes, just like they say it does. And the parts of my life that flashed before my eyes all had you. Moments with you, conversations, memories of us. It was all you."

I'm full on ugly crying now.

"It didn't matter if I closed my eyes or opened them, as the plane shook and smoked all I could see was you. And all I could think was that I couldn't believe I hadn't seen it. Seen that I was in love with you. And the regret, god the regret I felt in those moments was enough regret to consume me for a lifetime. Regret that I'd never get to tell you that *I* love you, too, that we'd never be able to see how it felt to really be together, that I'd never get to feel you inside me, that we wouldn't get to have a family together and travel the world together and do the most mundane parts of life together."

I put my hands on each side of his face. "Listen, my eyes were closed before and that's on me. But they're wide open now, and all I can see for a million miles is you."

I press a gentle kiss to his cheek, and when he doesn't pull away I slide over to his lips and press one there, too.

"I love you, Jake. I don't want to test the waters with you. I already know these waters, I've been swimming in them for a long time now. I want to freaking cannonball right in. Or flying squirrel, if that was your go-to move, too." He lets out a laugh and I laugh with him.

Then I wrap my arms around his neck. "I want all of you, every way, every day."

66

JAKE

And to think I'd been worried about Emma dying when apparently I'm the one who's died and gone to heaven.

I have the girl of my dreams in my arms, her own arms wrapped around my neck. It's heaven. Her lips on mine—

Oh.

Oh wait.

Her lips are...on my neck. God that feels good.

And now they're on my ear. And she's biting my earlobe. Yep, that *does* it to me. My pants tighten instantly.

And her hands...they're not clasped around my neck anymore. One is in my hair, the other is reaching down my back, lower...lower.

She brushes her hand over my ass and then grabs it hard and lets out a small moan.

Oh shit. I'm about to lose it and go absolutely feral on this woman. My willpower is shot. I've loved her all this time. She said she loves me back. That she wants me, too. And her hands are roaming my body while her mouth is exploring me. This is a green light, right? Please let it be a green light.

"Emmaaaa," I say in a low voice, drawing out her name in warning.

"Hmmm?" She asks with an innocent lift of her brows.

But her eyes give her away. They don't show innocence. I can see the heat in them.

I shift uncomfortably. I swear I think my actual pants are beating at this point. "Emma, my control is hanging by the world's thinnest thread." I squeeze my eyes shut. "I'm not going to be able to hold back if you keep doing that."

She nods slowly, like she understands. I breathe a sigh of... relief, I think. Then she blindsides me with her next words, peppering me with kisses every few words.

"Jake, I've been thinking about it, and I think to...*kiss*...take the pressure off...*kiss*...I think...*kiss*...I think you should fuck me...*kiss*... like I'm not your friend, like I'm not your costar, like I'm...*kiss*...like I'm someone you just met. Just the *first* time, to take the pressure off...*kiss*...because I feel like I can't handle much more either."

67

EMMA

"No."

"No?"

"No." He gently shoves me back onto the bed and climbs on top of me, propping himself up on his forearms. "No, I'm not going to do that."

He kisses my cheek.

"I'm going to fuck you like you're *you*." He pushes his knee between my legs and nudges them apart.

"I'm going to fuck you like you're my best friend." He kisses my jaw and rocks his hips into me.

"I'm going to fuck you like you're my favorite costar." He moves his lips down to my neck and rocks into me again.

Now I actually *might* die. Right here. In this very moment. And I'd die happy. Really, really happy.

"And I am most definitely not going to fuck you like you're someone I just met." He bites my lower lip and then licks it as if to soothe it. "I'm going to fuck you like you're someone I've wanted for a long, long time." He rests his lips above my chest, which feels like it's about one touch away from exploding, and looks up at me. "That okay with you?"

I don't answer. I can't. I can hardly breathe much less form a word.

He pushes his pelvis into me, hard, to make sure I feel him. "Emma. Look at me."

I lift my head and look down at him. He kisses all the way down my body to just below my navel and then back up again. His lips hover just over mine. "Is?" *Kiss.* "That?" *Kiss.* "Okay?" *Kiss.* "With?" *Kiss.* "You?" *Kiss.*

I nod.

"No, I need to hear you say it, baby."

Baby. Oh god. I love that.

I nod again.

"Emma." He sounds exasperated. "Open that pretty little mouth..."

I do as I'm told. I open it, wondering if he's thinking about what I'm thinking about.

"Good." But he doesn't move. "Now say it. I've waited this long for you and I can't do this until you say it." He brushes his thumb over my nipple. A current of electricity ripples through me.

At this point, I've forgotten the question. But I know I'd better answer something *and quickly* so he won't stop what he's doing. "Yes," I breathe out.

He doesn't move. So I buck a little beneath him for good measure. And that's all the confirmation he needs.

He pulls me up just enough to pull my shirt over my head. "I've seen you in my dreams so many times, Emma. And now I finally really get to." He nuzzles my chest and reaches to pull my bra strap down.

"Jake?"

"Hmmm?" I can feel his hum reverberate along my skin.

"Remember that thing you said about how you could make love to me while still fucking me senseless?"

His eyes darken. "I remember."

"Show me."

68

EMMA

I wake up happy, sated and *sore*.

Once we got in the bed, we never made it out which means we forgot to close the blackout curtains, and the natural morning light is casting a soft glow onto the room.

Jacob's arms are wrapped completely around me. I'm the little spoon to his big one, and it strikes me that I have never been in this position before. I've just never been big on after sex snuggling. But last night—or maybe it was this morning?—after the third time he was inside me, he pulled me close and told me he never wanted to let go. We drifted off together and I've never felt so safe.

Or loved.

I'm cocooned in his ridiculously strong arms, and all I can think is that I don't even know how this man can be real. Last night I discovered that he is the most incredible dichotomy—so tender and loving but also so fucking *wild*. He would be excruciatingly gentle with me one minute and then completely raw and rough with me the very next second. I *loved* it.

I feel Jake's heavy, rhythmic breaths and know he's still sleeping, so I let my mind drift and replay my favorite moments from last night.

Him kissing me so tenderly before padding my head with his hand and slamming us into the headboard.

My body tightens at the memory.

Him spending what felt like a full hour trailing feather-soft kisses over every inch of me, absolutely torturing me with anticipation, before finally slipping his fingers inside me and giving me the release I'd been begging for.
    Yes, *begging*.

I'd love to say I am above begging, but when it comes to being in bed with him, it turns out I am most definitely not. I'm a stone cold beggar. I begged him all night long. For more *everything*.

I close my eyes, letting myself relive the night a little longer.

Him wrapping my hair around his hand and pulling it just hard enough as he took me from behind.

A current of desire shoots through my core at the memory, and I'm suddenly very aware of how *empty* I feel. And how empty I did *not* feel last night. I squeeze my eyes and thighs together in unison, remembering how he felt.

Him pressing into me for that first time, and me gasping at the feel of him as tears filled my eyes.

I just had never felt so *full*, in more ways than one, and it made me emotional.

Him lowering down as close to me as he could and holding himself there, suspended in a low pushup, as he kissed my tears away. "Is this okay?" he'd asked, his cock buried inside me.

"Yes. I'm just feeling a lot of things I've never felt," I'd whispered back. He'd nodded and moved so gingerly, so achingly slowly, until the tears stopped coming and I'd moved past that moment of overwhelm and into an entirely different moment: one of pure, unbridled need.

"Jake, please. Now I need you to really give it to me." And god had he. Over and over and over.

I can *still* feel him between my legs.

And right now I can feel him at the base of my spine. I have a newfound and immense appreciation for the spoon position not only because it makes me feel protected but also because I love how I can feel his hard length pressed up against me. I push my ass back into him, hoping to stir him.

And that I do. "Good morning." His voice is gravelly with sleep. It's my new favorite sound. Actually, the sound of my name on his lips as he comes is my new favorite sound, but this sexy morning voice takes second place.

"*Best* morning," I correct. My own voice is hoarse and I know it's from how many times I screamed his name last night. God I hope the rooms around us are unoccupied. Otherwise, those poor people.

"Oh definitely *best* morning." He rolls me toward him, onto my other side so I'm facing him.

I press a soft kiss to his lips. "I've never snuggled with anyone like that. I liked it."

"Well, I *loved* it. And I'd like to do that every night, if you'll let me."

"I'd love that."

He strokes my cheek with his thumb. "And I love *you*."

And for the first time ever, those words don't send doubt shooting through me like they always have. They don't send fear. Or feelings of unworthiness. Or confusion. They don't blanket me in false hope.

Instead, they flood me with exactly what they're intended to.

Love.

EPILOGUE
JAKE

6 months later

We're walking the red carpet at The Emmy's and all anyone wants to talk about is Emma and me. Not the show, not our nominations—*us*. And I can't even blame them.

I clock each question being shouted out and look to Emma to see if she wants to take them but a subtle head shake tells me she does not. I have no problem fielding them and throwing out my responses as we navigate the photographers and interviewers on the carpet.

Were you two together the whole time?

"No."

Did you fall in love on the show?

"I fell in love before we ever started filming, but it took her until well into shooting season two to fall for me."

I hear Emma laugh beside me before she calls out, "Not true!

It just took me that long to admit it." She winks at me. That damn wink, undoing me since the beginning.

Are you worried what will happen to the show if you break up?

"Not even a little bit."

Emma's still holding my hand tightly as we continue weaving through the crowded carpet together.

Is your love story like Daniel and Annabelle's?

That one stops me. I look at Emma then back at the host who asked the question. "Remember when Ryan Gosling said *The Notebook* had nothing on his real romance with Rachel McAdams?"

The host nods. Because I mean, who *doesn't* remember that? It made *me* swoon and I'm a dude.

"Yeah...*that*." Then I kiss Emma to drive the point home and, as expected, everyone goes wild.

You're on hiatus before starting season three, what are you going to do next?

I pull my fiancé in closer and answer. "Her."

ACKNOWLEDGMENTS

I wrote this note to myself on Friday, May 26, 2023:

It's official. I want to be a romance writer. And I'm proud of that. From a premed biochemistry nerd to a mom to a marketing & website pro to a romance author. It would be easy to let the world make me feel "less than" about that. But I actually feel "more than." Because nothing is MORE powerful than knowing what you want.

And as a mother of two and a full grown adult, I finally know what I want to be when I grow up: a writer.

I had been dreaming of being a writer for some time at that point, constantly writing stories in my head and dictating them into my notes app as I developed the plots and dialogue. But it was just a *maybe one day* type of thing....until that day in May when I finally said to myself—*maybe one day can be **today**.*

I have several novel drafts fleshed out that I've dreamt up over the years, but I always knew I wanted to start with this one on paper. It has some elements that couldn't be more at odds with my life (I am the furthest thing from an orphan—my family is next-level amazing and genuinely are my best friends).

But a lot of it is rooted in my own reality of stumbling my

way into a stand-in and stunt double job, having to cut my hair, selling everything I owned and renting my house out to move across the country to Los Angeles...only to meet my now husband two weeks before my lease started in L.A.

Spoiler alert: I never moved. Well, I *did* move...right in with him. But that's a different love story for a different day.

I'd like to thank **you**—the readers—for being exactly that. I've loved seeing the resurgence of reading in a world where everything is so digital. LONG LIVE BOOKS. (And yes, eBooks are still books).

If you're a parent, encourage your kids to read *voraciously*. I think one of my greatest parenting wins is teaching my kids how to read quietly and independently wherever we are and whatever we're doing—at coffee shops, restaurants, the park, in the car, waiting in line, you name it. We have books in tow at all times, and that makes me so freaking proud of them.

I want to thank my family for being the best family a girl could ever hope for. I'm surrounded by love and support and humor and empathy and it's made my life what it is. Shout out to my sisters (also big readers) for being the BEST beta readers a girl could ask for. And for jumping from their preferred genres to explore my favorites (spicy romance and Romantasy, of course). I don't deserve yall. 🤍 Shout out to my mom for her epic voicemail telling me she wanted me to write whatever and however I wanted to and that she was so proud of me...*after* I warned her there were a fair amount of f-bombs and she wasn't exactly thrilled about that revelation. (Mom, I saved that voicemail to replay for when you read my books. 😉 You're my @.) She's also the amazing photographer who took the cover photo of my husband and me when we were on a family trip to Sedona. And shout out to my dad, who read every single newsletter and called after each one to tell me how excited he was for this book to hit the shelves. I don't know what I would do without yall. I love you. 🤍 And to my brother, I sure hope you can see this. 🤍

Thank you to my C'MON MAMA community—the OG mamas who have followed along with me for years since I started my C'MON MAMA blog and account in 2017. I've loved "doing" motherhood with yall. And imagine my surprise when I started talking about how much I loved spicy romances several years ago and found out SO many of you do, too! Thank you for being on this wild ride with me.

And to my ARC team—I had the best time launching this book with your help and am so grateful to have such rockstar women in my corner! Thank you! Hope yall are ready to run it back for Book Two!

To my kids, thank you for understanding every time I said *just one more chapter*...which was *a lot*. And for throwing that back at me when I would tell you to put the book down and come to dinner only to be met with, "*Mom*, just one more chapter. What do you expect? You know who we got it from." (touché btw) Thank you both for always encouraging me to find time to read—and write. And for keeping up with the plot lines of every book I read. And thank you for your excitement as you watched me write my first book. You both helped me with names, ideas, and gave great advice way beyond your years. I love that you both are total bookworms like your mama. Never stop reading. I love you both the mosterest no takebacks. 🤍

And to my real-life book boyfriend, my insanely hot and perfect husband—thank you for believing in me from that first moment I came to you and proclaimed, "I want to be a romance author." And for letting me say *just one more chapter* for like eighteen chapters straight—every single time. And for always holding it down when I needed to hole up and write. Anddd for being so patient all the times I cornered you with excitement over this book and wouldn't let you go. And now that I'm writing what I love and not just reading it, just know that our relationship is the inspo for *all* the love and spice. I love you. You're my real life muse. And being with you is living out my favorite 🌶️🌶️ love story every single day. ♥

Just one more chapter,

Christina

Keep reading for a sneak peek of Book Two...

ABOUT THE AUTHOR

Christina Capri writes what she loves to read: spellbinding love stories with a side of spice.

It took her a long time to figure out what she wanted to be when she grew up and she should've known sooner, if sneaking Harlequin romance books from the Winn-Dixie since she was 12 was any indication.

She lives just outside of Charleston, South Carolina with her book boyfriendish husband, two incredible children, two doglike cats and their golden retriever Queso.

She's one with coffee (and creamer), easily susceptible to hanger, and chooses Mexican restaurants based solely on the quality of the queso and not the overall food, much to her husband's dismay and children's joy.

She always has a romance novel in her hands or in her ears and is so happy to finally be sharing the ones she has in her head.

EXCERPT FROM BOOK 2
TIMBO

The absolute shit show of a storm that was just Jake has calmed, and we're finally able to talk without him threatening to kill me.

He sits down and leans back into the couch. But I don't trust his calmness yet. It's like that calm *after* a storm, when you're not sure the havoc is really over yet. No chance I can relax, what with the blind rage he just rained down on me. And turns out Jake's a scary fucker. I didn't quite see that coming, but I'd like to think it can be at least somewhat attributed to the beast of a physical specimen I've turned him into.

He's still peppering me with questions. But at least he's civil now.

"But wait, did y'all ever...date? Like secretly or something, since I sure as hell didn't know about it."

I sit on the arm of the couch, keeping a little bit of distance between us in case he comes at me again. I shake my head, "No. She hit it and quit it."

"Damn." He barks out a laugh. "So you mean she did to *you* what you do to everyone else?"

I nod.

"I do that to everyone else because everyone else isn't *her*."

FIND ME

For up to date news on my upcoming books and exclusive bonus content, including sneak peeks, join my mailing list at christinacapri.com

And find me on social media @christinacapri
I'm pretty fun.

And if you read my book with your book club, I definitely want to know! Tag me & tell me!

Last thing—if you hated this book please don't tell a soul about it.
But if you loved it please tell all the souls about it.
All of them.

www.ingramcontent.com/pod-product-compliance
Lightning Source LLC
Chambersburg PA
CBHW030226120726
47903CB00005B/1382